THE HAWKMAN

Jane Rosenberg LaForge

Amberjack Publishing
New York | Idaho

AMBERJACK
P U B L I S H I N G

Amberjack Publishing
1472 E. Iron Eagle Drive
Eagle, Idaho 83616
http://amberjackpublishing.com

Publisher's Cataloging-in-Publication data
Names: LaForge, Jane Rosenberg, author.
Title: The Hawkman : a fairy tale of the Great War / by Jane Rosenberg LaForge.
Description: New York, NY ; Eagle, ID: Amberjack Publishing, 2018
Identifiers: ISBN 978-1-944995-67-6 (pbk.) | 978-1-944995-68-3 (ebook) | LCCN 2017954112
Summary: Eva and The Hawkman, a vagrant, fall in love. Mortally ill, she transforms on their wedding night, leaving an empty body and an augmented widower.
Subjects: LCSH Post traumatic stress disorder--Fiction. | Veterans--Fiction. | World War, 1914-1918--Great Britain--Fiction. | Great Britain--History--20th century--Fiction. | Pianists--Fiction. | Musicians--Fiction. | Teachers--Fiction. | Historical fiction. | Love stories. | Fantasy fiction. | Fairy tales. | BISAC FICTION / Literary.
Classification: LCC PS3612.A3768 H39 2018 | DDC 813.6--dc23

Cover Design: Micaela Alcaino

For Patrick
and his people

Prologue

No ONE SAID anything about the condition of the body, though it was without the weight and rigor of death. One might not have detected its lifelessness if not for its skin. How pale it was: wax-like as if illuminated, a different kind of transparency. There was none of the blueness of it, of blood stopping at the surface. Nor were there scars from a struggle, illness, or the exit of a spirit. One might have instead remarked that the skin had the same cast as a quill, new and untested. Like the shaft of a feather, or bone made external.

But that was only what the ambulance men saw as they first approached the body in the wedding bed, to see what they would be disposing of. When they slid their hands beneath her shoulders, they noticed how the flesh there had taken on the appearance of another animal's: a bird's, specifically, dressed and ready for some sort of holiday presentment. Like a Christmas goose, perhaps, as though each follicle shuddered at its plucking, since the downy barbs that once secured feathers had been wrenched from their perches. Farther down the back, there were not scratches but marks more subtle; if magnified, they might have recalled the leather that outfits a bellows with its many folds, to pump out the air purposefully trapped within. To a physician's eyes, they might have seemed the marks that coincide with the end of a pregnancy, though there was no pregnancy in this instance.

The body was discovered where the bridegroom had said it would be, in the master bedroom upon the second floor. But the ambulance men did not know what to think of the room they had to enter, half in disarray and half absolutely settled, ordered, as though it had been just appointed as a honeymoon suite. The bedclothes were tangled and wet, the mattress partially rousted from its frame. The windows were open and the curtains blew about, but there was no wind. The skirt of her wedding costume swayed from the back of a chair on which it was hung, the matching shoes neatly stacked with the rest in the closet. Everything was light and dry, wrung out as though a gale had overtaken the room just moments earlier. But it was far too early in the season for such a storm.

The body was similarly insubstantial, without any of the bloat they knew to anticipate, and none of the smell they dreaded. Indeed, as they transported it down the stairs, out of the house, and into their vehicle, they felt as though the body's heft diminished, until it was something both men thought they could carry in the palm of their hands.

The morning following the death, and all the mornings

after, even after the body had been buried, flowers appeared on the doorstep of the house. Calla lilies, angel trumpets, moon-flowers—their petals the same crisp white as the deceased's neck and hands. They had nowhere else to appear, these flowers, as the bridegroom was immediately evicted from the premises. The house was owned by the Bridgetonne Women's College, which meant the local earl had a definitive interest. He took the death, as he took all opportunities afforded to him, to finally rid himself of the bridegroom, though the bridegroom returned, morning after morning, with his tribute. Had he been permitted inside, he might have left his offering in the bedroom, or set the flowers in a vase on the small table in what served as an entryway. It was such a small place, no more than a cottage, where he and his bride had lived chastely before the marriage.

The earl, meanwhile, congratulated himself that the newly-made widower did not parade the body for all of Bridgetonneshire to witness. Instead the bereaved had marched the length of the college alone, into the village, and finally onto the earl's property to notify everyone of the death. The earl considered whether he should be grateful for the man's behavior that afternoon: stoic, obedient, if still off-putting. He stood outside respectfully as the ambulance men fetched his bride from upstairs, and then as Lord Thorton and his attendants inspected the place for any damage. As they found none, the earl would have to admit to himself the slight disappointment he felt that the man and woman had been such dutiful tenants. The earl instructed his attendants to explain to the new bridegroom that he was heretofore prohibited from entering said structure permanently. Had they known the source of the man's discomfiting habits, it would not have quelled their suspicions, though many villagers had, by then, including the earl's wife and son.

The flowers the widower carried to the doorstep wilted in his hands somewhat, so that their trumpet-shaped petals approximated the crepe-like nature of his bride's skin, along her back. People said he chose those flowers because of their trumpet shape, as though he was trying to call out to her in some way or listen for a message she had left him on the wind. This made sense, knowing what they did about him, but it did not help him ever hear that message, whatever it might have been. By the day's end, those flowers came to take after the condition of whom they honored: deflated in texture and purpose. And the man who had brought them had been plunged into an ever-widening silence.

One

THIS IS A story about a man who thought he was a bird and the woman who helped him find his humanity again. But before such humble marvels might transpire, there was much talk about him in the village, though he did not live there. He could not be said to have lived anywhere, given the way that he lived. He had neither an address nor regular box at the post. He moved from alley to alley, bin to bin. The pubs would not admit him. Where he slept, kept his belongings, put together the wherewithal to walk, run, and keep on the move remained as a mystery to everyone. They thought perhaps he had a hunting ground, as birds of prey do, or a circuit, and he roamed it in ever-widening rounds.

What he did have was hair, a great blaze of it, on his head and face, and a look that the villagers found most disturbing.

He had two eyes, of course, but people could never see more than one at a time through the thicket of his appearance, and the one they could see never shut for sleep, nor for any instance of pain, fear, joy, or surprise; so much so that people thought he must have had a second pair of eyelids, just as some reptiles do. His features were buried beneath a beard that had grown so long it had collected things: leaves, twigs, bits of dirt, the gristle of what he ate—fish heads and the occasional hock from the butcher's shop. Yet it was his eye, or both of them, that attracted the most notice and gossip—their unnerving brilliance. It was hungry and restless; and it earned him his nickname.

It must have been the children who had given him this name, because of his eyes, the way he kept watch on everything, the coat he wore, and the scream that was his speech. The coat hid his clothes all the way to his feet, and, in the eyes of the children, when he raised his arms and ran toward them, it took on the look of a coat of feathers: a bewitching, smothering cape. He did not speak as a habit, but when tapped on the shoulder, or told that he had dropped a farthing, he would emit a piercing sound that might inspire one to weep. A screech it was, and it fell upon the village as though he had thrown a plea up to God or the angels, and it had been rejected. It hurtled back to earth so ferociously that those who had been in the Great War thought it sounded like the descent of a shell.

Though he walked as a man might if he had been broken in the middle, the children did not fall for this act and said his hands were powerful—creatures to be feared. He could catch a child with his long dirty fingers, latch onto the child's neck as a bird uses its talons to carry its prey, and feast on the child's neck before he took on the eyes, nose, and lips. His pockets were said to rattle with the molars of his victims, but the sound more likely came from the occasional coins he managed to collect.

The older boys taunted him, threw stones as he walked past, or they attacked him outright, smearing their greasy wrappings in his face. He tended not to fight back. One group of boys was known to have tried poisoning him, by slopping up waste from the street and disguising it in some rotting bread they handed him as he was begging. The Hawkman took to scavenging from behind the butcher's or the pub after that incident.

Bridgetonne was not without other misfits: old maids who, in an earlier time, might have been mistaken for witches, and bachelors who, likewise, would have been called out as warlocks. But by no means was the village haunted. It was a common village, with shops, cottages, a restaurant, in addition to the pub and inn, and all the requisite amenities of civilization. The Catholic church was the largest, in the size of its building, but only because it had been built before the Protestant. Its members had to compete with one another for seats in the pews or spots in the churchyard. The outskirts of the village, where the grand estate lay, hosted a women's college, which produced nurses, governesses, and other young ladies of use.

The college had been endowed by the fifth earl of Bridgetonneshire, and now it fell to the seventh, Arthur Thorton, to maintain the boarding school. Lord Thorton, as he was known, was far more proud of his uniforms and the decorations they had collected, through his service in the Boer Wars, than he was of his educational endeavors. He did not make it known how much of that service was performed from behind a desk, as he was a captain who organized and ran the refugee camps. The catastrophe that was those camps soured the young lord on many responsibilities and customs and the propensity of some women to upend the careful architecture of the world, as envisioned and made reality by their perfectly competent male counterparts. But duty is duty, and, at the urging of his wife, Lady Margaret, Lord Thorton affirmed his support for the cause of women's education, even if he was schooling teenaged girls.

For the most recent martial conflict, Lord Thorton fulfilled his duty in a number of ways, including through the most common route taken by men of his class and station. His only son and heir, Christopher, was sent in his stead, along with precise instructions to his commanding officers to keep the next earl of Bridgetonneshire far and clear from any displays of organized benevolence toward the enemy. Such affairs inevitably end badly, the lord lectured his son before his departure, and Arthur Thorton knew this as plainly as he knew the war would end by Christmas, which of course it did not. Still, Christopher returned before the war was far from over, though badly injured, and he quickly retired his military dress clothes. The old lord continued to wear his to the balls, parties, and picnics he hosted. He reasoned it was reassuring for the mothers, wives, and sisters of local boys who had been to war and were slow in coming back.

It was the most immediate goal of Lord Thorton, throughout the war and in its aftermath, to shore up the morale of the village. Aside from emphasizing his own small part in a victorious war of the past, he wanted to remove any other traces of the contemporary morass. He stocked the local grocer's shelves with as much of his own larder as could be spared, to avoid the rationing. If the resources could not be found to hold the annual flower show or a choral performance or some other concert, he would find them: a stage or musicians, the prizes, or even the audience. The black bunting hanging from his own estate and from the buildings of the college during the war he had resolutely replaced with roses, ribbons, and the other adornments of victory. He sent his daughters to the city, so that they might marry that much more quickly, and he rushed the nurses and doctors at the military hospital to bring his son home before his leg wound might have healed properly.

Lord Thorton did not necessarily believe the conclusion of the Great War signaled a new age for him, his family, or his country. He was too old for that sort of belief, having been introduced to the truth behind such triteness in South Africa. But he was most eager to dispatch with the concessions the British public had made at the home front to support the war overseas, and to hasten the return of normality. And, after having taken the initiative so ardently, Lord Thorton saw nothing between himself and his goal but for the presence of The Hawkman. The Hawkman smelled like the war, or perhaps more accurately, its refugees; his wanderings exuded a strange residue onto the walls and pavement of the village, which had to reflect poorly on Lord Thorton and all village residents.

The skulking, cunning nature of The Hawkman was peculiarly redolent of the Boer refugees who had tasked the young lord with alleviating their voluntary poverty, the tenacity of their communicable desert diseases, and their clamorous appetites. Lord Thorton believed that it was always the worst of people who refused to be helped, despite their proclamations that they are the most desirous of it. Tacitly supporting any beneficent enterprise to feed, clothe, and comfort a virtual Bedouin of the British countryside did not align with either Lord Thorton's inclinations or prejudices.

Lord Thorton had learned, through dealings with his superiors in South Africa, that it was far less deleterious to one's record and reputation neither to directly order whatever improvements he wished, nor to draft people in any specific cause. He instead simply made his feelings known at a meal, or some other seemingly insignificant gathering, and then he watched, with a glazed kind of amusement, as his wants were made into the real ambitions of those around him.

This was precisely his strategy as he gathered the more prominent villagers for luncheon at his home, just as the spring was returning to Bridgetonneshire. He wished for his daughters, upon their return, to freely amble over the grounds of his mansion and the fields of the county without fear for their safety; he wished the same for all the young women of the college, who would too soon end their training to begin their dour lives in the cities. Indeed, he wished for all women and girls to enjoy the liberty their brothers and fathers had fought for, without encountering lechery, thievery, and common depredation in their wanderings.

Lady Margaret congratulated Lord Thorton on his progressive view of womanhood once he announced the agenda for the luncheon to the guests assembled. The reverend and a visiting countess, a cousin to Lady Margaret, rumbled their approval, as did the president of the historical society. Of course the presumptive heir, the earl's convalescing son Christopher, was loudest in his compliance. But there was one guest who did not join in the preparations for applause: Eva Williams.

"There is poverty in this village?" she asked, as slowly and as deliberately as she could, because it seemed to her that whatever she said, being a foreigner, was met with a discomfiting surprise, as if she had spoken too loudly or boldly, no matter the topic.

"Perhaps not the poverty that someone like you has been exposed to," said Christopher, who felt as honor-bound to rush to his father's defense as he did to impress Miss Williams. "Here we are not burdened by the kinds of conditions you have in your Chicago or your New York."

"They are not necessarily my cities," Miss Williams said, as if she was repeating a phrase from an elocution lesson. Miss Williams was cordial but stiff for an American, and she seemed to invest a great effort in not being seen as another rude colonial—hence her tentative, if not diffident, manner. She framed each word as though as it was to be delivered on its own silver platter, then smoothed away by a silk napkin. "I could never live in Chicago, so large, so riotous. Yet in your own cities, I believe, do you not find ragged—"

"Perhaps in the cities," Christopher quickly interrupted, "but we are not talking about that kind of poverty."

"Poverty is the same everywhere," Miss Williams said. "Particularly in the eyes of the impoverished."

"Yet in the eyes of those who must provide for them— my father, for instance—" Christopher reminded her, "those differences are quite significant. A minority of the impoverished is quite deserving: a soldier who returns from battle, visibly wounded, unable to provide for himself and his family. But what we find most are lost causes, the inherited cases, the offspring of degradation or decadence.

"Under our—my father's—stewardship," Christopher continued, "Bridgetonne is no longer host to any unfortunates."

"Excuse me, Christopher," Lady Margaret quickly corrected him, once she espied an affirming nod from her husband. "One such unfortunate has been especially confounding. We have tried, but we cannot seem to be rid of him."

"Rid of him?" Miss Williams asked.

"Yes," the reverend said, and, although his voice was steady as he spoke, his glance toward Miss Williams seemed embarrassed, if not apologetic, for his luncheon companions. "We have approached him, in a manner of sorts, so that we might find out who he was, what he needed—to send him back to his family. But he screams, or runs, or disappears for weeks at a time should anyone approach him. He tells us nothing."

"'The Hawkman,' the children call him," Lady Margaret explained.

"Does he fly?" Miss Williams asked, if not a bit too eagerly. She caught her own impertinence, and tried again, "I mean: what is he, really?"

"He is a scavenger," Christopher said, with more than a

hint of warning in his voice. "Until one day, he will have scavenged all that he can. Then, he will turn predatory."

"We don't know that," the reverend said.

"This reminds me," Miss Williams began, and perhaps it was only the reverend who heard that a new confidence had entered her voice, but Miss Williams no longer needed to flit through her sentences because in her heart and soul, she was a pedant. She had come to Bridgetonne, at great expense to Lord Thorton, to teach at the women's college, for in America she had some renown as an author of small fairy stories and little poems. Those who listened to her story at that luncheon had been entranced during the tale: if not by her voice then the pantomime of her hands—the wrists that rose and fell, her palms acting out the shapes and gestures of the characters she created, the obstacles she had them surmount.

Miss Williams said the story she was about to tell had many variants, depending on the region from which it was collected. "In France and Germany, the protagonist is a veteran, starving for lack of work after the war; in Italy, he is a woodsman, wounded by an accident inherent in his profession. In Spain, he is a pirate, shipwrecked after a poorly deliberated decision," she said. "In all places, he is a man who has lost his faith in God and makes no secret of his apostasy. In some places, he is visited by the Devil; in others, it is a regional deity or demi-sprite, who reaps his satisfaction at recruiting the man by turning him into an animal.

"A bear, a goat, a great ram: this again depends on the setting of the storyteller; the mountainous regions, of course, give rise to rams and goats, and forests to bears. Whatever he becomes, he is a horror with horns or a gruff beard. His body is blanketed in fiendish hair. His breath is hideous, reeking of the lives he had eaten, and his teeth are spikes, like a giant's. He loses his human hands and feet; they turn into cloven-hoofed appendages or claws. He can find nowhere to sleep, to eat, to be among people, until he comes upon a group of children picking berries. They cannot reach the highest berries on the tallest trees. The beast man gladly picks the berries where the human children cannot reach; when they ask him how they might reward his good deed, he merely says, 'Pray for me.'

"He wanders to other villages and towns, doing good deeds only a beast can do: finding rings at the bottom of wells, waving away a tide of bees that a storm had dispossessed of its hive, rescuing an infant from a creek, finding a hunter lost among the most dangerous mountains, releasing a maiden held by a pack of wolves. For each of these deeds, the beast asks only that his fellow man prays for him: 'Pray for me. Pray that I see the err of my ways, and am returned to my once blessed form and soul.' As more people do pray for him, and more good deeds are done, the horns, fur, fangs, hooves, and claws recede, until, after a period of years," longest in Germany, Miss Williams noted, and shortest in Italy, "the transformation is complete. He becomes a man again.

"Because of this miracle, the sages and princes of every country want him for their own: as a leader, an advisor, a husband for princesses or noble women. But in every instance, the man declines, saying he merely wants to be a true champion of nature, because it is nature that has saved him: those berries on the distant branches. He wants nothing more than to serve nature and his fellow beings, and never again face the possibility of being so separate, so distinguishable, from them.

So he disappears: into a cave, the hollow of a tree. No one can say. Many have gone searching for him, but always he is illusionary."

At the conclusion of this tale, the reverend, Lady Margaret, the visiting countess, and Christopher applauded. Christopher withdrew his approval, however, once he saw his father, Lord Thorton, draw his mouth into a frown.

"That is not how that story is meant to end at all," Lord Thorton said. "You are neglecting the original purpose of the tale. This is a libel."

"One must never neglect the source material," the president of the historical society agreed. "A soul for a soul, I believe it goes. The man takes a bride, but the Devil—"

"A libel against whom?" Miss Williams interrupted.

"Against God," Lord Thorton said.

"What his Lordship means," the reverend volunteered, "is that in disguising the ending, you do God a great disservice," the reverend offered.

"I can see how that might be troubling, if one believes in God, and the Devil, and such things," Miss Williams said. Taking a breath, she looked about to see the discomfort of her listeners and amended her statement, "Or by affixing a potential good deed to the Devil, or to man himself, without God's intervention."

"Certainly God is in every story," the reverend continued, for which Christopher and Lady Margaret were grateful; their relief was audible as they exhaled, as if in a kind of harmony. "Particularly a morality tale such as this one, with the Lord's way set against the heathen's."

"There are some who believe Grimms' to be Christian

tales," Miss Williams acknowledged, "but I cannot count myself among them. Wilhem Grimm himself said—"

"I thought we were to discuss issues of the college," Christopher offered, "not its curriculum."

Miss Williams looked into the lap of her modest black dress, which suddenly seemed inappropriate for this event, as if she was attired for a far more serious gathering.

"I think I have had enough for an afternoon," Lord Thorton announced. As he rose to excuse himself, he was joined by Christopher, who nearly leapt from his chair, as if in deference to his father.

"Right," said Christopher, who, in his eagerness to second his father, had forgotten to leave his napkin on the table as he marched off behind Lord Thorton.

"It has been lovely," Lady Margaret said, rising to join them. "We will do this again, I promise. But for now," she paused, nodding in the direction of her absent family, "good day to you all."

There had been tea and cordials scheduled, sewing, cards, or possibly a salon. But it fell to the reverend to acknowledge none of that was possible, and he assigned to himself the job of escorting the remaining guests. "Right," the reverend declared as he stood. As he and Miss Williams exited the manor house, he suggested that the mention of Mr. Grimm, a German, might have proved most upsetting to his Lordship. Or, as one of Lord Thorton's servants claimed to later overhear, His Lordship was unconvinced the problem of The Hawkman would resolve itself as easily as the beast man of Miss Williams's tale.

Two

A FORTNIGHT LATER, as it was pleasant enough for a bicycle ride, Miss Williams pedaled around the village and back to the college grounds. She had been in Bridgetonne since the autumn of the previous year, but she had come for the spring. Although it had yet to make its full entrance, the sight of its green shoots and scent of its grasses would have to suffice for Miss Williams for the time being. Miss she believed the season inspired the best stories with their possibilities of renewal. Not that she hadn't attempted, in the autumn and winter, to think or use such emotion in her writing.

But she had not found the England she expected when she arrived. The place and its people were impenetrable in all aspects: the tart curve in their speech, the defeated fabric of their clothes, the sallow nature of their complexions. The war had done just as much in the States, but, in England, the heft of wartime still rode on the shoulders of both people and nature. The very atmosphere of the place, the fields and its pavement, even the space people afforded one another during conversations, was cumbersome, as if everyday tasks had become Sisyphean.

Miss Williams did not like such comparisons, between the contemporary and the patently mythic. The old legends of gods and demi-men were unyielding and afforded too little to transcendence. She preferred folk tales, old wives' advice, the magic and malleable. It might still be possible for a pauper to become a prince, or for a bundle of poppies or cowslips to loosen an old crone's embitterments. Those possibilities were all that were left in this rock of a world since the whims of the old gods, set to work on these descendants of Troy, seemed to preclude happiness.

But spring was inevitable; it always was, and winter was unraveling. She could smell it as she rode past the baker's, the grocer's, the seamstress's, and the millinery: the nectar of fresh bread loosening the air's hold on the dampness. The scent turned the village woolen and inviting. In the combination of warmth and bustle she felt and witnessed, Miss Williams thought she might unearth here what had always been such a font of wonder for her and discover, if not fairies living in the trees, then monarchies of a similar resourcefulness. The flowerbeds she would plant at her cottage; the bark on cedar and oak trees, lined with the impressions of frost and thaw; the soil that would part for roots and fresh stems, and then close around them, just as quickly. Was there a sound, a score of this minute, as when a breath is held in anticipation of joy? Miss Williams was determined to hear it. She must ever be on the alert, now that spring was within a reasonable distance. She pedaled on toward where the roads gave way to gravel, to pebbles, to the paths that were more like berms in the landscape, toward the back entrance of the college.

At a rise of earth she knew she could not surmount on the bicycle, she hopped off and saw him: his posture like that of someone or something trying to conceal itself, as if ashamed at its molting or some other natural process. As she drew nearer, he no longer appeared animal, but strangely human in how he attempted to disguise himself. A man, possibly, his hands and arms behind his back, walking with his head leading, pitched forward to the point of almost falling. He walked stiffly, as though he lacked joints that bent. The sum of this effect was a strange gait that accomplished little movement, other than an arduous shuffling. As a bird might try walking, although Miss Williams did not consider this association until she was much closer indeed, close enough to observe the indignity of this landlocked creature.

From the bundle of clothes, mud, and dust that composed this man materialized a hand, with long, fine fingers. Against the mass of filth from which it emerged, the skin of that hand was brilliant and ghastly, bright and scaly. The hand opened its palm and extended toward her, almost daintily. The man was begging. The skin of his arm was black, as if encased in a miasma. He smelled as a city does during the long, sultry nights: of garbage and excrement. He then leaned and paced, as if shuffling his pain between legs and feet, while supporting a great weight on his back: his wings.

She did not know how long they stood there, together. Miss Williams could have easily fetched a coin to join with his palm, but she was too taken with the skin there, so intricately cracked, a map of wells and creeks. When she placed nothing in his palm he withdrew his hand and offered her the other one, just as a bird ruffles his feathers to air them out, and then appears to have done nothing.

His fingers were like leaves, their reach toward the sun and meaning. She saw no harm in touching him, although she knew the dangers of touching birds, particularly the hatchlings.

Miss Williams had not known her own mother very well; the woman had been taken from her when Miss Williams was still a girl, and in the short time they had together, her mother was often bedridden, unable to show her daughter the acts and places of nature that she wanted her daughter to also adore. But her mother had warned her, once, on an afternoon when they watched the wrens splatter about in the bird bath: never, ever, touch a bird. The human touch permanently marks it as different, separate. The flock will reject it. Mother birds are particularly attuned to the scent of mankind. Should they discover it on their offspring, they leave them to the elements.

"Come," Miss Williams said as she realized this must be The Hawkman before her. To him she extended her palm. He did not take it, so she tried again, "Come. You must be hungry," but he remained perched as he was, moments away from her. She could see that the palm was scored and wrapped in calluses. But it was also white as paraffin, and as she took it, it had an almost lifeless quality. "I won't bite," she said, and it occurred to her that he might not have been able to hear her.

But she did not wish to shout.

"Come come come," she said. He relinquished her hand, dropped his arm and returned it to its original position, behind his back. He took a step, more like a lunge, as his posture required, but Miss Williams did not balk.

"This way, then," she said as she stepped back and returned her attention to her bicycle. She would have to walk it all the way home, if he was to follow her. She pushed the bike and took a step but did not look behind her, fearing how he might interpret the move. He might see it as a test of his civility or a measure of her hubris. She listened for the strain of his movements—human movements—the thaw in his knees and elbows, the stress in the soles of his shoes.

She walked the bicycle, and he lurched behind her: she could sense it through the dreadful rhythm of his footsteps. One foot gallantly placed forward, the other following in a tedious attempt to remain upright. He almost hopped. As if trying to avoid tenderness on either side of his feet, only to experience it in both, she guessed. The farther they walked together, the stranger they must have seemed, Miss Williams thought—master and servant or Mary Shelley and the physical manifestation of her imagination. She stopped walking, at uneven intervals, to make sure The Hawkman was truly there and not an apparition of her fantasies.

She got a proper look at him once they arrived at the cottage, and she could lay the bicycle on its side. He was faceless, having concealed his head within his coat, and he shook as if he was nothing more than a defeated husk of corn, waiting either for the wind or the vultures to take him.

"You might have to duck a bit," she said by way of instruction, as she opened the front door. "It's an old place, but very comfortable."

She led him through a short hall to the kitchen that had been added onto the original cottage, but it was hardly a kitchen at all. There was a sink, a washtub, an ice chest for preserving a small amount of food, and a pile of firewood beside the back door, but no stove. That remained within the sitting room, where it also provided heat for the rest of the first floor. Miss Williams explained that she took most of her meals at the college with her students, so the arrangement was quite suitable for her. The carriage of The Hawkman demanded a hot meal immediately.

She could not think of removing her hat, gloves, and coat, so quickly did she feel the need to retrieve the pitcher of buttermilk and pour out a glass for him. A hand and arm darted from his mass to take it; it disappeared in one long, vicious gulp. He wiped his lips on his coat sleeve when finished. His lips were left pale by the milk, and he held out the glass as if for a second drink. But when she motioned to pour into his glass again, he shook his head, and then nodded as she took it away from him.

"Would you like some tea?" asked Miss Williams, but The Hawkman did not respond. She was now confronted with the audacity of what she had begun. He stood oblivious and as still as his trembling would allow. She could hear his breathing, quick; the sway in his shoes; the swallow in his throat. "Please, please, sit down," she said, motioning to one of two chairs at the small table as if sitting would calm him, help him settle. "I do not keep much here, but I have a bit of chicken they roast for me at the college. I can make you a sandwich, or a plate . . ."

She left him there as she went to boil the tea. She tried to keep up a stream of chatter over the sounds of her preparations: about the college and the responsibilities of the days awaiting her. She spoke of lectures and luncheons and other meals; poems she had planned for idle moments she could capture; she spoke as if unfurling a blanket of birdsong, what mother birds use to envelop their sons and daughters.

"I keep busy enough so that I am not too homesick," she said. "The modern conveniences, a cook stove, I do not miss them much. I rather like the fire, as long as I have someone to help with the firewood."

She listened for any response he might make, but there was none. When she returned with the boiling kettle, The Hawkman remained unchanged except for his coat, which seemed to have been pressed tighter, faster, about his neck and trunk. Her kindness could be killing him.

"Here you go," she said, once she had served him a plate of chicken and sliced tomatoes. He held the fork not between his fingers but with his fist, as if it were the end of a spear. Miss Williams watched from too short of a distance, she realized, from across the table. She drank her own cup of tea, and wondered if it pained him to hold the fork in such a way that he had to twist his hand into such uncomfortable figurations to deliver the food to his mouth. He shoveled the tomatoes, not necessarily like a starving man would, but as one who had too long lived confined from civilization: in a prison, a hospital, or some other regimented environment.

"Were you," Miss Williams dared to ask, "in the war?"

He looked up from his plate and now showed her his eyes,

the yellow everyone had known and castigated. They moved together, his eyes did, first over her face, and then over their surroundings, as if he was gauging the strength of the walls, their dependability in a storm—or a fire fight. He did not nod or shake his head, but instead returned his attention to his meal.

"Should I get you to a Voluntary Aid hospital, then?" Miss Williams asked. This time when he showed his face to her, he shut his eyes and shook his head. His next object of concentration was on the last slice of tomato, which he pushed into his mouth. He edged the plate toward her once he was finished.

"Might I get you anything else?" she asked.

No, he shook his head again. He was no longer shivering, but both his arms still hugged the coat, as if to drive it deeper into his flesh. One eye had seemingly retreated behind the tussle of his curls, and the other appeared as fierce and bright as it ever might have been, stronger than the sun. A corona of stain spilled out, onto his eyelids and circles around and beneath, and he rocked in the chair. If he was still in need, he could not bring himself to admit it.

"You could have a bath," Miss Williams said, because her solution was to keep things moving—herself and him. She sprung up from the table for the back door. Just outside there was a shed with garden tools and odd pieces of clothing for what must have been the groundskeeper, for a time. A small man, Miss Williams thought, and those clothes were likely as dusty as her guest's; they would have to do long enough for her to wash and mend whatever he wore. Upon her return to the kitchen, she found The Hawkman to be dutifully standing by the table. She presented him with the old clothes, but he did not take them from her.

"It's all right," she said.

His one visible eye was honey-bright, and Miss Williams presumed the eye followed her as she swung around the kitchen to lead him up the stairs. He labored to climb the short steps, his breath was thick with nuisance, coughs, and phlegm. She left the clothes and the towel she collected from the hall linen closet on the side of the tub, and shut the door to leave him to his business.

Darkness had begun its walk on earth by the time he emerged downstairs. He found her at her desk, her eyes squinting into a book, through the colors of the approaching evening. She was not generous when it came to her candles and lanterns, lighting them had always been a trial; she could not adequately judge the distance required to light a taper to begin the candles, as if she did not know the reach of her own limbs. She would often find herself surrounded by nightfall before she would be forced to oil wicks and strike matches. She felt more secure in the darkness, as if it were a fabric, a net that would stop her falling. But she could sense him, see him, through Browning's words and the book's spine. His eyes were like a sentry, guarding his inexplicable history.

"Those clothes do you well," Miss Williams said. They even fit, to a degree; he was much smaller in the shoulders and legs with his coat removed than she had expected. He was, she was afraid to admit, substantially more delicate than a soldier should be: the mass of him almost doll-like, and his hands finely boned in length and width. If he had been a soldier, it was certainly not through his own volition. Perhaps he was a deserter, a conscientious objector who drove an ambulance. That would justify, in some minds, the villagers' treatment of him.

He extended his arm, the coat draped over it, and Miss Williams retrieved all the garments underneath the coat as well as the coat itself. Everything was so caked over with road dust and field mud that the cloth had a strange, second presence, beyond its bulk. There must have been a ghost in the clothes, within the fibers, where the soil and moisture had created something like vellum, important and delicate.

"Now, you should have a haircut," Miss Williams declared, to which the man took a demonstrative step backward. He shook his head—no, no, no.

"Oh," Miss Williams said. "I'm sorry. Would you like to rest now instead?"

She had to step around him, his last declaration was so rigid, to take him to her favorite room in the cottage. At one time it might have been a nursery, judging from its light and airiness. The room looked out over the open fields that buffeted the cottage, and the sun always rose first there, leaving it warmer than the rest of the house. Miss Williams imagined that the crickets and frogs that would live in the field during summer would be best heard from this room, a gentle infantry that carted children and troubled souls off to sleep most efficiently. This being still so close to winter, it was too early for those sounds, but the sweet green trim of the ceiling beams and moldings still enlivened the room, with its pair of twin beds and a nightstand between them.

Miss Williams turned down a bedspread and then a blanket for her guest, who could move no farther than the doorframe. Neither eye was visible. When Miss Williams finally turned to formally invite him into the room, she thought she might be hearing the verge of a sob in his throat. She had never considered that, having slept without shelter from both the natural elements and man-made harassments for so long, he might be afraid of sleep and the unique class of demons it might bring to visit him. "I promise: nothing to disturb you," she said, and she sat on the other bed, leaving a clear route for him to walk on his own.

He approached the small bed as if driven by contradictory instincts: one to rest, the other to remain vigilant. He could not tell the difference between an offer and a demand. His eyes revealed themselves, trained as they were on the sheets meant to match the trim and molding. He could sleep in green without it cutting or scratching. The fresh bedclothes, the mattress, the ache of his exhaustion—he could defy them no longer. He had fallen into the mattress.

As she stood over him, to tuck him in, after a fashion, she was taken by how large his eyes were, how they resembled packets of amber—clear yet intricate, but not symmetrical. Their irises did not quite match, the left eye consistent in its hue, and the right flecked with brown and green that lunged from the background. She turned toward the window to draw the curtains when he stopped her. He grabbed her by the wrist.

Miss Williams had long been in the close proximity of men: her father, for one, in the tenements where they slept, four families to a room. She had watched the backs of other men as they slept in their corners, the strain and pressure that their naked muscles could not relinquish, even in slumber. She had sat across from men at tables and in classrooms before lecterns. But she had never found herself so near to a man and his bald demands, and instinctively she resisted.

He put a finger to his lips, and with the other hand, he pulled her down so she was sitting beside him on the bed. She sat up straight, defiant, yet there seemed not to be a need. He merely moved his hand from her wrist to her fingers, and took the fingers into his own hand, then rested the pair he made on his chest. She thought he should turn his head, close his eyes, but instead he looked to her, boldly, without blinking. He meant for her to watch over him, she guessed from the wideness of his eyes, persisting despite his obvious exhaustion. She remained there until he fell asleep, his misery temporarily lost in the night. It had been an uncomfortable experience, his hold on her hand, the naked feeling in his eyes. But she did not protest as she reminded herself that she, too, as a child, had been afraid of the dark—the night could take more than her dreams, but her last thought of the day, the picture she might have made of her and her mother, together.

That night, with a candle at her desk, she listened for his breathing. Would he wake up, wander about the cottage, pillory the kitchen; would he shout out his story in a nightmare? But she heard nothing. When she was convinced there would be nothing more from him, she wrote in the book where she let her ideas run:

> Beast to beauty to beast again:
> all beasts have a soul
> but a human who loses his core
> to circumstance and language

is neither human nor creature

but a pinnacle of all the things he fears:

dirt and hunger, his lathered clothes and

the evening chill; the song that bleeds from
    nightfall

to daylight; a song of what he lost and cannot
    regain;

except for the moments in between when he
    remembers

the needs of an infant, and the gold of
    sustenance

offered to him in modest presentation.

Three

WHEN HER MOTHER told her never to touch a bird, Eva and Helen were in the Public Garden. This is what her mother knew: scents and ointments, waxes and fingertips, the consequences of her touch. She could set a demure string of curls in front of her daughter's ears, or one perfectly placed in the center of her forehead, with a bobby pin and dab of petroleum jelly. She changed her husband's appearance with a straight razor, scissors, pomade, and a hairpiece, when necessary. And it was, on many occasions, though Eva did not understand what brought these occasions about. She only knew that when her mother trimmed her father's beard, or elaborately waxed his moustache; if she ripped up one suit to amend another, with a leaner fit for the jacket, or new cut for the trousers, the family was soon to be on the move again.

On those days her mother would scrub the floor or polish the balustrade of the soon-to-be-abandoned apartment with a solvent that made her hands smell of mothballs, fiery yet chilling. The scent made Eva dizzy as her mother bore down to remove all the residue of their lives, so nothing might be dug up and identified. Talc in the air, hair grease that drooped from shoulder to floor, discarded handkerchief or bandage that stopped up the blood when her mother jabbed herself with a seam ripper or her father's nose was punched in an argument. A miasma must have been following them, like a stock of sore luck, and it marked them as a mother bird marks her offspring, invisibly but definite.

"If I were to touch a baby bird, I would confuse its sense of smell," Eva's mother said one spring afternoon, as they chanced by a family of wrens bathing in a marble bath. The air was luscious enough for breathing, as her mother said, and Eva's father had need of the flat for a meeting with a business associate. Whenever he had one of these meetings, Eva and her mother set out for the day with a basket that was mostly empty, with nothing more than an apple or a heel of bread inside. But, by carrying it, they appeared not as vagrants, but reputable citizens, entitled to a rest on the Common, or a wander around a busy market, or a quiet walk of contemplation through the Public Garden.

"If I touched a baby bird, it could be overwhelmed with my scent," Helen said.

From the side of the bath, the mother wren dipped her head into the water; then she waited for her hatchlings to perform the same movement, until they were equally rinsed to their necks. "The baby might think I was the one who hatched it, and preened it, while it was still wet and bewildered," her mother said. "Then it might follow me everywhere, and think my fingers are worms its mother stuffed down its throat." Her mother's hand took on the shape of a beak and pinched at Eva's cheeks and nose.

"But what if I touched the bird?" Eva remembered asking. She remembered smelling her fingertips at that moment, but she detected nothing remarkable there. She still thought of herself as not that different from the birds she and her mother saw each day. Small, hesitant, likely to be lost among the legs and feet of adults who did not notice the hue of another person's eyes, the dawns and sunsets in the coloring of their collars, and crowns of feathers on their heads. The birds also tired as Eva did when the day lagged on, so far away from their nests. They could not muster the strength to fly sometimes and simply jumped, or hopped, away from her approach. The sparrows did not bother to find water sometimes and bathed in the dirt alongside the public garden's paths.

"Especially if you touched the bird," her mother answered. "If you were a baby bird, wouldn't you want a little girl of your own to run with you as you learned to fly, to cuddle you when you were cold, to sing to you all the songs she knew?" The answer chagrined Eva further, for a bird could not "have" a little girl any more than her father could have one of the chickens behind their flat, or a carriage horse in the street. Chickens and horses, goats and sheep—those had to be bought, with money or favors, she knew, two things her father could never seem to hold in decent supply.

"When we are rich, may I touch the bird?" Eva asked.

"Oh, especially not then," her mother said.

"Why not?" Eva asked.

"Because that is the problem with the rich. They must own everything."

Her mother swept her up in her arms from the bench where they'd been sitting, and together they twirled in a tight circle. "But not you," her mother whispered in her ear. "You're all mine. I won't let anyone have you. Not a bird or the richest person on earth." Eva buried her face in her mother's neck. She smelled strongly of cloves this day; there were days she smelled of lemon, and orange, and sometimes of combinations of the three. Eva wondered how her mother might smell to a bird, like some kind of impossible flower or tree.

"If I can make you fly like a bird, you do not need to touch one," her mother whispered, "so put your head back, and look up."

Eva complied, and loosened her legs from around her mother's waist. Her mother quickened her pace, and Eva focused on the blossoming dogwoods above her head. Is this what a bird sees? she wondered, the white petals shaped as stars must have been, should she ever get close enough to the stars. Did birds find their way by the stars as sailors do, or were they confused by these petals in their color and balance? If they could be tricked by the smells of human hands, surely they could be fooled by white petals, or anything almost clear and very bright: the rings some women wore; their chokers and bracelets; and the feathers they wore in their hats, as if they were trying to lure birds into a false nest, a trap.

Birds must not be as smart as she was, Eva told herself, and her mother must be very honest, by not wearing jewelry or a hat with feathers. She was glad of both thoughts, and brought her head and neck back up straight so she could kiss her mother on the cheek, the color deepening on her mother's skin much like the cloves her mother used to make perfume: rich and exuberant.

"Will you take me faster now?" Eva asked after the kiss, to which her mother said, "Only if you promise."

"Yes, yes," Eva might have said, because she was laughing and screaming all at once, the amalgamation of fear and joy on her face; she did not want these sensations to end for, in a way, they depended on each other.

Miss Williams remembered how her mother extracted other promises: to learn to read and write, not throw rocks at squirrels, or feed the raccoons rooting about in the garbage, to also learn her figures when she was old enough. To not marry so young; or tell anyone where her pin money was; to never give up on her schooling; and find her own profession in life, because to be so dependent upon a man was dangerous. As dangerous as touching a bird or taking in a stray or living, as her mother did, at the elbow of a man always on the run and in need of disguises.

Yes, yes, Mother, I promise, I promise, Eva always relented, but whether she acquiesced at the moment these requests were lodged, as completely and affirmatively as her mother came to demand, Eva could not say. For then, as it was once she was on her own, Miss Williams was too enamored of the air when it was clean and exhilarating with possibilities for birds, and little girls.

IN THE MORNING, before he was up and about, Miss Williams sunk The Hawkman's clothes into the wash tub. She pinned his coat on a line where it could catch the air and expel whatever gave it such a terrible cast: a scent like smoke, damp soil, and the hides of any life that is neglected—fruit and live-stock, pets and vegetables. The wind might do well enough by the coat's lining, she thought, but the rest of the dirt would have to be beaten out of the coat, as if it were a carpet. She found an old wooden spoon among the kitchen equipment and whacked at the coat for a moment, driving out clods of dust in the process. She would have done more, except for the spitting and coughing it brought from her throat, and the feeling she had that she was hammering after a swarm of devils in the fabric.

She was feeding the fire on the stove when he finally appeared, a bit bewildered, from the nursery. Miss Williams glanced up from the furnace to see him at the bottom of the stairs, in his new clothes and bare feet, and she marveled again at how tiny he was—a wren or a finch—his hawkish shoulders and carriage diminished. He parted his hair from his face, as if he was unaware that she had been watching him, and she saw both his eyes, in concert, as they tried to remember the cottage, the kitchen, the sleep and dreams that now swelled on his eyelids.

"Did you sleep well?" she asked.

He tilted his head, slightly—enough to have the curtains of his hair draw closed again—and nodded. Then he slightly bowed his head, as if to show gratitude.

Miss Williams could not imagine what she might do with this odd bird, who was not only brief in stature but also in entire body. His bones showed through the thin shirt and his feet appeared immeasurably long, possibly because of the small width of his ankles. He was no longer the quaking mass he had been the day before, but she could see how a simple night of kindness did not strengthen him. It only made him more vulnerable. She did not know if she had done him a service or had helped to sharpen the tools with which the world was waiting to consume him.

"There is breakfast, if you like."

He nodded, and, in an instant, he seemed to have sprung up beside her to help her load the firewood.

"Then I must go to the college," she said, because she was not quite sure what to say. Should she have him stay, or drive him out—if he was her responsibility now, as much as any injured being becomes the responsibility of those who minister to it, regardless of how effective they have been? "Would you like to stay and wait for your clothes to dry? Of course, you are free to go, and I could still return them to you. We could make some arrangement. Or we could find you a place here, on the grounds . . ."

With a man now in her house, Miss Williams thought of how she was not opposed to marriage for others, but could not fathom herself making such compromises on where to live, how to spend, even whether to raise children. So she knew there would always be speculation as to her status, no matter how sparse or elaborate her household arrangements. There is always speculation where the sexes were involved, and as she filed out loud through their options, she felt something of a bird herself, running through the available scales and ensuring that she hit each one at the right interval. "Of course it is all up to you, of course," she said, as words became ridiculous to her, to both of them, because he said nothing as she ran through her vocabulary and etiquette. "The spring should be spectacular here," she went on, "if I could get a proper garden in. I've never been able to do that by myself."

Miss Williams went to the college that day, and she arrived home in the late afternoon to find him still there, to her relief, if not astonishment. He remained barefoot, and resolutely speechless, but he had swept and tidied, and he was in what passed for her library, in the main room. He did not smile when he saw her but rose from the chair and bowed his head, this time in recognition, Miss Williams supposed. When she offered tea, he went into the kitchen to fetch more firewood for the stove.

"I will have to have something to call you, other than 'sir,'" she said as they sipped at their warm drinks in the library. He grabbed at a piece of paper and pencil from her desk and carefully wrote on it. He showed her what he had written:

Sheehan, Michael Evan

before he threw what he had produced into the stove. He did not take his eyes off the stove until he was certain that the fire had consumed it. Miss Williams assumed he meant for her to say nothing of who he was, even if all he was now was that name, without a history or family or even an explanation of how he came to be in Bridgetonne.

And so they went on, in their way: Miss Williams leaving for the college on the days she taught and tutored; Mr. Sheehan staying behind to sweep and tidy, or to read from her library. When his clothes dried, Miss Williams tried to repair them, but they were no longer clothes, but rags not even fit for a scarecrow. She obtained other clothes for him, as discreetly as she knew how. To colleagues at the college she announced that she was collecting surplus clothing for impoverished soldiers. To the people in the village, she suggested an appeal for those in the workhouses. Through this ruse she was able, within weeks, to accumulate more clothing than Mr. Sheehan, or any human being, could conceivably desire. But having him settle on a few items was a trial, as the trousers were often too long or too wide for his attenuated posture. When Miss Williams finally decided to outright buy him some suspenders, she may have been too eager to inform the sellers that the purchase was part of her charity efforts.

Sometimes, in the evening, Miss Williams would espy Mr. Sheehan as he sat in a kind of strange conversation with himself, his glancing downward, toward his hands. Yet he would be looking just beyond his knees. His eyelids, when she could locate them within his hair, shifted and rested, as though he were tracing the progress of some slight occurrence, but of course there was nothing. His yellow eyes, meanwhile, seemed to fade in their crude articulation, into green and brown, as if they were leaves coming to terms with the autumn. Miss Williams wondered how many autumns Mr. Sheehan had witnessed, and how painful was the slow casting off of leaves for him.

When the weather became more consistent, if not thoroughly agreeable, Miss Williams took to planting the garden she had spoken of. Alone, she started, as Sheehan refused her almost daily entreaties. "Good morning," she'd say before breakfast. "Wouldn't you like to join me?" But she was gone before he could answer, out the door and around the side of the cottage, in a long jacket she wore to protect her clothes. She worked on several small plots, and he stood by a small window in the main room, where she might not notice him. She turned over dirt, planted cuttings: chrysanthemums. They were best planted in the autumn. But, as she explained later, the bitter scent of those flowers would keep insects away. She was a small woman, and the work made her smaller still. She was often on her knees, as though the soil demanded an exacting kind of attention.

He stood at that window and stepped back when he thought she might have caught a glimpse of his looking. He moved in closer as he thought he saw her struggling with the weeds, or the squirrels that threatened her work. She had to encase the pumpkins in wire she had found from a chicken coop, a favorite topic of hers on those evenings when she took her meal with him. She wondered if the plants could sense being caged within. Or whether they would feel doubly trapped as the pattern of the light that fell upon them would be like a net. Would the stems crane themselves into unhealthy postures, and the pumpkins come out lopsided or with some other sort of defect? In the end, she concluded that it couldn't be helped; it was a net or certain death at the appetites of the squirrels, which were charming but voracious.

"Would you take some air?" she'd sometimes ask, and he did not shake his head, no. But he was not leaving the cottage. He could watch the garden more directly after breakfast: once she left for the college and would not be back until long after the sunset. He watched the sun rise farther still, over the tree line before it poured itself into the garden; he saw how the soft, almost marshy, soil gathered itself together as though it was a soldier, searching out his gear after a spill in the mud. He resolved to go outside, to assist her, once he could be assured that the light would not deceive him. Once he was confident the light would not sear into his eyes only to disappear in an instant. Once the sounds the air must have made against grass, stems, and branches were secured, and he might actually hear them. Above the clanging and hum in his ears, he could listen for bees and dragonflies.

She was a diligent gardener. She worked through the sun and through the showers. She left the watering can out in the soft rain to collect the rainwater. If she found lady bugs in one part of the garden, she'd move them to another, to dispose of the ravaging insects chewing up leaves and flowers. She planted more cuttings, blooming plants, and on the weekend sat before her work, as if to admire it. "Won't you take a look?" she asked, with just a twinge of pride in her voice, but he could see just as well from the window.

The cottage was dark one morning, and there was no light outside, but a storm. The kind that brought rats out in the trenches. She said nothing as she plunged outside, wearing her usual gear, though her hair was loose, not piled into her hat. She ran to the shed to find a shovel and dashed back. She started digging around a vegetable bed.

He knew how the dirt would be heavy, uncooperative, slipping out the mouth of the shovel just as she raised it clear of the ground. The sound of the shovel landing in the mud, as if it were a cut of meat. She made little progress, gave up on one bed, and moved to another. He saw what she hoped to accomplish: a trench, or trenches, to capture the rain and keep it from flooding. The rain saturated her jacket and hat—a pelting rain that makes a froth of the dirt.

He was out of the cottage and taking the shovel from her hands. His palms burned where his calluses rose, but that no longer mattered. He worked through his runny eyes and nose, the risky footing, and the shiver at the small of his back. The rain, the dirt, Miss Williams pacing about him, or running ahead to sort out the next turn of the trench she wanted; he could smell and feel nothing. It was such easy dirt. The occasional root or stone that emerged was not much to wrestle; he could easily grab at it with his hands and toss it away.

During the war, in France, one might shovel on the line and find the missing, or their limbs. Joints, specifically: elbows, knees, the cut of the waist—material that allowed the body to bend and, therefore, crouch and hide. The shelling was hardest on these connections; the bombs shattered them, or made them to fly off, and sometimes buried them in the process. Digging into the mud freed them, along with swatches of uniforms, loose ordnance, rations and shaving kits, letters, locks of hair from lovers and children. If one dug in an abandoned part of the trench, the mass could come out as bricks, the human refuse like mixing material, the straw that grips onto sediment.

In the first reprisal camp he was sent to as a prisoner of war, at Sedan, one only dug latrines, those reminders of human frailty. But digging latrines was not particularly daunting. Only backbreaking and, if done wrong, predictably foul. They were merely holes beside other holes that were used up, filled in. The lime did not smell, but it burned the skin.

By the time he was made to dig latrines, the lime could only make a minor contribution to the wreckage of his hands. The lime added scales to the other offenses.

Sometime during that autumn at Sedan, he collected a gash to his left middle finger. He noticed the cut, which began in the finger pad and plummeted past the first joint, after coming off a *kommando*, harvesting wheat without gloves. It did not necessarily hurt, but that might have been the time of day, after his bit of bread and tea, when he was so tired he was drained of all sensation. He licked it clean as well as he could, and on the following days he nursed it with the hot water that was meant for his tea, and rags he made from his clothes. In a few days' time, his fingernail had turned black, as though a hole had been gouged all the way through. Then the finger swelled as if it were a lip, or an eye, or any other reasonable part of the body accustomed to bulging after injury.

His other fingers on that hand suffered through the extra burden he put on them to rest the injured finger, although what was suffering for them at this point? His hands were caked over in abuse, their skin like a prison. It cracked and bled in the colder months, as though it meant to restore itself, molt or shed, but failed in the attempt. When he dared look at his hands, he saw not his own appendages but the unguarded nails and knuckles of a heedless beast. Still human, though he no longer knew what human was.

Then the swelling turned blue, a much more virulent shade than in any bruise of his experience, and he thought he saw the deathly cast sweeping toward his palm. At night, as he lay in his bunk, he held his hands in front of him and tried to imagine how he would cope should he lose the finger.

He knew that he would still be able to play his piano; there were plenty of fellows playing with a fingertip sheared off, even some who'd lost a finger down past the knuckle. He'd seen them in pubs, playing tinny machines for tips with hardly a mark on their repertoire. The question was what would missing the finger do to his playing? How would his fingers traverse the keyboard without that one step, or curl; would phantom notes sound out like phantom pain? Would he have to have the same finger removed on the opposite hand, to keep his sense of equilibrium? Would he no longer be able to hear the keys that middle finger once graced; would those notes refuse a different kind of action, from a different kind of hand?

As he pondered all this at night, just before lights out in the prison camp's barracks, the unaffected fingers of the left hand seemed to move, space out from one another, as if the palm were stretching to accommodate a new arrangement. He would have just four digits, like a cloven-hoofed animal, or a bird and its talons. His hands then rushed to his face, as if to blot out the image, but he could not escape it. It followed him even as he kept the hand hidden through meals, marches, work on the fields.

A guard must have decided to take pity on him. Or perhaps there was no pity involved. The efficiency of the unit, the cost of losing another prisoner . . . somehow, the man was inspired to give Sheehan some turpentine and proper bandages. The turpentine turned the finger yellow, but tamped down on the swelling. Another limb salvaged, but for the Germans' purposes.

"You've done enough," she said; her voice through the

rain was real, in the present. They were in her garden. She was the woman who had taken him in, and she had one hand atop his on the shovel and the other beneath his left hand, its middle finger white from rain, the rest pink from exertion; the callouses on the palm facing upward as if they were eyes, blinded.

Their life thereafter may have been soundless, if not for the elements outside and the stories Miss Williams concocted for him. She did so in the late evenings, when she heard him shambling about the cottage, as if he was in search of something he had lost: a smoking kit, a button, or quite possibly his familiars—family or lost friends. On these late nights, from her upstairs bedroom, Miss Williams could hear his pacing, the physical execution no longer so difficult, but still distressed in its timing. Miss Williams would descend the stairs to find Mr. Sheehan in much the same condition as she had originally discovered him, and she would have to allow him to hold fast to her hand, as he had once required, and hear her voice, so he might be sent off to sleep and more tolerable dreaming.

She told him the story of the swan king, an imperious but handsome specimen, who, by day, ruled his flock with his grace and courage. By night, he watched helplessly as his subjects gathered in a body of water that had been forbidden to them. For it was in this lake, where the moonlight multiplied in ways that was said to blind, if not burn, swans discovered their voices. Anyone who has ever heard a swan knows how disagreeable their trumpets can be, but in this lake, swans could sing like gods. And it was for this reason, a much older and wiser swan king had forbidden his charges from venturing into that nameless lake; it also was where men went to capture swans, as they were singing and unaware of their surroundings.

But men did not come to this lake, as far as the swan king could tell; he was left to sulk in the reeds as he saw his subjects defy the word of his ancestors, and yet he longed to sing himself. He envied how the necks of his fellow swans stretched, as if to pluck out the stars, as they exercised what had been dormant in the sunlight. He also kept a keen eye out for the men who were said to be summoned by the voices of swans, to carry them away, to quarter, dress, and eat them. They were men, after all, and their own voices could not make up for the ugliness that they exacted upon nature. But the swan king could never see the men at the lake. They never materialized except, perhaps, as phantoms, dissolving as the sun rose and the swans lifted themselves out of the water to fly to their home waters by sunrise.

The swans went to this lake only under the light of the moon; on nights when the moon was in her repose, they remained with the king. Perhaps it was not safe on those nights, or their song was not possible in the impenetrable din. But on one of these dark nights, the swan king chose to see if he could make use of his own voice; to hear his own song, and to do so without criticism. He had to fly solely on his memory, since there were no landmarks visible without the moonlight; he had never concentrated so intently on the speed and flow of currents, how they dashed and then suspended above the lake shore. He dove into the water that no longer appeared as water. Now the lake appeared as a mirror, offering the familiar, which can be even more dangerous than what seems new and different. The fall of the swan king accelerated beyond his control until he crashed through the surface. Blood and feathers piped up from the lake and then the wind that had been missing from the lake reappeared, to carry feathers and blood back to the flock. And the swan king knew the real reason why his predecessors prohibited swans from this place: he saw it when he emerged onto the other side of the surface, to find his parents, and grandparents, trumpeting in welcome.

The next morning, the body of the swan king, perfect as it ever was, lay in the rushes, and the other swans mourned. Their cries had turned beautiful, like the voices of the clouds.

Four

Miss Williams took particular care to ensure Mr. Sheehan's presence in the cottage not be discovered. Because the Bridgetonne grounds hosted a women's college, the sight of any unfamiliar male in the vicinity, let alone the dreaded Hawkman, could be misconstrued as a presage to an invasion. So Miss Williams set to make Mr. Sheehan familiar, in the form of a servant. She ordered a gardener's boots and uniform, a straw hat to disguise his hair, and gloves to protect the near transparency of his hands. For the windows that did not have curtains, she found cloth in a notions store that she could sew into curtains herself, and hung them at night so the addition to the cottage would not attract attention.

She had not found this immediately necessary, for she thought surely Mr. Sheehan would soon find himself repaired in body and spirit, and would want to press on toward home. She bought for him a train ticket to London, leaving it on his place at the table as she spooned up a pudding she had brought back from the college.

"I understand that you might need to go elsewhere after that," she said. She expected Mr. Sheehan to look up as she addressed him, but instead his focus was on the ticket on the table. He picked up the ticket and placed it in the middle of the table, as if to say it was not adequate in some way.

"If you prefer another destination, I can return it and make an adjustment," Miss Williams said.

She brought the dish to him, and stood over him as he ate the pudding. His sight and mind seemed to have disposed of the subject; perhaps he had mistaken the ticket for a receipt, a piece of note paper, a bit of rubbish, something that had nothing to do with him.

"I would be happy to accompany you somewhere, if that would put you more at ease," Miss Williams said. But still, a casual yet resolved, nothing.

Her other overtures on the subject, whether they involved an offer of a ship's passage, use of an automobile, or a walk to inquire at the General Post Office after an address he might have, were met with similar disinterest. Miss Williams did not know what to make of his listlessness in this regard; whether "home," for him, no longer existed in spirit—so many soldiers lost their parents and siblings to the flu—or whether that home was in some hellish location. Perhaps some imagined humiliation prevented him from returning. It was also possible, she acknowledged to herself, that she was the source of the trouble, in her initial invitation that he accompany her to the cottage. She became wary, then, of speaking even of her own home, and her strange allegiance to it. While she had no immediate wish to return to the States, she knew she might be made to return from whence she came, and would, therefore, have to desert him.

So Miss Williams continued to teach her classes and mark her students' papers; she spoke at luncheons for village women about the books she had written, and the books they were reading. From the fields, she collected foxglove and heather, dog rose and pasque flower; she had come to favor the darker blushes, and acknowledged this was due to the risk she had taken on, in her circumstances. She did not necessarily fret over gossip or even the potential of losing her appointment, and yet she often thought she should check herself in the glass to see whether she should dedicate the time to powdering over the twitch that she detected now on her cheeks and forehead. She was more embarrassed by her concessions to vanity than by the petty morals of her so-called betters. She had nothing to conceal; Mr. Sheehan was so much the child, grateful to be permitted to roam in his own world, wherever it was: in the library, the nursery, or his own mind, in spite of the goblins he harbored in it.

Miss Williams thought she and Mr. Sheehan might have gone on in this manner in perpetuity. But Lord Thorton's son, Christopher, put an end to it. It was not, apparently, what Christopher intended, for he professed no particular interest in, or affection for, Miss Williams. Whatever attention he paid to her was to be expected of the son of the college's bene-factor. He did acknowledge, in his own thoughts, that she was unmarried and therefore available, but she was too educated and opaque in heritage. He was grateful that Miss Williams's flaws were so readily apparent, for otherwise his mother and sisters, and quite possibly his father, would be all too enthusiastic in suggesting he pursue her. He had been at a loss for courtship since returning home from the war, but he did not feel the immediate need for a bride. Indeed, the war had changed his thinking on so many issues, and the thought of obtaining a bride had grown detestable in his mind. He merely came to call on Miss Williams that day, as the spring term concluded, with the idea that he was looking after his father's interests.

He was welcomed to the cottage, as much as any formality was possible, by The Hawkman. Sheehan had waited until deep in the afternoon to risk some work in the garden, but still he heard an "Excuse me, sir?" as he was weeding through sweet peas and cabbages. The straw hat confined the riot of his hair, but not his eyes, and the infamous yellow irises positively glared at Christopher, or so Christopher divined.

"This is Miss Williams's cottage?" Christopher asked.

Mr. Sheehan returned his attention back to his work; it was best to ignore the stranger, as people had ignored him. It made them take their leave.

"Miss Williams?" he asked, again. "Is she here? This is her cottage, isn't it?"

Sheehan could have nodded. He even could have turned about, tugged on his hat, kept the wildness he knew to still be on his face to himself; for it had become engraved there. But he discovered in that minute that he too easily assumed blame, fateful responsibility. It had been the step that he had taken too loudly or assuredly; it was he who had taken too grand of a breath; he who had performed some other imperceptible function that now jeopardized his life and the lives of his compatriots. He was crippled, incapacitated by all possible outcomes: discovery, expulsion, harm to Miss Williams. He could neither cower, nor flee. So he kept to his tasks and listened for the approach of the man's footsteps. They marched up to him plainly, and Sheehan had no choice but to expose himself.

"You, you are?" the next earl of Bridgetonneshire asked, although Sheehan did not recognize him as such. The man had crouched down to meet him, though it was apparent from his clothes that he was not of The Hawkman's, or even Sheehan's, stature.

"You, do you know where Miss Williams is?" the young man now demanded. Sheehan clamped his eyes closed as if shutting down an unwelcome vision.

"Sir, you—I—have you done something with her?"

This accusation Sheehan could not tolerate. He found the motivation to move, to run, around the cottage to the back, where Miss Williams was recovering in the shade. The man followed him and observed how The Hawkman came upon Miss Williams and the gestures he shared with Miss Williams, as though they were portraying, if not speaking, a language. The Hawkman made a circle with his index finger, as if to say that Christopher had found him on the other side of the cottage. But he had not known that Christopher had followed him to where he and Miss Williams now stood. The sight of the young man sent The Hawkman into the cottage, presumably cowering. Christopher took this as a sign that he had no reason to be afraid, though as he walked toward Miss

Williams he felt a lack of resolve, remembering how he had observed this strange man and Miss Williams together.

"Oh, Sir Christopher," he heard Miss Williams say.

Christopher gathered his thoughts for a moment. "Yes," he said, "although no. I do not yet hold the title."

"Then good afternoon, Mr. . . . Christopher," Miss Williams said, and she too paused as if to register his white summer suit, crisp and spotless, while she, like her gardener, was steeped in dirt and cuttings.

"This is a surprise," Miss Williams said, as if to apologize for her appearance.

"Yes, yes it is," Christopher said.

"You have not met Mr. Sheehan," Miss Williams said.

"Mr. Sheehan?" Christopher repeated in disbelief.

"That is his name," Miss Williams said, and she cast an approving look toward where he must have been in the cottage.

"Michael is his Christian name," she said. "We all have one. Why wouldn't he?"

Her remark may have been meant to render Christopher Thorton speechless, but he refused to acknowledge it. He took steps, the authority in their cadence diminished somewhat, toward Miss Williams.

"Is this a formal inspection?" she asked between her laughter.

"There ought to have been one long ago," Christopher said. "Does the college know about this?"

"Just what is there to know?"

"If you insist on being coy," Christopher said, and his marching steps took him to the back door of the cottage, where he let himself in. Miss Williams followed. Mr. Sheehan stood beside the stove, as far from the window as he could manage. He listened as Miss Williams and Christopher spoke about him, even through him, although he could not make out exactly what was being said. Each syllable, though, seemed to undermine the ground on which he stood, so that he came to think of himself as floating, although not in the way a bird floats in the wind. This was a more buoyant, less predictable sensation, as if he were confronting tides and eddies, the patterns of water as dictated by the stars.

"But why must he stay here?" Christopher was asking.

"Where else might he go, I wonder," Miss Williams said, "considering the monster you have made of him?"

"It may be, in your country, permissible to address one's—"

"You said you wanted to be 'rid of him,' so I've done just that. He's no longer your concern."

"It is considered neither wise, nor polite, for a spinster to speak this way to her . . . hosts," he said, relieved to have found the right words, though he regretted them almost instantly.

"But I am not a spinster," Miss Williams interrupted. "Please. That sounds so dreadful. I am an old maid. There is more sympathy in that phrasing. Don't you think?"

"I think I will have to tell my father about this," Christopher concluded.

"I suppose you will," Miss Williams agreed, and Christopher embarked on his next mission: out the door and directly to the estate, as Miss Williams had imagined. For her part, she walked directly to where Mr. Sheehan was now crouching as if buckled over in shock or pain; the pain that comes not from age, nor even illness, but with responsibility of suddenly having to carry again those massive hawk wings.

Miss Williams took him by his shoulders to pry him out of his pose. What she had made sinuous and cooperative over the weeks with Mr. Sheehan had snapped and stiffened in only a few minutes of public exposure. Once she had him standing up straight, she fed into his ear: "I will take care of this, Mr. Sheehan. I promise."

She would repeat other such reassurances as the afternoon pressed on into evening, but Mr. Sheehan was not persuaded. He paced—although it was not true pacing, because his steps were so hesitant, as if he feared laying down some sort of pattern, a rhythm, that could be predicted. He scratched at his arms, his neck, his beard, but again he dissembled—deceptive in the force applied and the movements—as though he only meant to mime the effects of his nerves, not truly act on them. To do so would have produced a sound, abrasive, a friction, and now that his presence in the cottage had been uncovered, he required even more silence, a deeper quiet, to return to his disappearance.

At supper he refused to eat, and he refused to sit with Miss Williams. He stood, instead, in a corner of the kitchen with his back turned, as though he was intent on tunneling into it. But that would have meant poking, digging, shoveling, or any number of actions that could not escape sound, so he merely pressed himself into the wall, as if he could will its movement.

Of course he had always been strange to Miss Williams, but he now seemed intent on consuming himself, or being consumed. Between throwing out her promises and smiling at him as naturally as she could, Miss Williams thought it best if she continue with her regular routine, so that she might set an example. She could not eat her own meal, but made as if she did, amassing the dishes and silverware when she was finished, then washing and drying them. That he was so unmoved by all her activity was unsettling, but never more so when she finally had to leave the kitchen, and he did not follow. He was arrested in the terror he heard—in words, in nature, in the drone of the universe.

"Mr. Sheehan," she said softly as she re-entered the kitchen. It was too early in the evening for the moon to have any effect on the sky or the windows of the cottage. The small kitchen was clotted with night's pitch. She might have used a candle to find her way to him, but Miss Williams thought that even a flicker could frighten Mr. Sheehan. It was best to approach him as though he were invisible.

For at that moment, Miss Williams thought she under-stood why Mr. Sheehan had forsaken his voice. He had perfected a kind of shield around himself by remaining silent. If nothing need leave his person, nothing need enter. Obviously he was shell-shocked, thrown into a psychosis by some indescribable experience. Whatever it had been, it left him less than human, even if he had taken to the new life Miss Williams had provided him. Still, he could not withstand the slightest disturbance. For even a fish must bustle through water, or a rodent scamper through twigs. He took such pains not to be quiet but to perfect his silence: how carefully he turned each faucet, brought in the firewood, or removed a plate from the cabinet. It was as if he wished to leave no evidence that he had ever existed. The world would be deaf to him, and now it would be blind as well. In this way, he would eliminate himself in a manner that would be unnoticeable, undocumented.

"Mr. Sheehan," she repeated, and she sat on the floor beneath the door frame, sensing that Mr. Sheehan would want her to come no further. "I want to tell you something," she said. "And when I'm finished, I will leave you alone. But first, listen." Outside, the first movement of crickets could be detected, the initial preparations that their legs made with their wings and bodies. Some might call it a tuning up, but Miss Williams thought of the creatures as waking up the grass and soil with their practicing. Their song wove its way into the dark cottage as if it were a yarn, loosely knotted by the frogs that had joined in with their hooks and stitching.

"I am listening with you, Mr. Sheehan," Miss Williams said, because she realized that she would need these sounds to wrap The Hawkman in, as a man might use blinders or a blanket to lead a horse or some other petrified animal through fire or wind.

"I know of someone else like you," Miss Williams began, and as she built this story for him, she reminded herself to keep making room for the sounds outside to enter: an owl whose call might darn a hole in the fabric of the darkness or the paws of shrews and hedgehogs against the dew and grasses. These sounds had to be made necessary for Mr. Sheehan again, if he was to rejoin Miss Williams in this life, in the cottage.

"A boy who exiled himself because he thought he had done something wrong, something unmentionable," she said. "I try to think of what it must have been; had he stolen some bread? Had he been careless with a knife or an ax? Someone he loved? I do not know, for he fled his home and ran from his village, over a mountain, through a forest, as far as his legs would carry him. He came upon a meadow after all his wanderings, and there he stayed, convinced he was far enough away from people, even animals. He lived there without speaking a word, not even to God, you know. He forgot his prayers. He was utterly undone from sound, from angels, from what trails along with the movement of the planets. He wanted to disappear into silence.

"And he might have done just that," Miss Williams went on after a pause, during which she had found Mr. Sheehan's eyes in the dark, vibrant with their yellow fear, just as they had been the first night he had spent in the cottage. "He might have remained mute, if not for the wind. The wind tickled at the grasses in the meadow; it assuaged their loneliness, for, without the wind, each reed was silent and could not talk to its brothers and sisters. The grasses, you see, were young, still learning, and they wanted to share what they were learning, to sing out what they knew of the sun and its travels, the moon and its reflection, the habits of the animals that darted and hummed below the boy's notice: snails and mice, grasshoppers, a harmless snake or two. Did you ever notice how the tall grass will suddenly go flat, as if it expects someone to step on it, before a fox or a badger runs through it?"

Here Miss Williams left open a moment for Mr. Sheehan to picture it, and when she began again, she made certain her voice was lighter, so that Mr. Sheehan might imagine his own speech in place of her words—so that he might consider the questions she asked as his own. "Is it the wind that flattens it, or does the grass summon the wind to accomplish this?"

Miss Williams again waited. The words from the frogs and crickets were weightless, limber, with the ability to lift and carry herself and Mr. Sheehan out to a figment of a wood, the mountains and meadow of her own construction. The frogs met each turn in the crickets' song with their breath and fiddling, so that there was an either-or response to Miss Williams's question, a retraction as soon as there was a decision, the matter always open.

"Perhaps it is neither the wind nor the grass that moves," Miss Williams determined, "because, in this meadow, one day, the wind stopped, or the grasses stopped, and now the boy had what he wanted: a vacuum. He had air, and water, and food of some sort, I guess; but he had no beat from his heart, no blood in his ears, no draw on his breathing. And this frightened him, because he did not know if he was alive or dead.

"He did not want to die only to be so securely, unquestionably quiet. He was committed to silence—but only for himself, he realized. Not for the world around him. He thought if he could bring back the sound the grass made, he would know that he was not dead, and that the punishment he had imposed on himself was only for himself. He had not harmed anyone or anything further. So he began to gather the grass, to make it into a kind of instrument, something that could be played by the wind, if not himself. Something that could teach the grass to play itself."

In the space that she could barely see before her in the darkness, Miss Williams's hands reenacted the motions and actions her character made, gathering up swaths of grass and weeds, bundling and knotting them together. She mimicked the intricate pulling apart of individual reeds that was required if the story was to have proper strings for its harp, and the basting together, with ever smaller and thinner root strings, of those reeds so they would be the correct length. Finally, the harp was completed, and so was Miss Williams's private charade, and the boy, she told Mr. Sheehan, climbed a tree that was not so imposing that he could not carry his creation along with him.

"He waited for a string to sound itself, but he heard nothing. He blew on all the strings, but found the same result. Finally he plucked at a string, and then another, until he dug at the instrument because there was still no sound, and he was in a panic. He shook and knocked the harp and, finally, in his despair, he threw it through the branches. He did not care where it landed or what happened to it. But as he was about to jump out of the tree, he heard something—not from the harp, but from right in front of him.

"The wind had not returned to the leaves of the trees, to his skin, to grasses and ponds and rocks, but always it was right there in front of him, with him. For he was the wind. He skipped over the landscape. He heard the moans and whistles that his volume made. He rolled and delighted in the voices of bark and twigs. He could no longer remain silent, even if he had tried, because now he was the wind. He was a part of everything."

Then Miss Williams reached out to Mr. Sheehan from where she sat on the floor, just as she had once risked extending her hand to him that morning off the main road. She did not have to wait long for Mr. Sheehan's long fingers to take her own—to take her hands and raise them to his chest, where he held them in solemn contemplation as he bowed his head, as if the gesture could convey both gratitude and regret, without having to own up to either one.

"We will fix this," she said, "but it will take some doing." She put her hands to his face, her forehead to his. "I will think of something."

WITHIN A WEEK's time, Sheehan found himself the recipient of gifts. They came from a London catalogue Miss Williams could now openly consult, as word of his presence in the cottage had no doubt spread at a lightning pace. She watched as he cautiously relieved her hands of the four white boxes and then just as delicately unpacked their contents. The first held a single-breasted jacket with a one-button closure, and he ceremoniously laid it out on his bed. The second contained a tie with a white day shirt, which he placed atop the jacket. He ran a hand over the length of the clothes with some trepidation, as though he was an undertaker inspecting the wardrobe his newest client was to be buried in. With the third box, the trousers, Miss Williams thought she had gotten through to him: he held them up to his waist. But the shoes he would not remove from the box, as though he quickly confirmed they were either too tight or too fine for him to wear.

"No, no, no," she said, as lightly as she could manage, as he proceeded to return the clothes to their boxes. "We have an important social engagement." And with that bright message, she excused herself from the nursery, so he might dress himself in his first set of new clothes in . . . she could not try to calculate the length of time.

The suit made him walk that much more carefully, as he stepped out of the nursery. Miss Williams smiled her approval, though there was also a good deal of relief in her expression. She said nothing, however, for if she had ever thought of him as her creation, for her to outfit and amend, she realized that had been a frightening and distasteful notion. She returned to her usual composure, vaguely but faithfully cheerful. Sheehan took this as pride in what she accomplished, which made him feel uneasy only because the potential now existed for him to bring her disappointment.

"Lastly, we must do something with your hair," she decided. "Unless you wish to keep it under your hat, even inside." From another box she pulled out a new straw boater, but Sheehan held up his hands, as if to stop her; he was not going to take to it. "Well then, we need not cut your hair, just tidy it up a bit," and then she was gone. When she returned, she had lifted the chair from the kitchen, and brought it into the room. "There," she said, trying to sound authoritative.

"I will not displace a single curl," she said, and she held her hands up to him open, empty, as if to show she would use nothing more than her fingers for the operation ahead. "I keep my promises, don't I? I've been doing fairly well so far, right?"

He bunched his hair with both hands into a ponytail, and made certain it covered his ears.

"Shhhhhhhhh," she said, and he felt her hands upon his head. He could neither hear nor see what was being done to him, as were the circumstances in the last such interrogation he underwent of this nature.

"Hush, hush," she said. He felt something pulling at his

scalp, and he was on his feet. He had jolted up with such force that the chair fell beneath him. There was the sound of an accident, a shelf breaking under the weight of the teapot it held, or an open window forced into closing. Miss Williams hopped backward, her hands in the air as if she was ready to surrender her fingers.

"It's all right, it's all right," she said, her hands still in the air. "If I'm to deal with the knots, there will be some pulling," she said. In her eyes and mouth, she appeared more curious than scared, he told himself, although there was the possibility he was more imposing in the new suit, a more threatening figure. He spied the chair, on its side at his feet, and set it right.

"All right?" she asked as she approached.

He returned to his seat without a glance.

"All right," she said. "Easy, easy," and returned to his hairline, and the gentle tension they shared between them. Her hands moved slowly, assiduously, through sections of his hair. She could have been testing the pages of an old and treasured book as she worked. "Ready?" she asked, and he knew he need not answer, because everyone—the prisoners of war and their guards, the commandants, the Red Cross monitors—knew what was to follow in the camps, when these plagues set in, how they began: the small discomforts that ratcheted themselves up invisibly, at night, during the day, whenever the initiative struck them. A tickle that leapt to prickling, then a searing brand, the body devoured by insects, from the crown on down. In the Holzminden prison camp, there were rumors of men who took kerosene to their scalps to stop the itching. In their sleep, they were consumed by fire, the fumes catching any spark they could react with.

"Steady, steady." Miss Williams's small reassurances came with more irregularity.

In their place was the imperiousness the Germans deployed as they sought out the offending creatures. The Jerrys used four commands in bleak and naked delivery, though their timing was perfect.

"*Setzen Sie sich*," was the first, barked by a guard, so that the "sister"—how the English called the nurse—could go through their necks, collars, cuffs, and lastly, hair. She was pale and seemingly virtuous in her bright uniform, from where they could see her queued up in the infirmary. This being Holzminden, no one was permitted to pace in the queue, shift his weight, crane his neck or engage in any other natural human behavior that would have suited instinctual curiosity about the awaiting interrogation.

"*Nach unten*," the guard continued, and, if a man didn't understand, the sister took her hand to the back of his head, and pushed it downward. It was a trial, to sit so exposed, as if one's neck was suddenly out there for the taking. Sheehan might have felt the hesitancy in the sister's hands, as she lifted, tugged, peeled away his hair, looking for signs of infestation. The sister's hands then scurried through his scalp and something flashed through his skin, from his forehead to his ears to the back of his neck, as if an unusually tight cap was being made to fit head entirely. He lifted his arms out of instinct, to touch what had been placed there. But the guard shouted, "*No Berührung!* No touching!" and the impulse was rescinded.

"Do you understand?" a guard shouted.

"Insecticide," explained Lewis, their sergeant, who stood

beside the chair. "Got it?"

He had to answer, so he grunted a curt "Sir," and was done with it.

"*Fertig! Aufstehen!*" the guard shouted directly at him; then "*Nächste,*" to the man who had cued up behind him. "*Setzen Sie sich,*" the guard repeated, and the process began again.

"Take a deep breath," Miss Williams was saying. From his new jacket, she extracted a handkerchief, and unfolded it so he could see his initials embroidered at its edge. When he did not take it from her, she blotted the cloth on his forehead, the back of his neck, to staunch the sweat. She then restored the fabric into its usual composure, before handing it back to him. "We are not quite finished," she said, or perhaps he thought she said this. The clanging in his head had taken on the rhythm of his pounding heart.

His hair fell far past his shoulders; at Holzminden and the other camps, it had been rigorously maintained at regulation length. The Holzminden bunk sergeant saw to that, even if assigning the rank of "bunk sergeant" was an afterthought. They were all afterthoughts, as the camp had been staged for officers of the British Empire. The enlisted were assigned to living quarters of improvised huts; then they were assigned to serve the officers. Still the sergeant demanded they take pride in their appearances, the bunk as their own sweet soil, their uniforms and comportment the finest of examples. They were to take pride in their tasks: sweeping, dusting, pouring tea, and refreshing glasses, as if they had been born to service.

"Lice," the sergeant informed them after the day's inspection, although Sheehan and his fellows had already figured as much. By 1917, there was hardly a camp where lice had not made an appearance, if the talk among prisoners was to be believed. And Holzminden, they were told by the new arrivals, was the worst camp in all of Germany. It was a miracle they had not been infected elsewhere. Sheehan had been in three different camps. One for each year the war was supposed to end.

"You know what that means," the sergeant said, and he pulled what passed for a mattress from his bunk and dragged it to the hut's center. He threw his bedclothes, all his possessions—his kits and keepsakes, what he had of a wardrobe— atop the mattress.

"Now everything goes," he said. "Everything," he repeated loudly, although the emphasis was not necessary. The men, Sheehan included, immediately followed his example, though they knew such housecleaning to be a futile effort. Still they added their own bedclothes, the spare sets of undershirts and pants given to them by the Red Cross. The guts of packages from homes—jams, cigarettes, books and photographs— spilled to the floor, to be swept up with the rest of the contaminants.

"You'd rather I found it, than one of them," he said, and he'd plunge into any suitcase, duffel bag, or bindle that somehow managed to hang onto its shape through this routing. The sergeant whipped out news clips from baggage, or a stack of playing cards; photographs of girls and mothers from mattresses, and sentenced all to the pile. "Everything of mine means everything of yours," he continued. "Come on, then. Don't be stupid."

The insecticide that had been smeared into Sheehan's hair and skin bristled in his nostrils, tart and antiseptic. He sat on the frame of his bunk, folded over into himself. He was an egg, or one of the bugs they found in the potatoes they were given: locked in a ball and doomed to roll in whatever direction he was prodded. Except Sheehan had no wish to be swept up, poked, set on any course, even if it was escape.

To the pile, Sheehan had already contributed his few letters from home, though the lot of them had been blotted out: first by the Germans, then by the English. Hello, prayers and love, easily committed to memory once filtered, thanks to the censor's pen, of the messy business of being Irish. The thermals and the wool socks his mother had sent were also dispatched. He could hear, in the dreadful quiet, the procession of other men's goods and earnings: cigarettes, empty tins. Books, pencils, caps, falling like grief onto fresh snow; so light as to be soon forgotten, unnoticeable.

They were sequestered in the bunk until lights out, when the Jerrys arrived with carts and wheelbarrows. The conveyances held the new clothes they would wear once they surrendered their current uniforms. The guards had them relinquish socks and gloves; anything that put a layer between their skin and the out-of-doors—pants, too, it turned out; the blue scarf the aviator next to him wore and folded up into his arms each night as if it were a pet or some other beloved object. Once satisfied there was nothing left, the Jerrys had the prisoners load their old clothes and the pile of artifacts onto the vehicles, and march with them to the yard.

For three days they were quarantined, dismissed from their duties, denied the privilege of washing, the duty of eating, except when the Jerrys felt obligated to cater their meals in the bunk. The Jerrys had sealed the bunk by locking the shutters over the windows. They didn't want anyone to see in, apparently, or the men to see out.

They slept on the frames of their bunks the first night, and the sergeant forbade them from speaking from the start. Lest anyone would hear they were infected, he said, though the men exchanged notes, whispered opinions, and alliances. Altman told him there was no use for this confinement, unless the Jerrys meant to halt an outbreak of typhus. For lice it was just melodramatic. Everyone bloody well knew how diseases worked, Altman insisted, and it wasn't like this. He was a tailor from Belfast, the only Brit who would deign to speak to a practically mute Irishman.

No one could tell it was evening when the commandant appeared. The Americans, newly arrived at the camp, christened him "Milwaukee Bill," because he spoke English, Sheehan guessed; though he spoke fretfully, as if he was the recipient of the punishments he pronounced. Now that the Americans had entered the war, the war and his imprisonment might go on forever.

"This day, today, finally, and now," the commandant said, and Sheehan would have complied but for the men around him. Through the shell he had made for himself, he could see the men looking to the sergeant. The sergeant did nothing, and the men maintained at ease.

"And now!" the commandant began again. "Today! We finish with this! *Bei dem erstem Auftrag die Koepfe rasieren,* Medical Officer. Now, I said!"

The sergeant rose, but to address the commandant directly in his ear.

"*Nein!*" the commandant shouted. "Today! *Jetzt!* Now. I

hate *sprechen mit ihnen English, bitte schnappt Sie, schnappt Sie!*" and he stomped his foot, but in a controlled way; that was what scared them. Had he been having a tantrum: they knew how to react to his fits, by shouting their English at him. Now they had nothing to arm themselves with.

"*Achtung. Montieren.* I don't give a damn if you don't understand. *Herren, herren! Herein,*" he called to his own men. With the guards, they were marched through the shuttered camp, back to the steps of the infirmary; the sergeant had asked for a word before they were to assemble inside. But they were kept outside, in the roaring of the night: insects in the surrounding trees, the rye grasses, the birds and their vigils, for they would take the insects at first light. The other prisoners were shuttered in their bunks, banging their tins. Men were forced through the infirmary doors, but never out. The final transformation.

The men issued forth from the infirmary as Sheehan eventually did, bald as if brought naked into a new world. The Germans had changed him from a soldier to a prisoner, from a man to a creature, and now they had executed a branding, in case he ever had the means to change back into a man again. The night air was devilishly bitter, a battering of his ears and scalp that next sought out his extremities; he put his hands to his head, in a permanent state of surrender. Altman in particular was unnerved, something about his religion, he heard the others muttering. Sheehan might have approached him, had he the courage. Their bodies could be next on that pile. He resolved, if not for himself, then for Altman, to never alter his appearance. If he lived to grow out his hair, a beard, his fingers and toes to claws, until he was ape, or bear, or anything more natural than he was.

Vain creatures, they had been revealed to be, and the only cure for such vanity was to parade them through the open air, or so the punishment seemed. Surrounded by a new coterie of guards, the bunk was marched to where they had abandoned all their possessions a few nights earlier, to find them re-configured into a pyramid atop tree stumps and branches. Two guards escorted the sister to the pile, and she emptied the bag where she had collected their clippings and stubble.

The sound of the blaze was mesmerizing, a tremendous gasp and trampling, as if voices were being pressed into the ground. All they had accumulated in their privation and endurance: parts of themselves flattened by fire. For the walls of the pyramid, made with their mattresses, it was a slow collapse, punctuated by the puckering of tin, the crackling of bark and paper. Sheehan thought he had heard worse in the war, though being forced to listen to this was a far crueler score; the anatomy popping, final gasps and pleadings. The lice snapping, as if they were phalange and knuckle.

"Am I hurting you?" Miss Williams asked.

Sheehan had been returned to the cottage.

"Hold your breath if it hurts," she said. She had taken up a comb and was pulling it through his hair, perhaps as a swan's beak sorts through the feathers of her cygnet. On his head, his scalp, he felt warmth, the light that must have been funneling in through the window. He preferred to sense it rather than see it directly, with its noise and riotousness.

"There," she said, resting her hands on his shoulders. Her touch through the jacket was muted through the suit's layers. "You look imminently more handsome. See for yourself."

She stepped away as if to give him a wide berth before the hand mirror she had brought from her bedroom upstairs. He did not take it, and merely stood at attention. "Yes, yes, we'll go now," she said, and he could see that she was unnerved, suddenly, by the prospect of what she had planned. "Let me get my hat, and perhaps a parasol, it is warm, and we don't want any fainting . . ."

Five

Miss Williams explained that they were to walk to the estate of a Lord Thorton, to deliver a book of poetry Miss Williams had inscribed. "Were there an empire of conjurers, of little worlds and fairy places, let it be here in this green soil, in the high sweet grasses the mares sort through for their colts and fillies, in the blue fire stoves with their hushed smoke, an island of pears and other orchards, generous with their shade and hours," she had written; she recited it as they walked arm-in-arm. She prattled on about the birds they saw, the trees that hosted them, the smell of the air. Alfalfa and periwinkle, as she identified it. The sky was a deeply-seeded blue, she said—"a profusion of blooms in sterling." This was how she wrote her poetry, she explained, auditioning lines to hear how they took to the atmosphere. She was not certain about that last one, and asked him to remember it so they would not have to stop for her to write it in her book. She fell slightly behind, as though she had stopped to listen to it again in her mind. She used his arm to pull herself forward.

She fell behind again as they walked on more tenuous surfaces, particularly the polished stone that marked the walkways of the Thorton estate. Sheehan had not imagined she would tire so easily. When she stopped speaking in her trilling voice, he found it more difficult to muster any bravery. If he was not afraid as he had been in the war, it was only because he had so thoroughly drained whatever stores of fearlessness he had once accumulated.

"Listen," she said, nearly breathless, as Lord Thorton's manor came into sight. "Our feet on the rocks, like bells quickly stilled."

He was sorry when the walk was over, for walking, or more properly, marching, had been a respite for him during the war. On marches, there was light, air, and when it rained, fresh water. In the camps, there was the darkness of too many men who no longer knew themselves; they did not know whether to be grateful for being removed from the front, or to be ashamed at having been taken away. There was space and distance on the marches, sometimes exquisitely maintained; in the trenches, there was no such guarantee of movement or privacy, given the mud, vermin, and men that stood at less than an elbow's length. On the marches, there was quiet, the discipline of keeping up. In war there were whispers, men weeping, a raft of speculation breeding in the minds and bodies of his colleagues. Even after his capture, marching through a gauntlet of German towns, he had been more comfortable than he had been in other circumstances, knowing for the next stretch of moments what was expected of him. There were times townspeople spit on their parades, or threw their bed pots in their hair and faces, but they were to keep marching. He could even accept this abuse in principle, as he and the growing cadre of prisoners were anonymous. The fear did not begin until he reached the camp, and the hatred and deprivation would be slow and obvious.

Once incarcerated by the Germans, he found there was more marching to be done, and marching on those *kommandos*, whether to a farm or a factory, was the safest of all. Sentries barked and men sickened; diseases and gangrene could not be outrun. But there was no need to prove loyalties, which is where zealotry and competition begins. There were no rumors, since there was only the marching to get through, even if they were to be taken across France, to build new camps for new prisoners, due to overcrowding in the home-land. On the marches there was no crowding, five-hundred men to a faucet, or a thousand. There was only the next step, and at some points not even the one after it. To place one foot ahead of the other so squarely, with the proper rhythm, was quite enough to accomplish.

He was able to march as a prisoner of war; to walk, to wander as a beggar after the war, because he did not allow himself to think of a destination. But today, with Miss Williams on his arm, he most purposefully had an objective, even if he was not entirely certain as to the nature of their mission.

Miss Williams knocked on the tall door, and they were met by a butler in full dress and polish. The butler escorted them from the atrium to a second floor sitting room and library. Miss Williams thanked the butler, and then asked him if he might show her to a wash room. She was panting, as if only able to collect flat, shallow breaths, and her face showed the red of her exertions.

"I only need to cool down a bit," Miss Williams said to Mr. Sheehan. "You'll be fine, and I will be back in seconds."

When she left the room, he remained standing. He calmed himself by thinking he'd just let this Lord Thorton speak whatever gibberish his mind meted out for the occasion. Then Sheehan saw his own reflection in the ebony finish of a piece of furniture. But it was not merely furniture, though it may have been to His Lordship, his family, and their servants. Sheehan knew it as something else entirely. He might investigate the piece further, to help him compare himself to what he had been, before the war, and what he could be again. He wanted to approach the piece slowly, but rushed ahead, as he found that he could not keep still in its presence.

A Blüthner. Sheehan smiled, and inhaled that smile. German. He would have thought a man such as this lord, or his predecessors, would demand nothing less than a Broadwood, though if they had, it might not have spoken so well of the family's musical acumen. But he also knew the accumulations of an empire are inherently self-aggrandizing, and Sheehan posited there must have been someone in Lord Thorton's lineage who imagined going beyond the whims of a dilettante, so this piano was obtained. How it had survived the war, and Lord Thorton not taking the patriotic action of destroying it, was nothing short of a miracle.

Sheehan did not immediately sit himself at the bench, but

instead randomly put his fingers to keys as he imagined the mechanics he was setting off, the hammers and strings, and the sympathetic notes Blüthners were known for. The Aliquot string. He was more accustomed to the Bechsteins that made their way to Ireland, the Collard & Collards; a Blüthner, such as this, he did not encounter until University. There were none in the music school; they were the instruments of symphonies. He had always been curious about this extra string, its indirect life, at a remove from the keys and yet closer to the source of the music. It was said to produce an effect more tender, romantic even, than other pianos. But what would it do to his beloved Satie, with its silences as integral as the chords and dissonances? Would they be erased, as if silences could be made mute? Would the echo destroy the original?

He sat on the bench, placed the book of poems to his right. His hands fell as if they were still soft and ready, denuded of years and experience, but he mimed the *Gymnopédies* at first. His hands felt small, shrunken at the expanse of the keyboard. Perhaps they had shrunk from misuse: shoveling that kept them in an abbreviated grip; weeding in which his fingers plucked and grabbed, without reaching their full length. Digging, molding, patting, all the actions that transformed fingers from free agents into implements of more immediate elements: earth, water, and wind. Or perhaps he had no fingers, only the slight differentiation of digits that a pawed animal uses to grasp and scratch. His fingers had retracted, and as he played now, in actuality, he felt initially as though he was using his knuckles, with his span so diminished.

The sparse melody, the 1-2, 1-2, came easily enough at his

right hand. The haze in his ears almost parted, but he could not be certain. The agility of his fingers in the left hand was quite rough. But the wrist and arm could make up for some of the handicap, and he listened as the notes took longer to finish than he remembered; whether it was the tantrum of noise in his head, or the truc production of the instrument, he could not determine. It made him stumble, poorly time his transitions. But the keys themselves were still like the prow of a narrowboat, taking in waves and eddies. They just did so at odd intervals as he struggled to make them respond to finger-pads. They felt remote, trussed up in the insults to his skin he could not prevent.

Yet he was on the verge of mastering something; a kind of control, mainly of his expectations. Since he could not assume that he possessed as much control as in his earlier playing, he had to be more solicitous, less demanding of the instrument. He had to find a balance between what he knew of its theoretical possibilities, and what was the actual result of his senses. He hesitated, repeated himself, balked at notes and phrases that struck him as incomplete, unburnished. What he could hear, make out of his performance: he did not know if it was his performance of the room, or his imagination. He was working from memory that he had alternately tried to preserve and discard.

The collar and sleeves crisp against his skin. The length of him cosseted by what had to have been made by hand, attention to detail in every stitch. He was close to being properly outfitted for a performance, although perhaps not a recital. That would have required more confining, formal dress. This was like an afternoon of tea, or a luncheon, a garden party where the flowers and fascinators would draw all the attention. In his new clothes, his still awful hands, he faded into the furniture, and only the notes baited the limits of the room and its decorum. He had not always been a monster: a bird shorn of its repertoire, a reminder of lost souls, and a lost nation. Once he had been a kind of caretaker, one who ferried the moments before sunset as the sun drips down, the deliverer of water in its rebirth from the grip of a dead season. He once plodded the earth to place seedlings in a field. All he would leave behind would be bright, if anonymous.

He had not played at this length since his training, when the NCOs would set him up on Saturday nights in a make-shift concert hall. At 1700 hours, after the last meal, the men were shuffled from the junior mess to the rec compound, where the only instrument available was a doddering old thing with a brassy sound. He discovered on one of these Saturday nights he could play "Je Te Veux" and the "Valse Ballet," if he was not too particular about the piano's defects. The men waltzed with each other, there being no women available to partner. He played it over and over, and at the end of the night, the men, still standing, gave him a bracing round of applause.

He had kept his eyes open so as not to lose himself, but now he could not stop thinking of other pianos, his own at the third studio in the music school; the hours that he spent with her, hours that spilled, dissolved, scattered before they could be measured, like the distance between planets. He could not avoid how his playing had changed, how cautious and timid it had become, unable to capture those moments. But he could revisit when he tried to rescue time, the music like moments when diamonds are first exposed, before their light turns garish. He could find a way to be in the world, after the war and too much time away from the instrument. He could provide each note with the isolation it deserved, before it was grafted onto the next; he could make way for the slip of an instant, so the phrase could be savored, without his crushing it. This was a compromise, between music and vacuum, and he would jeopardize neither if he could keep what his hands and body had suffered away from the instrument. With this pledge, he exhaled; he was finished.

He bowed his head, then glanced away from the keyboard to Miss Williams. Instead he found a crowd, with Miss Williams in front. She was tightly holding the hand of the woman who must have been the lady of the house; behind them were the maids and footmen. The lady of the house looked pale for the season, although he detected a kind of blush pulsing through her neck.

"Please," the lady said. "Continue."

Sheehan stood. The servants, it seemed, retreated with shuffling. Miss Williams took a step toward him and Lady Thorton, if he was correct in his identification, turned around briefly as if to invite the servants back. But it was too late. Sheehan had stepped away. From the bench, then from the other furniture. He thought of grabbing Miss Williams as he bolted, but it was best to leave her out of this. He leapt as if he were a goat or antelope, then ran as he had when sighting a flare, a firebomb, a grenade. His gait accelerated once he was clear of the house, on his way toward the college.

His breath was ragged by the time he reached the cottage, his vision blighted. By the hair that fell over his eyes, the sweat that fell into them; the wind he had to press himself into, to run without stopping. He took to the nursery, secured the door with a chair. The door that he and Miss Williams had made a habit of leaving open, so he might know he was neither confined nor unwelcome here. The curtain he pulled shut, the child's chest of drawers pushed against the door as well. A barricade: all he needed now was to find the room's darkest corner. He stripped off the new clothes; in his pants and undershirt, he waited for reinforcements.

Six

HE NEEDED WATER for his face and throat. He was hot with shame, trembling with anger. He could leave the nursery to sate his thirst, subdue his humiliation, but he could show himself only to Miss Williams. Yet he could not allow her to see him in this state of abject failure. He could have been shot, a fitting consequence for his stupidity. Soldiers lose their vigilance at their own peril, and he had lost his at the Thorton estate, just as he had lost his timing.

He had believed, wrongly or not, that he could hold onto his timing in the trenches through his finger exercises, through his imagining the immediacy of sound to result, action to sound. The music his hands made had always been immediate, an indivisible logic that drove his mind, fingers, the keyboard, pedals, hammers, and strings, as if all acted in concert, by instinct. This was what Sheehan had striven for as a player, a flow and current in his playing that he recognized he could very possibly lose without practice. But if he kept a hold on the way he had learned to perceive cause and effect through the ruminations of his fingers, through music, then he might get through this war, and go back to his instrument unfettered. With this in mind, he gladly took to the regimen of arching a single finger, holding it steady, applying pressure from the tip and then squeezing back against it in an instant. Shooting: shooting would preserve his sense of order, of direction. The shooting drills made sense to him in training, simultaneous time, reaction for action, a sinuous chain of sound and movement: an arrangement.

But war also requires a certain kind of patience he hadn't anticipated, like the patience called for in the launching of a grenade. In the launching of a grenade, there was a moment of waiting—of praying as if God had taken His glance away and shifted it toward someone else, if not the enemy—until the device landed, so one could be sure it landed on its nose and detonated. When the rifle delivered its kick to his side and shoulder, he had to learn how to wait for the jabbing sensation to fall in his shoulder so pain would not interfere with reloading of the weapon. These vigils, which he thought he could measure, would have to be inserted, worried over, calculated with a ferocious rigor because one measure off could mean the difference between survival or death. But then came the harrowing interludes between light and darkness in the trench, the light that did not hold to any schedule but to its own indecipherable purpose. Flood and flare, a surge or a disturbing trickle, light ruled a soldier's movements, his decisions and gambits.

The training officers warned them: their first firefights would be chaos. Yet each man finds his own way of coping. Look out for yourself and your fellows, Sheehan and his unit were told. Look elsewhere, and you may not live to tell about it. Sheehan thought he might cope by orchestrating the chaos, at least to his own mind: he would build out of the chaos a chorus of light and thunder, light and percussion. He knew light announces sound, and thought war could not reveal too much more in this regard. He knew lightening announces thunder, and the gas lamp and taper escorted that sound of air surrendering to fire, the sound the candle made, like sating a thirst or drawing a breath, within its wooden chamber. A parade of light and sound he would make of the firefights.

His father, on candlebox rounds, hadn't prepared him for anything more than a lost vocation, it turned out. But Da did prime him for these principles of sight and feeling; he applied them to buck up young Michael against stage fright. "They'll see you first, sitting out on the stage with all the other students," Edmund had said, "nothing you can do to stop that. Once they've got a look at your mug, what more is there to worry over? Play your heart out."

In a firefight the object was not to be seen, but to make one's impact felt. To affect the advantages of darkness while exercising the privileges of light. To no longer count in such docile measurements but be prepared for weights and tonnage, regiments and battalions: the only signatures of time he would have at his disposal, but only in the sense of time lost, time squandered, time given over to the enemy's advantage because there was no time for frivolous counting, unless one was prepared to be liable for more carnage, more destruction.

Sheehan entered his first firefight with more of a sense of what not to do than any particular reaction he should have, or action he might take in response. He was not surprised by the demand the light from the shells made on his eyes, nor the convulsive dialogue between trenches that followed. But the persistence of both light and sound together, the sound slapping over light so that it became impossible to ferret through which flash of light was responsible for which explosion: that unnerved him, because it made all the calculations he had practiced irrelevant. Smoke and cordite poured through the light, prolonged their heat and scent as if aided by the force of the explosions. Everything was echo and source, then echo without source, the elements pulled apart and yet not independent. The light continued to insist on seizing distinguishable moments, plumes of smoke, the bewildering whiffs of cordite: they leapt from nostrils to behind the eyes as if a frigid wind meant to blind a man, though the odor dispelled as soon as one thought he might identify it. The light froze soldiers in action so Sheehan could not be sure if grenades had been tossed or shots successfully fired. The man that was hit—the men—had they been taken away, or would he find them underfoot? The sounds that landed together forced earthen walls into collapse, remade trees on the battlefield into torches, their trunks torn open, their branches a scaffold for fire.

Was it the light that did this, or the collusion of light and sound—not sound, but petulant, unschooled noise—with a velocity that had been armored and sharpened so that when it made contact, it ruptured, gashed and mangled. There was a sound as metal rent its way through tissue, like the amplified landing of a butcher's knife. In the slaughter and confusion, Sheehan aimed his Lee-Enfield where he could see bursts of white dust coming from the opposite trench—enemy fire. More light, and the object was to snuff it, quickly, as if sweeping away candles like they were dominoes refusing to yield to their comrades.

In that first firefight the batches of light and sound seared Sheehan's retinas and battered at his eardrums. Against his legs he felt weight falling—initially at the ankles, then up to his knees. The weight kept piling on, and he kicked it aside—when he could. He was sinking below it, and he would have to climb atop it if he were to keep his focus on the bursts of white dust from the other side, the reports of German rifles amid the intervals of blinding light and deafening noise. He found he had to hunch lower, shorten his posture, to keep his aim without getting himself grazed or worse; as though the bottom of the trench was rising. At sunrise, as the parapet of the opposite trench became visible, the shooting halted, and Sheehan and the other men were ordered to shovel out the mess. And there, they discovered their colleagues.

Gorham, the shopkeeper's son, was the first Sheehan recognized. Face down, mud in his eyes and nostrils, his neck elongated at an impossible angle. Had he died of a broken neck from the fall, or was a bullet responsible? The fabric of his uniform had been dug away into an arrangement like the rays of the sun, as a child might depict them. Perhaps Gorham had turned around to look at something, and this was how he was hit, but what could he have been looking for? There was nothing to see but one's own men, and less than that, in the slew and punctuation of the firelight. The blood from the point of impact to his uniform was sticky, black, probably because of the cold. The chill and dampness accentuated the darkness in everything.

After Gorham, they would find Arden, the dairy man's son; Collins; Owens; Douglas; Rogers; the Scotsmen, Ross and Thomson; Armstrong and Gardener—they were musicians, a violinist and a coronet player. They had studied at Manchester before him. As they continued digging, Sheehan's hands blistered inside his gloves at the dorsal muscle between index finger and thumb, and the faces appeared more furiously clotted over with mud and trampling, though no less recognizable. Palmer, the footman in service. Hughes the miner. They died in the same way, if not by the same cause: they slumped upon impact of some ordnance, whether it was inside or beside them. How they flailed before falling, their arms and torsos arrayed in the contortions of acrobats: this would be the only inquiry made to distinguish them, if any inquiry was made at all.

Rooted beneath the pair were men Sheehan could not identify; since he had never seen their faces, he could not imagine how death might have distorted their natural features. He knew them solely by how their mouths were torqued open. It chilled Sheehan to look upon their eyes, and yet those eyes took on the appearance of being feverish. Eleven men they counted, and the cause of their demise could have been anything. Had he known them, Sheehan thought, he'd be able to separate those who succumbed to the broiling churn of shrapnel through their insides from those who surrendered to the accrual of filth they had to eat and breathe, or the crush of boots and panic. Had he known them, he'd be able to distinguish those who were the kind to attempt speech at their deaths, and those who embraced their fate with a wink, or a kiss. But as it was, they were all in a state of slight awe, speechless and befuddled, as if they were in the midst of deciding whether they were the instigator or the brunt of some grand trick.

There were men they could not immediately retrieve because of the tangle of their limbs and would have to wait until afternoon. By then maggots had consumed their cheeks and hollowed out their chests. Sheehan looked at the cratered landscape of his palms and thought there had to be something else in the mud, with a far greater appetite, to do what had been done to his own flesh and men.

Over the days that followed, there were replacements for the men who ran the big guns at the parapets, and those that fed them ordnance; there were replacements for the men who cooked the meals, sewed the wounds, oiled the rifles; there were replacements for those who carried clipboards and counted the men, the weapons, the stores of bully beef and biscuits. But there would never be enough men who counted men, or men who maintained the ammunition, or those who carried away the dead, or patched up the near-dead; there would never be enough men to replace those who had been on watch. There would only be jobs to fill, and numbers, not men, to fill them; Sheehan understood this as the line felt looser at every evening assembly. The new men had been trained in the same manner as Sheehan's regiment, in mud and marshes, in uniforms and boots made heavier by water, in the pulling and pushing, tugging and shouldering, in the bearing of their fellow men and equipment until they moved with the same studious detail as a train of pack animals. But they were new men, and, although they were trusted implicitly by their more seasoned compatriots, their fresh eyes and bright complexions did not appear to possess the same alacrity and confidence as the fallen men had displayed, to hear the stories of those men circulating about the trenches, like high water in untested channels. For Sheehan, as he was staking out a position where he could sharpen his aim on those exploding bits of dust, the feeling was paradoxical, as though he had been set down to play at a keyboard made softer by moisture, yet the attending mechanisms, the strings, had been pulled tighter.

The first flash of each firefight was a gust of fluorescence. Long after it had receded and was replaced by other flashes, the noise of explosions, and a gamy, beefy scent like what he remembered from Summer-hill Dublin, the echoes of that light resounded against his eyelids. If he looked to his fellows, he saw their faces framed by a gloaming redness. Across No Man's Land, the fire and light surged not from the trench, but from what seemed to have been a smelter of ore engaged in a blistering escape. If Sheehan could not pick out the cooler bursts of whiteness that were his targets, he would crouch down, shake his head, and will himself not to see the streaks and pulses blasting through his vision. But concealing himself in the darkest reaches of the trench only accentuated the light that popped around his ears and taunted him at the eyes.

Once Sheehan caught the image of a hand above his head: was it a flesh-and-blood appendage, still wedded to its bearer's arm and body, or was it another shadow made by the light, a shadow and its report in memory. Sheehan saw the fingers on a trigger, then the pistol released, the fingers bloodied, the hand immediately vaporized, as if it had never existed. A face and that same face seconds later, converted by terror and pain, and in the next flash, death had taken it over as the face detached from its neck and left a distance there, one not thought capable of existing. The light broke down movements, inserted blackness into reflexes, drowned everything in a spasmodic wash that wrung the logic of what one saw progressing before him.

Somewhere in the division of seconds and instances, Sheehan heard orders shouted: "Get up, get up, keep on, keep at it."

Sheehan could put neither a date nor number on the firefight that consumed his hearing. He could not place which rotation it was when the sound came, how its light might have hollowed out the trench before conveying the sound; the light had to hollow out the trench, for otherwise the sound would not have been so effective. A sound re-doubled, layer upon layer of vibration and damage, a sound that was more properly noise, but noise could not describe its volume and impact, its fatal musicality. The sound and noise shoved through his ears, into his other organs. He was knocked off his haunches, displaced by its pitch. Voices, orders, balance: he tried but could not get back on his feet. There was a ringing in his ears, though the sound persisted. It was bottomless, and did not echo. It shook the interior of his hearing. He had hardly a moment before the sound pushed its way out, from his ears to his throat and out of his mouth. He vomited. His mouth tasted hot. Mottled. He buckled over and clenched his jaw. But it was too late. Uniforms, chunks, and swaths: the identification said Peterson, Lansdowne, Waterson, the Jew. They had gotten on, the Jew and Sheehan, the Irishman. Sheehan looked for the man whose uniform switched about him like rags, but he could not find him. Sheehan was on his knees again, in his own sick, in guts and dankness. The orders came again: "Stand up to it men! Don't let up, don't let up."

Sheehan grabbed at the grenade on his belt and lobbed it over the front of the trench. The cloth streamer on the grenade spun out like a flag behind it, and Sheehan could be assured the device would hit its mark and explode. But there was no explosion, or could he not hear it—his mouth tasted dirt that fell like hail around him. He spit his lips clean but just as soon tasted what must have been his own stomach lining, an acidic curdling. He watched for the cloth streamer that would tell him that his grenade had landed on its belly, on the wood planks atop the opposite trench; the Jerrys were sure to throw the thing back at him, and he might be killed or maimed by his own instrument. Dirt rose again, in fountains and gullies, and he was on his knees and again retching. "On your feet man!" someone shouted, and Sheehan was up like a rabbit, quick and startled, but unable to maintain equilibrium. From where his throat connected to his chest a cough unrolled in a blunt motion, and the infernal flavor of his own decay pushed against his teeth. He was vomiting again. He could not stop it.

"Get out of here, man," Sheehan heard, and arms were suddenly around him from behind, under his armpits. The pandemonium of limbs pulled away from him, and while the light and its echoes pursued his vision, the sound lessened but did not quite fade. It wed itself to the beat of his heart, each intake of air he could trace. A pain in his head became noticeable; it seemed to stopper up the sound, forcing it deeper into the ear canal, to his skull's dead center. He was dragged away from the front, but only temporarily. A sergeant held a number of fingers in front of Sheehan's face and then asked him something. The only question Sheehan could hear issuing from the officer's lips was the same blasted hum that had overtaken his ears moments earlier. Yet it was clear the sergeant held four fingers up on one hand, and three on the other. Sheehan did the same and the sergeant smacked him on the head. He yelled something too, Sheehan couldn't make it out, but he got the message as he was shoved in the direction of the fighting. Someone put a rifle—not his own—in his hands.

The white bursts from the enemy line kept Sheehan occupied, as they were no longer presenting themselves cohesively. They darted and dropped when they were not climbing though there was nowhere for them to climb at the front of the line. Sheehan fired; each time he fired, the noise added a nail into whatever was choking off sound in his ears. He would have thought by morning he'd be completely deaf, if not for the jagged cries of men calling for help, for their mothers, for water as their fluids and organs flooded over their skins and uniforms; those did not subside, even to his suffocating eardrums. They struck Sheehan as clear and frenzied as if they were aimed at him personally, with no space between himself and the dying.

But men did not pile up on his feet as they had during the last firefight, and a notion grew within him, as he fired and re-loaded and his hands blackened with gunpowder and the cries of the men climbed in pitch and shrillness, that he had been left by his fellows to fight on the line solo, that he was the last uninjured man standing between the Jerrys and all of Europe, and he would have to carry on without orders. He did not know what to anticipate once the dawn came and laid its bright shroud on the battlefield, but he would not allow himself to consider the possibility of sleep, of shutting his eyes. Was he to hold the trench forever or until his unit's return? How would he recognize his unit, since its composition had been wholly swapped or killed? Would it make a difference which unit he fought with, just as long as he shot from this position when he was not ducking to cough, or heave, expectorate the last of his fluids from his mouth?

For all the fretting he had done over his hands, maintaining their pliancy, the muscle memory that connected notes and chords to reach and fingertips, he had not given a thought to his ears—and he was paying for it now, in sweats and dizziness. In the plumes he coughed out, onto his uniform, his boots, whatever throttled and gagged beneath him, on the ground. He had made the mistake of assuming his ears would survive what might scar his hands, so long as he kept his head down, his steel on. Even with the swirl of the firefight engulfing him, Sheehan could not conceive of even noise causing such damage, yet the destruction was all around him, voices that were immensely large and inflamed snapping at him in one moment, reduced to a chilly reticence the next. He could not conceive of the potential for damage because sound was so diffused as to be a spray; it was ambiance and obstacle, what fell through bones and membranes. But those obstacles had deserted him on the battlefield and what routed through his ears now was raw and merciless, the passions of lost men intent on pillaging what they wanted but could not have, because they were at war and were being made to desire what could not be held, molded, or forced into subjugation: the beating, bloodthirsty hearts of other men.

With all obstacles removed, from the trees split by mortars to the intricate anatomy of his own hearing scorched to coals and embers, Sheehan knew he would have to rearrange what he understood about noise and sound, and the blows struck between these categories. He would have to rethink everything he thought light was capable of touching and transforming, and the purpose of any sound that came after. Certainly it would not be to confirm the time of day, or announce a job well done, or to entertain, or distract, or any of the actions his hands had once been capable of, if they were ever to be capable again. Sound was only for war, as light was only for war, as were trees and flesh and dirt and any earthly material that remained in steady supply of opposing groups of soldiers, himself against the Germans, the English against him. If he was going to be deafened, by the Jerrys, by his own compatriots, he would never stop firing, supplies and the exposure of daylight be damned.

He would fire until his fingers were wedded to the trigger, until the only sound they could make was the click of the mechanisms, ignition to gunpowder to shell. He'd keep firing even when the sergeant tried to grab his rifle and shouted something Sheehan could not make out for all the fury and might the sergeant unloaded in Sheehan's direction. He'd wrestle the sergeant for the rifle as the sergeant yelled, "Cease fire," and repeated it endlessly until another man corralled Sheehan by the waist and lifted him up as though he was so much rubbish, the bales and mounds of it they threw out of the trench, hoping it would land on the Germans. "Cease fire!" the sergeant may have said, or "Clean yourself up, man," for all that Sheehan could dig out from his ears and the look of the sergeant, disgusted by the vomit, if not the blood, on Sheehan's uniform. "Get a hold of yourself, or we'll send you up for a court's martial," the sergeant said as the other man released Sheehan and stood at attention. "You bloody stink, you Bog Trotter," the sergeant concluded upon leaving with the corporal obviously assigned to protect him. Sheehan spat after the pair in the mud before collapsing into it.

From the bodies that could not be salvaged with gauze and medicines, Sheehan found a bottle of the dressing that, though opened, still had the look of sterility about its contents. During the day he pulled out strips of the dressing and worked them between his fingers until the material resembled a plug, a ball of cotton to barricade his ears against the next assault.

At night the light came again, and the sound that chased it, and Sheehan, his hearing no less rattled from the explosions the night before, found himself debating the plugs' effectiveness. Until he saw blood shoot out from the chest of the man next to him.

Sheehan did not know the man. He must have been a replacement, though he could not find any rank insignia, no name or other identifying information readily on him. The man was slumping, the fount of his blood weakening, and Sheehan caught the man before he could hit the ground. The man's blood quickly smeared over Sheehan's arm, the one holding him at the back; he was bleeding clear through the chest to the spine. A bullet might very well have done this, but for the volume and the persistence of the blood; Sheehan

97

thought it must have been shrapnel that twisted and drilled clear through his heart. He lay the man down beneath the grooves and shifting of the bullets, and tried to watch the man speak, but through the flashes of light, he could hear nothing, and discern only the ghoulish hold the light imposed on sense and movement. For this man, there would be no final words.

Sheehan knew nothing of the man's life but could predict how his death would play out that night. The public spectacle the body would become, with everyone trying to ignore it; they had to ignore it, if they were going to keep themselves going. They had to ignore the neglect, the smell, and the rot, and possibly the maggots—though the flies would come in the night, they always did—if they weren't going to get their brains blown out. By the first morning's light, people would try not to watch as the ambulance man tried to retrieve him, but he'd be stiff as a pallet and would weigh as much as unexploded ordnance, and they'd struggle with the body like a couple of drunkards getting their man home. Then they'd stack him up in a pile of other corpses as if his body was now so much timber, and it would be left out for inspection, perhaps a warning to the men as they circulated through from billets to battlefield and back out again. Next, the race was on, to sort him out from all the others, find out where he came from and who was to be notified though it was all a formalized transaction. The clerks typed names into boxes and stamped the signatures of commanding officers at the bottom. Sheehan knew this because he had heard other men tell of it. They spoke of it when they thought they had made a friend in their unit; in impolitic whispers, they'd beg the newly saddled friend to provide more than the curt form when their survivors were to be alerted, so somehow someone would tell a better story of how they met their end. At worst there'd be someone to light a wick of truth attached to the official notification: that they died with their courage intact, or their intestines, and had not fouled themselves upon death.

With the plugs in his ears Sheehan remained fully aware of each explosion, but their sounds fell at his shoulders as if their impact was delayed, shortened before they could tear their way through his concentration. Now it was the light that most affected his perception of the battlefield, what he could separate from other constituents. A pair of eyes for another pair, uniforms torn from limbs, mud that flicked around skin, teeth, fingernails, foreheads. The shells were unceasing, and their reverberations shifted from the bodies and air around Sheehan to his sternum. His arms became useless, immune to how he might have directed them. The light was renewed in its brilliance, another shell launched, and, in the flash, Sheehan could not catch the sergeant, blood on one side of his neck, pumping out in distinct globules. The sergeant's wounds would be blocked soon enough with trench beetles and worms, come to feast on his skin.

To be covered in insects—he dreamed as much, in the daylight after the fighting, or perhaps on another day. He was not keeping track. He was not counting. He dreamed that if he were covered in insects, with their skeletons outside their bodies, his limbs would be transformed into castanets. Chittering, clattering, percussive yet reedy, the insects' hearts beating against their string-like skeletons, a grand mobile piano, glittering in the distance. As a child he watched too intently at his hands as he was learning; his hands were too soon to jump to the next measure, the next note. His teacher thought it rushed his playing. So he had Michael, the boy, close his eyes when practicing, so he would have to complete each section firmly and roundly before feeling his way to the next; to play like a civilized man, the teacher said, and not a child trying to get through his Hanons.

He could live with that, being covered with insects or waiting for this metamorphosis. He would wait for sounds to take over his lungs, his blood and bile, and when he had to be quiet, he would be merely a resting instrument, and be wary not to have the wind influence the voices he had within him. It was preferable to be this way, to dream this way, than to play as if he was a dead leaf in the trench, looking for traction. It was preferable to be the languid sound of a summer evening than to be a dead leaf in a pile of other dead leaves, with nothing to hold onto.

He knew it was a dream because he was awakened by the sergeant, a replacement for the first one, or the second one, or the back-up who stayed behind at the billets. The new sergeant was kicking Sheehan in the ribs. The new sergeant was shouting something as Sheehan hopped to his feet and saluted. He yanked the gauze out of Sheehan's ears and clocked him on the temples.

"Damn Irish," the new sergeant said, "and God damn their musicians."

Unlike the other men who found themselves deluged by the spins once their hearing had been torpedoed, Sheehan found himself adept enough at maintaining his balance. He was steady enough on his feet that he was rotated off the line for training with another unit, a special detachment. They practiced jumping and crouching, hanging on during the furious tailspins that would characterize No Man's Land and their attempts to cross it. It would feel as though one was being throttled against the horizon, the training officers promised; one must not merely stay low, but sprint and parry through the bodies and barbed wire; and one must do so not like some rodent. Patience again was required; no scampering or darting. That's the way to get lost, become a target, tumbling this way and that. Stay cool, stay fast, collect one's thoughts to see a clear stratagem through, then dive into the labyrinth and into the trench. Take on those Jerrys on our terms: man-to-man, hand-to-hand, grappling and close combat.

Into the German trenches Sheehan fled. Found the German men before he was found himself. If he could not find a complete German to grapple with through the sound and the light, he would find some part of a German and hoist it on a bayonet, fling it over as if it was rubbish. Sabotage their burials. Steal the Jerrys' weapons, break the barrels, fill them with dirt. Take the uniforms from the dead, wrench the sleeves off arms, trousers off legs, scoop up the boots, helmets, and even the rings blasted off fingers. Anything that could be salvaged. It was a scavenger mission. Or it would turn out to be. Because if the Jerrys could anticipate the incursion into their trench, if they could play dead or act dumb long enough and fool the Tommys, lure them into a false confidence about picking off enemy soldiers like an afternoon's shopping, only to spring awake and alive with all barrels blasting, it would mean more than death for the invading British. It would mean the beginning of recriminations, the death of British careers in intelligence. Not that the shock troops would ever know who or what led or misled them, what kind of punishment would be meted out, or if there had been any bother to assert discipline against the higher ups. They'd be dead, or near dead, begging for the enemy to finish them off. But if they lived, if they survived their own rotten intelligence and the foresight of the German officers and came out of the campaign whole and in great humor, it would be for the British officers to sweep in later and grab all the congratulations. It would be for the officers to run over that trench like moles and opossums as they were hailed by the Allies for their victory, a major coup despite the trap that the Jerrys had set up for them.

The Jerrys screamed on that first ambush. The third night, Yates and Johnson were gone. A farmer from Dorset, Reeves, was brought in to replace them. The Jerrys screamed but it was all nonsense and language to Sheehan. They screamed even as they gritted their teeth and ratcheted their blue eyes wide open. They all had blue eyes, or it was the reflection of the grease they had put on their faces to make themselves look angrier, wilder, less in control of their faculties. But there was as much white and red on their Jerry faces as Sheehan wore on his own. White like the fear that overtook the red: fury, ore, and blood. The Jerrys' necks bulged and their arms flailed when they were shot. They pissed themselves, into the trench that became a canal, a sunken causeway of horrid outcomes. Sheehan had to slump into the disgusting silt when he ran out of ammo during one raid. He had to play a corpse himself, be as still as a stone against cold-cocked necks and faces with the butt of his rifle warm beside him. If anything moved in that pile, he would beat it senseless. He had not kept count of the men he had killed, but as long as they were men, it did not matter. So long as they were not boys, though German boys were outfitted the same as he was and were likely his equal in soldiering.

He was coming to prefer these attacks over stewing in the mud in the trenches, breathing from the wounds in the dirt. If he kept moving, he thought, he might outrun the sky as it opened up above him before it plunged headlong into his ears, his throat. He volunteered for subsequent assignments, every other night, then every night. He did not know which night it was when they lost Reeves and the rest. He only knew he did not vomit, though he had been plunged face-first into the sluice, with bits of uniform and tobacco, the excrement of rodents, their scales and fur separated. He did not vomit though they lost Reeves and the rest. The following nights, he fought with men he did not know in the least, and found that he preferred that the most.

In the trench, he could feel the earth buckle and slant beneath his feet; his vision askew and the men pirouetting around him. But once ordered out of the trench, he could fly over No Man's Land faster than the Jerrys could load their ammunition, and he made it through each time as though he were meant for traveling such fraught distances. A rat with wings, he was, at ease in the piles of other men's leavings he found for landing. Digits, torsos, pairs of feet: he could tell they were pairs by how precisely the footwear had been issued. A foot came to his face; he felt something wet at his eye. He raised a hand to the wound and saw what was below him, a ghastly figure slopping, drowning, as it tried to kick him again. He let go of his own bleeding, grabbed an ankle, wrestled it still in the muck, and then the light began. From his side. He held onto the drowning man's ankle though he knew what was coming: the sound and confusion. He held onto his trophy, so his valor would be proven, when his body was retrieved by his own side. Now his own side was trying to kill him. His unit must have given up on him. Given him up for lost. Or dead. Or he was the enemy, disloyal to the crown. He held his breath, put a second hand to the man thrashing beneath him and crouched deeper into the pit. He tasted slickness and alloys disintegrating, and the sound fell. It filled his nose, jutted out of the bloody place on his face. The ankle he gripped between his two hands went limp, like a chicken with a broken neck. He had to begin counting, now, if he was to get out with his prize. He had to get out before the next round of shelling. He had to get out before the light began again.

The distance between events was seconds, then moments less than seconds. Then no distance at all, light and sound concussed into each other, which meant there was no escaping, which meant discovery and imprisonment, discovery and death. If he could be tied to the manual execution of one of the Germans; if he did not let go of the dead man's ankle. He could not get his hand off the ankle, he could not find the distance between light and sound, and if he did—if the light briefly showed a way out of the trench, then the sound crushed it. And yet this lack of distance was like music, hands atop the sounds, fingertips manipulating scales, wrists in control, gathering chords and rhythms, sorting them out, into measures and melody. In the mire, between explosions of light and sound together, inseparable, a disastrous kind of miracle, Sheehan slipped away from his kill and considered the taste it swabbed throughout his mouth, since his other senses were dead to him, at least temporarily. Too dark or too bright to see, too uproarious to hear, but with a taste of blood in his nose, and the salt he had absorbed from the dead man's flesh—the taste of death transferred—this was the only empathy Sheehan had left in him. The shells were British; his own men were firing upon him.

He could die like this, suspected of treason, hiding out when he had indeed been savage in his duties. Or he could die a hero, as his father predicted; so much for the doors that would be open to him, Irish no more to the masters and mistresses doing the hiring at music schools, the conductors at orchestras, benefactors seeking to have their wealth and generosity made immortal through tidy, even acquisitive compositions. Or he could do something about it, something about everything: to remove the muck on his person, though seeped through his clothing. He could strip to his undershirt, scythe it clean with the blade of his bayonet, turn it inside out, find the remaining brightness of the shirt, and wave the slop of white flag he had retrieved from his own body. He could surrender to his own people, stop the shelling; he had the power. Now it was a matter of ability. Stop the war for only as long as it would take him to get out of it, and then return to the spot where he would be most comfortable with the killing.

HIS TIMING SACRIFICED, his hearing surrendered, Sheehan could still say he had hung onto his vigilance through the stalemate that was the front at Laventie. Even with the movements of the shock troops, there was no country worth conquering on the French border; the Jerrys had replacements too. For every night Sheehan and the others dove into enemy territory, there were battalions of new Jerrys in reserve, ready, if not anxious, to be deployed to re-take the feet and inches their dead comrades had just occupied. In the trenches, soldiers wrestled over mounds of dirt, walls and exits. On No Man's Land they tussled over holes and pock-marks, and a crater that was a world unto itself. Grappling to the death, for they had certainly already killed the dirt by tunneling through it, bombing it, exercising the unwitting impulse to re-arrange, to destroy what they could not have outright. The men blasted shells, which wrenched the holes in the ground; the men filled the holes with the bodies of their enemies, as they aimed and fired at look-outs, turrets, and sometimes just in a vacant, general direction. The clouds above filled the holes with water. Unexploded ordnance turned the holes rancid. And over these cisterns, through channels attempted and culverts abandoned, Sheehan's regiment and the Germans had been tangling all summer.

Until the silence that landed over all of them.

It was an unsettling, confounding silence. But it did not mean a truce, Sheehan could immediately tell, because of how steep of a silence it was, sudden and even careless. The battalion, having had no communications to verify a truce, he thought he could hear the intentions of the enemy ringing through it, as if a crack in a piano's soundboard, the felt pulled off its hammers. Or his ears, still rattled from the shells, had been clouding his hearing, and the quiet was actually the noise that pulsed through his chaotic eardrums. But the other men said they could detect no speech from the opposite trenches, no cheering or boasting of superior positions or rations. The sky no longer opened up in flashes to demand the lives of men, as if it were a furnace. And men no longer flung themselves into the light and called it lucky when they came out as something other than rag dolls. The hours became loose, if not unguarded.

Men roved about, stepping out to hunt rabbits. They played cards and re-read from their letters home, first to themselves, then to the men who didn't have any. On the third day, they retrieved their dead from No Man's Land and buried them. On the fourth, they hurled the rubbish into the Jerry's trench. But still no response. On the fifth, the officers decided the silence warranted investigation. It was mid-July, and the flies were into everything: their eyes, ears, wounds; Sheehan thought he could hear them, especially. They looked like green bottles packed with soot. The sky was a pale, almost white blue, as if hot metal was being poured over them.

"Private!" an unfamiliar voice shouted from behind his head. "Sheehan, Michael?"

Sheehan turned to see an unfamiliar captain standing before him. He saluted, and the captain started talking at him, quickly. The captain's voice occasionally toppled through the racket in Sheehan's ears but too often it did not, and Sheehan felt as though he was being made to listen through a pair of shells from the beach, mourning their detachment from the ocean.

"Come with me, Private," the captain directed, and Sheehan followed him through the trenches named for places back home—their home, not his—Cheltenham Road, Eton Road, North and South Tilleroy—to the officers' billets. Because it was summer, the officers held fans, and hid the gin they drank in a fine porcelain tea service. Only the platoon's lieutenant was not among the drinkers. He was standing, and the captain, whose name was Jones, approached the lieutenant within a breath of his face.

"You didn't have the balls to pick one of your own men, so I have," Captain Jones said. "Why not this one?"

"You mean Beethoven here?"

"Why not?"

"He's got sharp eyes, and he's fast enough on his feet. From the shock troops, though the kickback on the rifle doesn't always suit him," Lieutenant Eason said. Sheehan stood at attention and felt oddly liberated from the commotion in his head, to be able to hear their back-and-forth, combative on one side and resigned on the other.

"He's a good man for this sort of work," Captain Jones went on. "Look at him. Swift, quiet. Knows his way around a Jerry trench."

"Good enough for a Paddy," Eason said, and then the captain and his lieutenant looked to Sheehan as if measuring his height and strength, his efficiency and allegiance.

"Yes, sirs," Sheehan answered, because every statement an officer makes is not a statement, but a question to be answered in the affirmative.

"You want this assignment, Private?" Captain Jones asked.

"Yes, sir," Sheehan answered again.

"It's a mission, really. Dangerous, if you're caught. But you won't get caught, I trust," Captain Jones said, and then the captain's voice dropped off, into the ocean wallowing back and forth in Sheehan's hearing.

"Yes, sir," Sheehan said for good measure.

He was made to sit down at their table with the pair and the other officers: a major and a lieutenant colonel, by the look of their uniforms. The higher ranking men did not speak. Sheehan was shown a map of the battlefield and surroundings in exquisite scope and detail; what the crows must have seen while scavenging. He could see how the farmers sorted out their plots of land before the fighting, like the keys on an organ, he couldn't help thinking. The trenches made such shallow marks on the earth. The crater they had fought over, named Duck's Bill, was indelibly large, like an eye gouged out of a face. Despite the specificity in names for the impassable streets, the demarcation of farmhouses and cottages the Jerrys had sacked, a barn where they might have kept supplies, the distances were haphazardly calculated. The battlefield may have been ten miles in length. He need not walk all of it.

"Now you need only go this way," Captain Jones said, his index finger sweeping over the map, "and then that, to get behind the enemy, past his bunkers, maybe to as far as La Bassee." Jones then rolled up the map, and Sheehan put out his hands to receive it, but Jones kept the map, using it as though it were a baton, to keep both hands occupied.

"We want to know if their convoys have already come in—armaments, food, fresh soldiers, anything—and how many. And how much damage has been done to the countryside, and what's with this blasted silence . . ." Sheehan already could do that. He could describe what happens to the mind when the mechanism of the human ear is blighted.

What happens when the ear is pitched open to the world, and the world cannot stop feeding it. He could tell them of the bleeding numbness, the pain that was static. But Captain Jones had gone on to another point in his scheme by the time Sheehan could balance the captain's voice in his head and be ready to shout about his deafness.

"He'll need a washing," the lieutenant colonel said. "A shave, at least, before he gets into civilian gear."

"He'd make a fine French peasant," Captain Jones observed.

"Turn him into a civilian and he's captured, he'll be prosecuted as a spy," said the major, who had finally taken the initiative to speak.

"Executed," Eason said, nervously.

"Can't have the Jerrys executing soldiers, no matter from where we dig them up," the major said.

"Why not?" the lieutenant colonel sniffed.

"Because," the major said as he tossed away a piece of paper he had been studying into a pile of what looked like telegrams, briefings that appeared to no longer matter. "You want to get into the business of executing soldiers, we'll have to find a few Jerrys to pop off. You can't even cull through your own stock, you want to pick and choose those targets?"

The remark had silenced the officers; Sheehan said nothing. He hoped they would give him the map in Captain Jones's hands. A soldier is nothing without directions. But nothing that could identify the source of his mission could be on him, Eason explained, in private. Eason had led Sheehan to a cot, in a corner of the billets, so he'd be fully rested for the mission.

"Though I suppose the uniform will do enough of that," Eason said.

"Yes, sir," Sheehan said.

"There now," Eason said. "You'll be back by dusk, or . . ." Eason said, and the lieutenant turned his face away from Sheehan, so that Sheehan could no longer hear him.

"A night out in a field never hurt anyone, right?" Eason said for reassurance. He had turned to face Sheehan again, and he was smiling, though it was a worn down smile, tired from so much rehearsing. "The shooting's supposed to be done in a month, if the politicians are to be believed. Your mission will confirm it."

On Jones's orders, Sheehan left the billets at dawn to walk into the sunrise. In the billets there were mornings, but not in the trenches; in the trenches, there was only the extension of the previous hours, into days and weeks and years, so Jones had to remind him, thick and Irish, what a sunrise meant. He headed east into a vinegary mist, the kind that comes from too many men in close quarters. The summer wind carried it beyond the battlefield to where the non-combatants subsisted.

The land was rough going, as if it had been churned and spit out, then churned again. Mud and mountains. Barren forests, the limbs of cherry trees curtailed by fire and shelling. He could smell it, a sulfurous vacuum. He pulled his shirt out of his trousers so he could raise the collar over his nose and mouth, and quickly realized he'd have to find a new way to walk, to conceal himself, in a world ripped open. He might have to adopt the viewpoint his British masters had of him, become their creature more fully, so he might be a barely detectable residue, carelessly kicked underfoot. At his feet were the remains of past fighting: pieces of wire mixed with twigs, bones dirtied and pocked so they might be indistinguishable from felled branches. He sorted through the debris with his eyes. He had become the scavenger above, lingering, balanced upon nothing.

The air was a blank wash of high white clouds and blue, as though it had lost its purpose. The soil was white with ash. No crops to feed, fruit to grow, or birds it might support on its streams and currents. He scooped up what he could and rubbed it over his face and hands, his legs, and the trunk and arms of his uniform. Now he would be a ghost, or an object without human qualities, skittering from blanched tree to tree. In the widening stretch between himself and the front lines, he was certain he heard the big guns going, but in such daylight, that would be impossible.

He watched for shadows by which to tell the hour, as he was certain he had long passed the parallel of Aubers, and figured he had five wild miles to get through before La Bassee. Five miles for him to find something proving the war was at its end while he was stranded in the middle of it. Not in the fighting, or even its aftermath—that would be peace. The defeated trees, rooted at their posts—a ghastly army refusing to acknowledge the fault of its strategy. He stepped on charred bits, branches that cracked open under the weight of his shoes, as though he were torturing once animate beings. The final insult, the shot that put them out of their misery, that was his feet. It was loud, tremendously loud. He leapt behind another tree, put his back to the bark, held his breath. He did not move until he realized his weight might push the tree out of its berth.

Where the trees ended, there were fields in all directions. He spotted a gathering of buildings: a hamlet, it was,
forgotten by the mapmakers. He crouched and trotted across
a field to get to it. The shops had their windows smashed clear
off their frames, the glass in beads on the dirt walk. The town
hall boarded up, the cottages sour and gutted, nothing officers would commandeer for their headquarters. The enclosures
for the animals had been consumed by tanks or lesser transport. The only difference between this wasteland and the rest
was that there was a church. From the outside, it appeared
untouched.

The bell tower would afford a view that could help keep
him off the ground, or the more dangerous parts of it. So he
gave himself permission to enter it, and in the vestibule, came
upon a massacre. A pile of faces, hands, feet, the statues of
Jesus, Mary, and unidentified apostles dismantled. For which
spoils he could not fathom, although he could imagine possibilities, for cement and the steel rods used to reinforce them.

He spied into the sanctuary, and saw it, straight ahead in
the balcony above him.

His legs took him up the stairs, to the balconies, much
more quickly than he himself could have commanded them.
He was only going to look out the windows, he told himself,
but the rest of his body, the parts that were not saddled with
war senses, had other designs. And there, they found it—
an organ. Or where a pipe organ once was, the ramparts of
the instrument and its remains within. It had been gutted as
expertly as each house, every shop, the apple and pear trees:
what more was there to steal? The manuals, the individual
keys of the five ranks, and the stops on the panels, had been

separated from their bone and wood coverings, as if they were fingernails torn off, in an act of ceremonial torment.

He had not had much experience with organs; he had chosen, at an early age, to devote himself to pressure and strings, and organs were about release and air. He thought at the time he was making a great distinction between noise and sound. Noise was what imprisoned him in Dublin, and sound was the way out of the slum. The piano was sound, a clean instrument that allowed for the silences that spellbound him. Between the notes were measured intervals, moments so rare as to be numinous, if he could properly time and arrange them. He had to learn all of it: dry theory, composition, exercises that tested the resolve of his wrists and knuckles; not much came naturally to him, besides reticence, which the broad chords and bombast of the organ foreclosed.

A church organ, it would have been for him, and that meant staying in Dublin, burying the children he'd father in his own lifetime, in ground that had failed generations. One could not grow anything in rubble and cinders, and one could not be assured rubble and cinders were enough to keep the dead quiet, for the church organ seemed to celebrate their haunting and howling. If he had chosen the organ, perhaps as his mother Catherine had wanted, he would have to keep to the Summer-hill road, the lower street, Number 13-16, submerged in its chaotic noises of families and near-famine. No pauses, no patience, only the perpetual quest for scraps, each morsel less satisfying than the last. There was neither time nor room enough to draw a breath privately, be reminded of the beauty of one's own beating heart, or the music it might inspire or remind one of.

What there was on Summer-hill was the mass of frantic clamoring, cattle yards and chicken coops crammed behind the forlorn plots of tubers and the street view of the buildings. Before the men would head out to the pubs, they'd slaughter what they could salvage from the beastly soil and load it up in a jaunting cart, one used for English passengers in the daylight. But at night, as the English were tucked in for their righteous slumber, the cart's wooden wheels raked against cobblestone and dust, and the men threw what carcasses they could pass off as healthy inside.

As a boy, Michael could keep time by the halting cadence of this schedule, the bleats of dying animals, the slap of flesh against the cart's benches, its departure and then return in the morning, the dousing of the cart with sluice from the gutter, and soap made from ashes. Michael awoke to the slap and battering of the cart as it was being made habitable for the day's unsuspecting passengers. But to Michael, to anyone with enough sense to look around the surroundings, the scent of blood and concussions had long since insinuated itself into the benches and wood, and made what little food any family had to eat nearly impossible to stomach. Browning meat or yellowish fish—largess, it was said to be—from the households where the girls and women toiled, if they weren't employed by a laundry. The vegetables tasted of mud and fungus, what lived on the walls, the dirt in the street, dust that chalked around the children's feet and hands, under the noses of his parents and siblings.

Michael could not know where organ-playing would take him as a boy, but it did not take him long to recognize the shambles, the amalgamation of noises that could not be teased out or untangled, so that it was always too much noise to consider, to swallow. The piano he found far more orderly; its distinctions between scales, the calm and separateness of its sounds, so much more readily deciphered. It would take him far, this kind of dignity and control; what his countrymen lacked, his father Edmund said, not quite into his chest so Michael might still hear him in the single din of the room where they lived. "Get to England, or Canada, the New World," Edmund would say when in his cups, which was comparatively rare for a man such as him, in a slum city with a passel of children and dire prospects. "Enough of this huddling despair and circus." Edmund went on to recount other Sheehan men, uncles and cousins, legitimately farming in Manitoba and Saskatchewan. There were stranger places for planting and homesteading, stranger names for sober earth, names as unfamiliar as their own Gaelic, for a right young man to take on. If Michael Sheehan could be a man about it. He needn't bother with that ladies' church music.

To his credit, Sheehan got himself across the Irish Sea, only to find himself engulfed by the English, the Germans, the maelstrom of an organ that had been dismembered. The keys were mere splinters, nubs, suggestions of the levers that had once been there. He checked for the bellows, and found their leather reinforcements in shreds. The pipes had been yanked off the walls only in sections, but all the connections between them and the instrument had been severed. For lead, he guessed, but he no longer felt such explanations logical. His hands found the keyboard, and he pressed. He pressed hard, and heard dull thuds, like the sound of oars in a boat, banging into one another, upon landing.

He remembered what Mozart had said, what a grand instrument the organ was, how it nearly played itself. But his hands could only ramble and bang at the air. He understood how the instrument's anatomy had been summarily junked, to be melded into shot; to shore up the walls in trenches; for casings and shells and barrels and bayonets. He understood, as a soldier, that there could never be enough raw materials in war. But no exercise of the mind could explain the zeal in this destruction: the removal of bone from the organ's stops and manuals. Why strip beyond the skeleton, in a beast that was perhaps the only remaining proof that men were superior to animals? Why gut it so thoroughly—surely not for survival? But war was not a time for abstraction. The operating principle was that they had done it, the Jerrys had dismembered the organ to within an inch of its being unrecognizable. And he would have done the same, if he were in their position. He knew that much about himself.

His hands accelerated, his feet were stomping where the pedalboard had been ripped out, as if he was demanding wraiths to produce music. He heard nothing as he played and then he heard a scream in the air, a siren, and he played on this nub, the one surviving connection between the pipes and the manuals, the only mechanism of the organ that had withstood the punishment. He played on that horrible note that only half came through, with the clanking and admonition that overruled in his ears, so he searched for other notes, other connections. In his mind the racket was so loud he thought he could destroy the entire building.

"English?" he heard a voice, and he thought, no, I am not English, and he kept up his playing, the Bach he decided he heard through the human syllables and the sirens, the screams and the drums. No, I am not English, he hummed to himself through his own hatred, and the human noises became only louder.

"*Du!* You! Deserter?" the voice persisted because it was a complete voice, more even in tone than he had become accustomed to deciphering.

Sheehan stopped to see a German soldier aiming at him. A man younger than himself, but far more steady with the weapon. He swallowed, as if he might shrink himself into his stomach, disappear. He raised his hands in surrender slowly, as instructed, to give himself time to guess at the most suitable answer, in a language his fellows thought he knew too well.

"*Deserter, nein,*" he said. "*Aber Englisch, nein.*"

"*Ja, Englisch, du,*" the Jerry said. "*Du bist prisoner, jetzt, genau.*"

Sheehan shoved the clothes Miss Williams had so decorously presented to him, just hours earlier, beneath the bed. It was still a warm day outside, the air possessing a width and height that flooded over the nursery. Yet the chill on Sheehan's flesh was intolerably cold, and he swaddled himself in the coverlet from the bed without bothering to return to his regular wardrobe. He found the corner of the room that afforded the best surveillance of the door, and placed himself in it as though he were a clandestine sentry. If anyone dare move the handle on the door, he could dash under the bed or out the window, though he did not wish to leave. He did not wish to ever leave the room, the corner, the comfort of walls pressed against his back and sides. He wished he could back more deeply into the corner, until his sweat and flesh could be subsumed by the walls—the bones of the cottage—their quiet and implacable embrace. He wished he had a will to make it so, rather than the hopes and curiosities that Miss Williams had awakened in him.

Whether it was the riot of distractions in his ears, or Miss Williams's effort and trepidation that kept him from hearing her return, Sheehan did not know. This being the height of summer, the nights were lax in their arrival. The darkness, in its nightly apportionments, could not deal out its merciful pieces to Sheehan quickly enough. He waited until he could be assured that Miss Williams was no longer awake before he rose and eventually stepped out of the room to breach the kitchen. There he found a plate of cheese, bread, tomatoes, and fruit waiting for him, with a note in Miss Williams's hand:

> Beast to beauty to beast again
> unless he is told what he cannot
> explain will not be asked of him;
> unless he is told there is art in
> silence, for it allows us to listen:
> In the tilling of dirt, the divining
> of water; in the work that is not
> industry, but the private, joyous
> toil; in memory that is not relaxed
> but held fast, so moons and orbits
> neither drive nor dislodge it; in the
> stillness he might perfect, in tending
> chestnut trees and peonies, and
> his own sainted breath.

Seven

As THE WEATHER grew slow, thick, and, in its own way, treacherous, Miss Williams noticed a twitch in her throat. She was not ill, or she did not believe herself to be ill; it was the air, she thought, how stale, thick, and mean it had become. In the length of the days and the intensity of the heat, Miss Williams felt as though the earth had stopped turning, and if she was not attentive, she just might fall off. The twitch worsened into a catch, an occasional cough, and her extremities seemed to wilt from the suffocation. Her desire for the garden, for writing, for rising from her bed in the morning flagged from day to day. She sought out sleep as a cure, but found none, only more fatigue.

She could not hide her deterioration from Mr. Sheehan, who had sustained his own kind of injury from his visit to

Lord Thorton's. This she surmised from the handicap that returned to his movements, the great mass of grief added to his composure. And in his eyes, now, that yellow scrutiny had returned: he watched her as her own timing broke into a protracted agony. He took to pacing, to delaying tasks in the garden; and when he fetched Miss Williams a cup of tea or glass of water, he did not simply hand them off to her. He waited, as if expecting an explanation for what was overtaking her.

Miss Williams thought of that day in the rain, when Mr. Sheehan first ventured out of the cottage, and whether her shivers and discomforts had commenced soon afterward. Perhaps she had ignored the strange displacement occurring in her lungs, as though the air she took in had to work its way past an obstacle, and could not find its way back again. Inhaling a great draught of air was still easy enough, but when she exhaled, she was puzzled by how little air there was to dispose of. The natural impulse was to take another deep breath, to force the old air out, but that only quickened the disruption, and the shudder in her chest would demand to be let out. She coughed and was unable to stop. She didn't have much in her symptoms, whenever they presented themselves, to be an indication of anything serious. Her ribs ached with the effort of breathing.

The worst of it, though, was how her obviously temporary illness blighted whatever stock of confidence Mr. Sheehan had built up over the months. This was how Christopher and Lord Thorton found the pair, dull and in an anxious retreat from the world, when they came to call a week after the impromptu piano recital. Miss Williams feigned surprise as she answered the door to find them there. She invited them in as graciously as she was able, but they refused to sit in the main room. They stood as if to deliver a final message. They said they would keep this affair mercifully short, but she already knew the course of this affair before they spoke. She saw in how Christopher paced at the window, keeping watch on Mr. Sheehan outside.

"I—we—will try to make this easy for all involved, and be simple, and direct," Christopher said. Lord Thorton, dressed in a summer suit that was the color of what Icarus might have seen falling away over his shoulders just before the flames began, had traded places with his son. It was for the earl to keep watch over The Hawkman.

"Of course," Miss Williams said. She had placed herself at her desk. If they would not sit down, she would, because she was not leaving.

"That man—" was how Christopher finally decided to refer to Mr. Sheehan.

"That gentleman," Miss Williams corrected.

"Your—"

"Friend."

"He could very well be mistaken for your paramour," Christopher said.

"But no one has ever remarked on it," Miss Williams said. "So you are the only one who is so mistaken."

"What is he, then? You cannot truly know him," Christopher said, and his voice was high with frustration. "Is he some kind of project of yours, a social experiment? We have heard about you, you Americans; you will try anything."

"It was one of your gentle ladies, sir, who came up with

that idea. A man as man's creation, not God's."

"Yes, yes," Christopher said, but he was distracted and could not continue. Miss Williams imagined Lord Thorton casting an exasperated glance from behind her, but that was not enough guidance for his son. "In any case," he recovered to begin again. "I—you are aware of the—incident. The incident he was involved in."

"Yes, yes. I was there, after all."

"Right," he said, and he might have looked for room to begin pacing in front of the desk. A bad lecture always requires pacing, Miss Williams knew. A good one does not require such theatrics. "As you might imagine, we—my father and I—cannot have trolls wandering about, terrorizing our staff, to say nothing of our family, or His Majesty's subjects."

"The only person he terrorized was himself," Miss Williams answered. "He realizes his error, and he is suffering now, through his deep regret."

"Which is our—my—point," Christopher Thorton rejoined. "He needs to go back to his family, or to hospital, where he can be cared for, professionally; where he can be cured, if possible."

"He can go to the hospital, or to his family, or anywhere he desires, on his own initiative," Miss Williams said. "He prefers to stay here."

"Of course. Why not? Here he has everything he needs: food, shelter, your delightful companionship," Christopher said, and Miss Williams wondered at the last surge in his voice, if this was simply jealousy, until Christopher continued, "And all at our—my father's—expense. And once you, your time here is—once it has ended, he will be released, to prey upon a population of souls with which he is already familiar, to beg, to harass, and chase them from their peace of mind, their way of life. Since he has already demonstrated that preference, naturally."

"Mr. Christopher," Miss Williams said, and upon voicing this error in title, she heard how ridiculous it was, as if the man before her could be reduced to a mere boy who was only known by his familiar, first name. "He takes only what I give him," she went on, "and I do not give much, considering what I earn, according to a contract signed by the dean of this college. I have done nothing to violate that contract, so I will continue giving what I want to him, because he is my guest. Finally," she said, rising from the desk to move toward the window so that she could see Mr. Sheehan more clearly. "Mr. Sheehan is neither an unfortunate nor some lesser being, neither a bird nor a trophy animal. He is a human being."

"But what do we—do you—know of his background?" Christopher ventured. "Do you know where he is from, how he was raised? Do we—do you—know if he has family; a woman from before the war, possibly? If they had reason to send him on his way, a very practical and understandable reason, which might quite possibly be beyond your . . . your comprehension?"

"I know that he is a human in need, as human as you, me, or even your father," Miss Williams said. "And that is all I need to know. His humanity qualifies him for my care and sympathy. "And his humanity has been injured, gravely," Miss Williams continued, although now she had to use her arms to support herself against the windowsill. Her weight seemed to have expanded in the heat and the closeness of the library, as if her mind and bile conspired to sabotage her throat. "Through that war of yours, probably, or some other imperial ridiculousness. He has served in some way, I am certain, and it has broken him. Why do you require more?"

"Because I require decency," Lord Thorton said. Christopher turned on his heels, astonished as she was, if not at the entry of his father into the conversation, then the volume he applied to it. "I require it of you, of those most directly in my employ, of everyone in my family, of Christopher, here. This is not Paris where you can take up with whomever you please. This is the world my son will inherit, will steward through his generation. He was injured in the war, but we do not see him begging on street corners, horrifying his neighbors."

"Yet still, Mr. Christopher does profit from your advantage," Miss Williams said plainly. "That terrifies me, if not more than Mr. Sheehan. He is unable to speak, but your son is unable to speak for himself."

"Now, Miss Williams," Christopher began, but his father hushed him. Christopher tried a second time, with a gesture, the start of something, but Lord Thorton, through gestures of his own, put an end to it. Lord Thorton swallowed, as if whatever he had intended to say escaped from his lexicon. The earl of Bridgetonneshire removed his hat and raised a handkerchief from his pocket to his forehead. Upon removing it, he studied the sweat he had gathered in the cloth, as if he were expecting to find the same mud droplets that used to stain his wardrobe in South Africa.

"I have some experience in these matters which you do not," Lord Thorton said.

"Which matters?" Miss Williams responded. "Turning

people out when they're down?"

"Helping those who cannot be helped," he said.

"Mr. Sheehan has blossomed with my help," Miss Williams declared. "I thought you would be grateful that he is no longer begging on street corners, which, for him, you obviously deem preferable."

"I do not have time for a lecture," Lord Thorton declared. "But other women, so much like yourself, have tried to rescue these irredeemables—"

"So much like myself how?" Miss Williams interrupted, because she knew how to make a man veer off from his case and into another topic for which he was not prepared.

"Abominable, is how—"

"Father, please," Christopher intervened.

"No, please Mr. Thorton," Miss Williams addressed the earl's son. "Please, let the man say what he means."

"And ignorant," Lord Thorton picked up as though there had been no delay in his speech. "If you deign to familiarize yourself with the truth of situations like these, you may contact my secretary for a meeting. In the meantime, I trust you will inform Mr. Sheehan of this decision," Lord Thorton said. "He is to be gone by tomorrow evening."

"Why not inform him yourself?" Miss Williams said.

"Why—" Christopher began, but his father took him by the shoulder and turned him away from Miss Williams. Together they walked out of the cottage without a farewell. Miss Williams shut her eyes, tightly, to stop time until she could hear the slam of the front door and know that they had left, entirely.

In the library, the day had compressed into a burden

and density more suited for the night. Miss Williams badly wanted to collapse. To cry, to cool off, to bathe, to lie naked beneath an open window within the fresh sheets of her bed. She did not know if she was shaking, but she knew her fever—if it was indeed a fever—had climbed to a new level. Now it was symmetrical, equally divided over the left and right of her back. She felt as though the pain tried to escape, just below her shoulders, and, once thwarted, it had begun to sprout flame through her skin. Her legs felt like stones, as one might find on the haunches of an animal. She tried to move away from the window, but found herself too heavy to carry on her feet. She bowed her head and forced her way, balancing the new weight on her back, with the fever spreading as it locked around her neck.

"Mr. Sheehan," she called. Her voice was weak, and she could not be certain she could be heard. But she could see him. He was a flicker of a wavering candle in the air that melted and waved back at her. She stepped onto the grass, and she remembered walking through those waves, or so it seemed to her as their pull and power sealed her every movement. She fought against the air, she fought against water, she fought against the stones in her back, the flood in her lungs, and the drought in her limbs. He might have seen her falter. He might have rushed up to steady her by her arms, the small of her back. He might have seen her eyes widen in grief, narrow in listlessness.

He might have thought she had fainted from the heat. As he lifted her in his arms, he calculated what would be the easiest distance to carry her: up the stairs, to a doctor in the village, to the college from which she would be sacked soon enough, particularly if she was seen profiting from his assistance. Those minutes he stood there, studying the breathless, spiritless Miss Williams, they crested into hours, days, an entire existence. She lost all corporeality, and when she awoke, she was drowning in a pool of silence.

Eight

BEFORE HE CAME to Miss Williams, Sheehan had trouble, as it was, thinking of the war directly. He could only touch on the differences between what he knew before and what he had learned. What he knew best, of course, was his hands, the sonatas in which they excelled, the symphonies they could endure; he knew the temperature of water they favored, and the number of hours of practice they required. The rest of his body worked as servant to these appendages. And he knew, once he volunteered, that the war could change them irrevocably.

"You. Always with the hands," the training officer, Everett, complained. Sheehan tried gloves—wool, silk, canvas, cotton, leather; the cotton and canvas provided no protection against the moisture, and the wool and leather caused too much friction. He thought he could treat his hands, and from the kitchens he might procure a lubricant to soothe the skin as it chafed and thickened. Butter might have worked best, but there was no butter to be had. Shortening and cooking oil would have to suffice, although they did not. They did nothing other than attract insects. From the infirmary he begged for tape, that he might wrap his fingers, but the infirmary was in the business of extending the lifespan of larger extremities: arms and legs. He spliced leaves for their oils and pounded bark for its powders, but, like everything in a soldier's existence, they were too decimated to provide any comfort. On leave, his compatriots promised him a visit to a whorehouse. He agreed so that he might steal away a splash of rose water, a smear of cold cream, a sprinkle of talcum. He offered the woman additional money, if only to get at her potions, but she refused, and threw a chair at him so he would leave.

Before the war, he knew hands: bones, ligaments, and tendons, and the hard beginnings of new bone, burrs and swelling, that occurs between knuckles. But the war made him consider the rest of human anatomy. War made him consider the flaws beyond the reach of fingers: the weak points where the body separates, hips from the abdomen, the chest in several different directions. War made him consider colors when before he had only to worry over a spot of blood from a blister; now he saw the full spectrum, pink descending into the sickening yellow, and other liquids, clear, botched, speckled with infection. Finally, war made him consider what he must have known, what he must have felt, in theory: soreness, exhaustion, bruises. It turned these things into a rude blooming of the liver, the kidneys, the contents of the stomach, once they have been blown apart by mortar.

Now, when he thought of the war, he could see the battle-field, but only from above. He saw it rise up to him, as though he were coasting down toward it, as if he had always been a bird, The Hawkman, with his talons extended. He could spot the trenches as they replenished themselves with new soldiers; the last batch not having been removed, but carted to the side, denuded and dismembered. The trenches made mazes in the dirt, like webs ripped from their scaffoldings. That was his job, shaking the lines free and assaulting the men who held onto them, so they'd surrender their grip and plummet onto his bayonet, beneath the toe of his boot. With his arms and legs, he had killed or injured dozens of men; with his back, he had dug graves for his fellows. The war made him know those other parts of himself—those that filled shovels, hammered blanks, screwed nails, shot rifles—so that he might take some-thing of nature and turn it into something unnatural. He had transformed men and their world into a mechanical rendering, a creation only recognizable as abominable.

The war was his creation, far more significant than any music he might compose or play. People closed their eyes when he played, as if to jot out the interferences, to get to the essence, the purity of a melody or a particular phrasing. They not only wanted to hear it, but to see it in a kind of approx-imation, in their imaginations. But people did not close their eyes to distill war. They insisted on keeping them wide open, to digest the newsprint, the lists of dead and injured; they kept their eyes open at the lectures in the prison camps and at home to hear the testimonials, speeches for and against. The war and its confusions were so much louder than any misplayed sharp or flat, louder than bassoons and percussion sections, or whole orchestras ill-supervised and lost in their own turbulence.

He heard it again, the war with its anarchic noise, as he carried Miss Williams from the cottage's garden to the college in search of help.

Out in the broad sunlight, Sheehan's head rattled with the sounds of the fields that separated the cottage from the college. The insects and grasses drummed on in an uneven, electric hum that strengthened when the sun glanced out from beyond a cloud. The college's acreage stretched so far out that he found it disorienting; the grasses moved ahead of him as if affected by a rumbling underneath, sorting themselves out like an ocean not entirely under its own power. He scoured the fields for shadows or trees for shade; she was so hot, or she should have been. The sweat rose on her lip, her forehead, her throat—the emergence of each bead an agony like the birth of a tide, unwelcome but necessary.

"See here, fellow," Sheehan heard from behind him. He swung around to find a short man outfitted as though a fisherman, Wellies beyond his knees and all types of gear hanging off his belt. "Just what are you up to?" the man asked and he continued talking, or his mouth was moving. Sheehan could not hear over the electric clamor seemingly at his feet.

"You did this to her now, did you?" the man asked, and Sheehan was grateful for that question, for he could answer it with a robust shake of his head. But afterward he was at a loss to explain the unearthly sheen and silence on Miss Williams's face, and his carrying her around like a Bluebeard dumbfounded by his bride's reaction to his wiles.

"Miss, Miss," the groundskeeper said as he peered over Miss Williams, waving his hands, snapping his fingers, finally clapping his palms above her face. "Like a light out, she is, eh?" he asked, and Sheehan nodded. He tried to look beyond the man, a groundskeeper or perhaps a plumber or some other trade, but the man dashed about and kept up with the questions Sheehan couldn't quite hear.

"Tiring, are you?" the man said, and he moved in closer, with his arms extended. The man was going to take Miss Williams from him, and Sheehan shook his head, stomped his feet. He stepped back; he was walking backward and surprised himself by coughing—the sound that came easiest to him, raking his throat of mire and panic. He pointed at his own chest as well as he could, still holding Miss Williams, and kept on coughing. He shut his eyes as tightly and breathed loudly through his mouth, to make a sound like wheezing.

"A fit?" the man asked, but Sheehan did not know how to respond. "An episode? Fainting spell?" Sheehan felt numb in his face. Whatever hope he wore, thinking he could find a doctor for Miss Williams, withdrew its encouragement. "Good Lord," the man said, "something worse?"

The man turned away to march off somewhere, but he motioned with his arm. "This way, now." And he checked back, after every third step, to see that Sheehan was following. "Not much farther now," the man said; his Wellies kept him from running outright.

Once a building was in sight, Sheehan began to run toward it. "That's it, that's it, in there," the man shouted after him, and he continued shouting directions, what to do once he was inside, but Sheehan could not make them out. He leaped up a set of steps and pushed through a door into a darkened hallway, and began coughing again, to herald his arrival.

His cough rankled the air and his throat, like membrane on metal, honed and serrated. He kicked at doors, coughed again, and the doors opened. The men and women who emerged from classrooms and offices were quick to recognize an unconscious Miss Williams, and quicker to be horrified by the man who held her in his arms. "Where are you taking her?" one shouted: a man in glasses and too much clothing for the summer. "Miss Williams, Miss Williams," another voice said: a woman, perhaps a secretary, her fingers stained black from typewriter ink. She scampered like a duck so as not to trip over her skirt. Still others said nothing and put their hands to their mouths in shock and disdain. Voices and faces came at him as though he was running a gauntlet, a human equivalent of berms, craters, and fragments of barbed wire. Each time a door opened, it unleashed a torrent into the hallway that smeared his vision, like an attempted blinding.

Finally a pair of double doors were thrown open to reveal an infirmary. The beds, five of them, looked dispiritingly small. The man with the glasses, nowhere as tall as Sheehan, tried to wrest Miss Williams from his arms. Sheehan swung away, refusing to relinquish her. The groundskeeper appeared; more people followed, the swinging of the double doors like a valve in a church organ that could not hold a note consistently.

"Set her down, son, set her down," the groundskeeper urged him, and the crowd of people rushed him toward the first bed, where he gently placed Miss Williams, her clothes now fouled and twisted as though she had been fighting a storm, a downpour unexpected.

"No air," Sheehan scrawled with pencil and paper that was handed to him. He wanted to write more, or to have the option of writing, but the implements were quickly taken from him. Sheehan felt as though he had to shove through a crowd of swaying heads of barley, downed branches and weeds, to reach her bedside. They were hollering, fanning her with whatever they could find, but Miss Williams tossed her head back and forth, as if to avoid their calls or say no to their entreaties. Sheehan put his forearm and sleeve to her forehead to wipe away the sweat. He thought he saw her lips tremble, his name forming there; but then she swallowed, and sunk deeper into her exhaustion.

"Give her some air," Sheehan heard a new voice, a woman's, command the others. "Get her out of these clothes, they're soaked," the woman ordered. She might have been the headmistress or some other lofty figure. She appeared at the other side of the bed and pulled Miss Williams up to a sitting position; Miss Williams slumped. The woman pushed her up again. "You—all you men, out!" the woman said. The groundskeeper and the man with the glasses immediately complied.

"You need to go, sir," the headmistress said to Sheehan, who shook his head as he grabbed at the bed's metal frame above Miss Williams's head. It felt greasy, resistant, like the mud of a trench wall.

"Is there something you don't understand, sir?" the headmistress continued.

Sheehan did not know whether to shake his head no, because he understood everything or yes, to indicate how badly he needed to stay.

"Sir! Are you also unwell?" the headmistress shouted.

No, no, no, he shook his head. He clamped his eyes shut at the sight of Miss Williams's nakedness. Her skin appeared blue as though thinning. It was no longer skin, barely able to contain pulse and oxygen. The light hairs of her arm stood separate and scared; she was all goosebumps and flailing, like waterfowl that did not comprehend its injury at grounding. The headmistress took Sheehan by the shoulders and shook him fitfully. It was the only way she could get him to look at her directly.

"Something wrong, sir?" the headmistress demanded. Sheehan took to the ground, his knees pressed into wood floor that refused to yield. He clasped his hands together as if to beg and shook them in the headmistress's face. But she was unmoved. She was calling for assistance. The men she had just banished from the room would soon return, to draw and quarter him. "We need some help here," the headmistress said in their direction. The groundskeeper and the man in glasses had to be nearby, otherwise she would not have been shouting after them. "Come on now. A pair of strong men I need. Quit cowering."

Please, Sheehan thought intently to himself. Please.

"Sir! Sir!" The headmistress's ire was more fully directed at him, yet she was backing away as if she were frightened—perhaps by the remoteness of his features, his size and posture.

Sheehan drew his hair away from his face. He motioned for the pencil and paper back, but no one responded.

"Ma'am," Sheehan heard above his head. "The doctor." A graying man had entered, though not in a doctor's garb. He carried a medical bag, his shoulders seemingly tamped down by transporting its bulk. Sheehan rose, out of deference, but slipped one of his hands between Miss Williams's fingers.

"Now then," the doctor tried to say reassuringly, but the warmth drained out of his voice as he saw the strength of Miss Williams's convulsions. Worry tugged at his eyelids, as though he wanted to shut his eyes to her distress. He put his palm to her forehead and shouted, "Blankets! A hot water bottle! Something! Bertie!" He was addressing the headmistress. "Can't you recognize a fever?"

"I'm trying to be rid of this menace here," she said, nodding at Sheehan.

"You?" he said to Sheehan, who cast his eyes downward. But he did not remove his hand from the patient's. "Who is he?"

"We don't know," Bertie said.

"And I can't care much, at this minute," the doctor said. He had removed a stethoscope from his bag and placed the earpieces in his ears. Sheehan held his breath and shut his eyes, as if to stop the churn of orders and whispers around him, to hold the infirmary still as the doctor listened. "And I can't concentrate under these conditions."

"I said—" Bertie began, but the doctor somehow stopped her.

"How old is this woman?" he asked.

Sheehan opened his eyes and raised his hands, then two fingers on one hand, and five on the other.

"Seven?" someone asked.

"Twenty-five," the doctor said. "Obviously." Sheehan put his hands down, as if he had been too forward with the information.

"You, you brought her?"

Sheehan nodded again and put his hands to his throat to demonstrate choking.

"She choked on something?" the doctor guessed, and he looked to Miss Williams, as if for confirmation.

"Why must you ask him?" the headmistress said.

"Who should I ask then?"

"He's dumb, obviously," the headmistress said. "And there's no place for him here—"

"Bertie," the doctor said firmly. His voice was hoarse, disrupted, but Sheehan believed he could feel the force the man used to clear out the croup to make his point. "He's mute," the doctor guessed, as he took in the full measure of Sheehan. Sheehan knelt to wipe away the ropish strands the sweat had made of Miss Williams's hair.

"The man has a fetish," Bertie despaired.

"You in the war, son?" the doctor asked.

Sheehan nodded, but did not take his eyes off Miss Williams.

"Obviously a reactive psychosis, Bertie," he said to the headmistress. Before she could speak, the doctor declared, "Now's not the time to debate it." He returned his attention to Miss Williams, lifting her eyelids as he tilted the lamp downward into her eyes. "She's responding to light," the doctor said to Sheehan, "though I can't see how."

"Please, Richard—" Bertie started in again.

"No," the doctor said. "He's all we've got to go on. It's as though she's had a stroke, but she's obviously too young. You—" he addressed Sheehan directly. "Go about and make yourself useful. Fetch us some water and towels."

Sheehan would not have moved from his position if the doctor hadn't pointed where the sink was, in a far corner; Sheehan needed to be certain that this was no fool's errand. When Sheehan returned, the doctor was listening to Miss Williams's lungs again, the stethoscope inserted beneath the bed sheet. The headmistress was fashioning some sort of bed clothes out of linens, and the waddling secretary reemerged, her arms holding blankets.

"Has she been ill in any way?" the doctor asked Sheehan distractedly; he seemed to be counting breaths or heartbeats; his hand had taken hold of Miss Williams by the wrist. "Has she been exposed to anyone with an illness?"

No, Sheehan shook his head again, unsure if anyone was paying attention. The doctor withdrew the stethoscope and discovered the groundskeeper beside him. The groundskeeper handed him the paper Sheehan had written on.

"No air," the doctor read. "You mean she couldn't breathe?"

Sheehan nodded, as he would to a superior officer.

The doctor crossed his arms. "Her lungs—" he began, but could not finish. "Her heart's a bit fast—from the fever, I'd expect." he said. "This is delayed, for a case of the influenza. You must have seen a lot of that."

Sheehan shook his head no several times, and raised his hands in surrender. As the headmistress and the doctor's eyes were upon him, the groundskeeper's, and the waddling secretary's, he felt all the fury and nerve that had brought him to this point dispersing. They had taken him for a carrier, the source of infection. A quarantine would be next, questions would be put, his explanations insufficient. Unless he could write them on paper, and he began pounding his fist into his hand. He put his index finger to his palm, to motion for the pencil and paper again.

"This?" the doctor asked, slowly returned the paper, with a pencil, to him.

"Influenza not in camps," Sheehan quickly wrote, and when he returned the paper back to the doctor, he found himself breathless.

"Camps?" the doctor asked.

Sheehan nodded.

"Prisoner of war?" the doctor continued.

Sheehan nodded again as he reddened, drenched in sudden shame.

"How long?" the doctor asked.

Sheehan kept his focus on the ground but lifted a hand to display four fingers.

"Right," the doctor said. Miss Williams was finally being covered with the blankets. "Someone get this man a chair, for God's sake," the doctor asked of no one in particular. "The name's Weir," the doctor said as he offered his hand to Sheehan, but Sheehan could not take it. He had returned to Miss Williams's side, his hands busy with the water and towels he had brought to make Miss Williams a compress.

The chair appeared; the doctor placed a hand on Sheehan's shoulder, and Sheehan sat as if he had been commanded to do so. But for the doctor, the rest of the world fell away for Sheehan, as he had secured a foothold beside Miss Williams and had no intention of ever giving it up.

She had not contracted influenza; this was something else, a denser disease, its prognosis impenetrable. Sheehan knew from the war, the camps, and the trenches, how a body was put together. He knew how it could fall apart, whether it be a gradual collapse, through strain and starvation, or a violent sundering. In her bed at the infirmary, Miss Williams seemed to be enduring both conditions. Her breath shortened into a terrible panting as if her lungs had been stolen, wrenched cleanly from their perch with a furtive precision.

Nine

As THE FEVER bent and jerked at her body, Miss Williams believed she was quite well, and years younger, at the children's asylum where she had lived as her mother approached death. St. Joseph's of the Desert, it was called. The sisters gave her a simple bed in a convent room away from the other girls, so long as her mother lingered in the sanitarium the nuns ran across town. Eva felt fortunate in her room, to be sinking beneath the blankets with the buffalo grazing in the woolen hem, and coyote howling at the summer doldrums. Winter had beset the landscape with bitter winds. From outside she could hear the wind searching for objects to scour, for the bungalows and adobe could not satisfy it. By the end of the night, it would find its power solely applied to the sand, bright and unabashed in how it threw reflections into the horizon.

Each morning the world was white and new again in the distance, and her mother was that much closer in having the dry salve of the desert absorb the thrashing waters in her lungs.

Eva had a hand in this process, accompanying the wind on its nightly visitations. She did not fly with the wind in her imagination, but listened as it rose and fell, rose and fell, redoubling its resolve with each ascent. She cheered it on, in her mind, because the sound kept her company; because should the wind tire, should it go lax in its routine of self-cleansing, her mother would be lost. *I need you to be as strong as you've ever been*, Eva said in her whispered conversations with the wind. *I need you to make my mother better so we can look for my father, together.* At daybreak she was anxious to look through the frosted panes just above her bed so she might see the wind's work, the sand ablaze with the signal for good health and the return of her mother's hardy constitution.

She was about to leap from underneath the blankets the nuns had piled atop her when she was suddenly in a larger room—the dormitory in the children's asylum. She had been stripped of her blankets, and given an anemic substitute that did nothing to keep out the consuming winter temperatures. Her hose were black like her undergarments, and, for working in the laundry, she had a white smock. For the kitchen, she had a white apron. She gathered all her clothes for warmth before returning to her cot. Each cot was placed at just over an arm's length from the next, so that no girl might reach out to comfort the girl next to her. The legs of each cot had been sawed down so no one was able to stand on the bedding and see out the windows. The cots were arranged in a dreadful seniority: the oldest girl slept in the cot closest to the exit, for she would be turned out as soon as she came of age. Eva was the second girl from the door.

Her mother was gone now; this was something she knew in her dream, though no one had explicitly told her. Helen had finally diminished so greatly that her hair and skin might have been easily confused with the lime that was used to curtail her scent, the unraveling that was both salt and metal, at burial. Eva had missed the funeral somehow; perhaps she had been prevented from attending. She was made to hang the laundry or sweep up the grit that besmirched the white sheets and gray habits. As she worked, she thought she saw flashes, pulses of light, that distinguished themselves from the dance sand performed before it climbed into the mountains. These were not mirages but the last panting breaths of a woman who was brighter than glass, her flesh and bones blanched by time in the sun, its relentless polishing. They had come to the desert, which had supposedly made the Pima men, women, and children impervious to disease. Sun, air, and stars appeared as though they had punctured the night, so urgent was the need to bring light to it.

Still these curatives failed her mother, and Eva was about to be turned out into the infinity that blinded those who could not penetrate it. She was kneeling at the feet of the abbess, though she had not intended to place herself in such a position. The abbess had grabbed her writing hand and yanked the fingers like she was cracking a whip. Eva's hand stung as though an electric current had been run through it. Eva withdrew her hand and coddled it to her chest; for weeks she nursed it as though it was an injured wing with time as her only medicine. But for this excruciating, interminable moment, she was freshly wounded, huddled against her pain and the nun's rapacious need to punish her. Eva had been telling stories to the girls that evening.

She wanted very badly to recall just what she had said to the girls in the dormitory minutes earlier. She believed it was the story of the girl who ate her own hand. She had written it for one of the other girls in the asylum, a younger child who chewed on her fingers as a nervous habit. The nuns considered it a vicious tendency, evidence of an insatiable nature, and warned it would lead to further and far more horrendous sins in adulthood. They wrapped her hands in bandages that left her unable to dress herself. Nor could she feed herself, though her place at the long table remained empty; she was to be given no food, since she had too long feasted on what God had given her for other purposes—for work and prayer.

What was this girl's name? Miss Williams first searched the dream, then what she could peek into of her memory, for the nuns had truly done this. They had pulled the bandages so tight the girl's skin had begun turning, just as leaves do, the ebullience in their coloring drained away as the sun chooses to ignore them. Miss Williams could still find nothing of the girl's name or fate in her re-dreaming, her remembering. But she could not forget how the girl could not work with those bandaged hands, and because of that, she was not to be fed. So Eva brought the girl food, biscuits and porridge. The other girls followed suit, and they took turns feeding her as though she were a baby. They helped her to wash at night and dress in the morning.

But the bandages declined into brine and rags, as cotton

does, when left on the boll to go rancid. Eva could no longer tell the younger girls how the bandages were like cocoons, and the girl's hands were at work on a spectacular metamorphosis. A miracle Eva had promised them, fingers and thumbs molting into joints as strong and mighty as a forest. Not only would the girl be able to work again, but she'd find herself the recipient of new talents: she'd heal sick animals. Eva was about to explain how the girl's fingers would bear fruit for the hungry, provide shelter for the dispossessed, when the nun who ran the laundry pulled her away from the others to bring her to the abbess.

"You," said the nun, whom they called Sister Tuber; she was rewarded with this name for the divets on her face. "I always knew you were dangerous."

This was how Miss Williams found herself in another country, listless in another narrow bed. She did not so much resolve to escape the children's asylum, the Arizona territory, and the whole of the United States, as she allowed the winds to carry her away when they beckoned. The abbess could have been said to have welcomed them onto Eva's path that night, declaring that Eva's sins—her wildness, contrariness, intransigence, and unmanageability—would ultimately deprive her of a husband. "We'll see how well you write stories without your fingers," the abbess then said as she wrested Eva's hand like a farmer's wife might take to cracking a chicken's neck. "The next time, the Lord will see fit to do this to your teeth," she said, dismissing Eva into the custody of Sister Tuber. Wild, contrary, intransigent, unmanageable, and willful, she was; Sister Tuber repeated the benediction and added that final amen.

In the dormitory, the girl whose name she could not detach from the swirl of her recollections gave Eva the sweaty, gruesome bandage the nuns had tried to emboss on her skin. Perhaps her name was Katherine or Elizabeth, something that carried with it a diminutive: Kate or Becky. On that night, the girl came into her name, and was no longer greeted as a girl. A hand for a hand, a girl for a woman. Eva's name, trim and finished, could not be stretched into another connoting arrival, a more polished status. The bandages had lost their tautness, their pull and acumen for healing. Eva thanked the girl, and said neither of them had any further need for the binding.

But Miss Williams did need it, the restorative protection a bandage might have provided, in the narrow bed where she strained and twisted against the linens and her nightmares. Her mind insisted that she engorge herself upon these disordered thoughts, as though there was nothing else to sustain her during sleep.

She was willful and bullheaded, also provocative, and she liked the sound of that word. Eva smiled to think of the potential it conferred upon her, to which the nun they called Sister Monsoon responded with tears. Sister Monsoon wept copiously, Eva was able to observe, when confronted with her own impotence. Unlike the other nuns, she had been raised at St. Joseph's, in the same asylum that impounded Eva and the others. The girls were supposedly not to know this, but Sister Monsoon had attested to as much in one of her many tearful binges.

For the abbess and Sister Tuber and all the other sisters, Monsoon was the unspoken proof of what could befall the stubborn, the dim-witted, the unruly, or the overly joyful.

Worse than mere spinsterhood, she represented but the ruth-
less, indomitable expansion of the present day for the child
inmates into an infinite permanency. To become one of them,
the undesirable, undeserving, unmarried, superfluous females
for which there was no other tenable existence but assuming
the habits and wimples of their tormentors. Eva surprised
herself with her lack of concern over which personal failing
had ensnared Sister Monsoon. She was concerned only with
evading a similar inculcation for herself.

Eva's hand healed after that night; it returned to its
natural state and dexterity over the course of days and
frequent dunkings in the laundry's cold water washings. But
the wind that the sisters depended on battering and bedeviling
Eva lifted her up and brought into her view another way for a
woman to live, especially since she had been deemed unfit for
a future in the domestic arts. The sisters would have to send
her away for training, wouldn't they, since sins clung to her
like a baby at the breast. "The Father will have you sucked dry
as bones," said the nun they called Sister Root, as she seemed
to be in the thrall of Sister Tuber. "The only children you'll
be fit to nourish will be in a classroom." Eva answered Sister
Root's petition with the most flagrant sin possible: another
story, which the wind would conduct to the most wanton
magazines that publish such things. And then an entire book
of stories, to be sent to the printers of such volumes. And
on to any school, anywhere, that permitted women to study
literature and languages. And, finally, to the mailbox of every
Catholic nun in America, if she could manage it.

Miss Williams often did this: try to write the course
of her own dreams into something useful. She'd apply the

streams of what could be remembered with what her dream was teaching her, and come up with words and pictures suitable for a public audience. As the fever slid deeper into her muscles, diaphragm, and lungs, she regressed back to her mother's pearls, how soothing their cool skin would be against her hot throat. Her mother had said pearls were much like the shot, like the lead poured for the air to shape; but pearls lacked the threat of violence, unless one thought of their removal from their mothers. That must have been why her mother's pearls felt so cruel and indignant in her hand, once Eva was made into an orphan. The abbess had promised to return the pearls to Eva upon her manumission from the asylum. The pearls were not restored to Eva until she had long since departed St. Joseph's, as one of her professors intervened after hearing Eva speak of them. The professor needed only to write to the abbess, asking after their worth. The inquiry was enough to warn of the consequences.

Helen had once told Eva that she was much a pearl, formed as she was in bellies and warmth, and from a deliberate act of love, whether it be a union of light and seed or a protective reflex against an irritant. If a pearl is taken too soon from its mother through some inadvertent act, it will never mature into what it was meant to be: a teacher, a physician, a titan of a humane enterprise—a settlement house, perhaps. A pearl is a spinning compact of minerals and luminescence and therefore not meant for human ownership; it can be owned only by itself, like a star, or its reflection streaking through water.

Miss Williams decided in the midst of her dream and fever how she would have her pearls conceived: through their mollusk mothers as they opened their mouths and hearts to the father of their children, the moonlight. Once the mollusks captured enough of this light, they sealed themselves against the darkness of the sea, and balanced their babies on the edge of their tongues. There they grew, as interwoven layers of frost and radiance. In this way, the pearls were much like the needles in a pine tree, each requiring time and freezing to set properly, so as not to die off immediately with the coming of spring. To keep their children, their mollusk mothers could not speak, lest their offspring be jettisoned into water, into waves, into another existence that would find them as servants, rather than the masters of brilliance they were bred to be. A pearl was born only when a mother was asked to speak too soon, for purposes of profit or human indulgence.

But perhaps there could be a girl, an orphan, young and solitary: a pearl diver who might believe she could forge a family out of the water that was her most consistent companion. She might steal a pearl to love and nurture, so that it might grow as large as herself, to become her sister or at least a cousin. They would share a grandfather in a conch shell, and their parents would be fish and birds, koi and doves, that met in the ebb and flow of air and seaweed.

Yet this story did not wholly make sense to Miss Williams. Though she was either sick or dreaming, she knew where such stories truly came from: from Africans who wanted their children to understand the origins of their world, where there is not necessarily good and evil, but intentions and consequences. Yet it was also a world of plains and deserts, trees that did not wear leaves as much as they could balance head dresses. The world of pearl divers, of stars and orbits and their effect on bodies of water, belonged to another continent. Asia: China, the shores of Indonesia, and the island of Japan. Every civilization must have beliefs or its practices will devolve into superstition, Miss Williams had learned through her studies.

Miss Williams thought she had stepped out of her dream, into consciousness, and tried to open the palm of her hand. She wanted to find Mr. Sheehan. He was at the cottage gathering flowers or harvesting peas, or perhaps he was reading or studying the space just beyond his hands, as they were poised at the edge of his knees. She wanted to sit him down, her hand at his back, and tell him the story she had written. She believed she felt someone's hand in hers, between her fingers, but she could not say to whom that hand belonged. The skin of this hand was cool, almost like a pearl's, perhaps Mr. Sheehan's when he was young, before he had taken whatever trade that gifted him with the calluses that had hardened on his fingertips and palms.

She strained, to thank him for the comfort he provided, but felt that too much of herself was alternately melting and hardening into new forms. She felt the hand within her fingers cast a pearly brilliance over her skin, a weightlessness that she wished would transpose itself into her limbs, so that she would have the ability to float, to glide, to fly away from her illness. Perhaps she had died, she thought many times, and had failed to make arrangements for Mr. Sheehan.

IT SEEMED TO Miss Williams that once she awoke, in a number of days she could not count and no one would help her to quantify, she was suddenly without her most basic faculties. She could no longer sit up, or speak, or drink from a glass. When she tried to accomplish such tasks on her own, her body felt light, insubstantial, almost foreign, and there were no arms on her body to lift herself into sitting; no mouth on her face to take in the water. But Mr. Sheehan was there, adjusting her pillows, encouraging her to swallow. He could do nothing as she strained to accommodate air within her ribs, but he ran his hands up and down her back, as if clearing room for the oxygen to come in.

She had to relearn to walk, to talk, to laugh, and smile when prompted. Since the mass of her body seemed drained of muscles and blood, it was her chest, the flutter in her lungs, that powered her every move. If she spoke, or sat up, or stood up, her legs and feet free from the mattress and blankets, it was her lungs that propelled her forward, and her lungs that curdled with exhaustion in the following minutes. She had lost trust in her feet, and when she held her arms out for balance, they might as well have been webbed to her sides, for they could not be lifted instinctively. Like a broken fan, they would extend unevenly, one over-confident at half-mast, the other listless in defeat, no better than a flap of excess skin. Mr. Sheehan took to rubbing her arms in oil, as he was directed by the infirmary staff. He rubbed her feet and ankles too, though there was a weightlessness to them, almost an ecstasy that Miss Williams dare not reveal to her caretakers, for how could they understand her belief that some day she may no longer require her legs, that walking for her would soon be outmoded.

Miss Williams also had to learn how to see again, for what

was closest at hand now was distant, whether it was the glass of water Mr. Sheehan kept filled on her nightstand or the handkerchief that somehow always wound up knotted in her fingers. And what was remote, either across the room or far beyond that, in between the blades of grass outside, was now as close as her own bedclothes. It would be nothing to pull her hand from under the blanket and discover a ladybug drowsing on a leaf, or taste the juice of white bark and birch leaves.

Only in the distance, and in the stretch of days, did the awareness of her limbs return, as well as her ability to direct them into motions and movement. It was as if, after leaving her body, the fever had been succeeded by a rime of ice. On some mornings, that frost sprouted anew. Mr. Sheehan would have to raise her in bed, and move the drinking glass closer so she might more easily reach it. On those mornings, Miss Williams felt the teeth in that frost, primed and hungering. She would have to be heaved out of the bed, the muscles in her legs locked as if undecided in their thoughts and determined against all resolution.

On other mornings, which were far more rare, on those days when Miss Williams glanced upon a feeling that eluded all chances to capture it, bolt it down, and stretch it from seconds to minutes, Miss Williams still felt the preening in her lungs, but not the unfurling of their agile qualities. There was no ice to break through, nor was there blood, her heart stalled in its purpose, but all of her—shoulders, knees, ankles, hips, and elbows—immediately and immeasurably heavy. She would have to beg off her daily strolls on the arms of the doctor or one of the nurses. She would consent to lean only upon Mr. Sheehan, who took her into the corridor, where they could carry out their march in relative privacy. If this was death, she did not wish to complete it in as lurid a fashion as before an army of nurses and doctors bemoaning the haplessness of their profession.

Her mother had died in just that way. A spectacle the nuns had made of her, as if they thought they were teaching Eva a lesson, or providing a warning to their other patients. There was no shouting, no dramatic last testament to be taken upon a demand in desperation. And there was no deathbed conversion. The last rites, which her mother did not request, were conveyed into Helen's ear somewhere below a whisper, as far as Eva could make them out; perhaps it was the Latin. Nevertheless, the priest and the nuns and the novices and seminarians and orderlies and the undertaker and anyone else who could be summoned for the pageant made quite a production out of her mother's death. Eva asked for a screen, a curtain on wheels, to at least shield her mother from gawkers: all of her, cheeks to feet, swelled near to the point of explosion. But the request went unanswered, and people kept fusting and swishing around her mother. Taking her pulse, her temperature, lifting her nightdress so they might listen to the gale that would submerge her organs. It was anything but dignified, her mother transformed into a doll or a medical seminar.

Miss Williams did not want to die in this manner. She did not want to die with regret. But the resistance in her joints, the wear and weight of remaining upright, even in the bed—she was certain she was larded with regret and the slippery reminiscences that accompany it. She wished that she had been quieter as a girl, that she had devoted more time to studying her mother's face. She did not want to die without being able to remember that face, the curls on either side pouring over her ears, the high bun pulled tightly to the back, the wave of hair above her forehead. But the face: it was blank, almost, except for the requisite features. But the contours, their reception of the light, were vague; her lips: were they thin or generous? How they might have curved as she smiled or thinned in anger? When she cried, did her mother conceal her tears by looking up, as though balancing them before they dared to trickle out and make landfall upon her cheeks?

Out of the myriad of facial features Miss Williams had observed in her travels and teaching, she could not decide which ones might have fit her mother, who was certainly a pretty, if mostly unadorned, woman. Helen had no jewelry, but for a tawny wedding band that turned Helen's finger green beneath the metal, a pair of earrings and matching string of pearls she rarely wore. Helen kept them in a pouch she secured to her wrist, and took them out only for "occasions"— when her father had a contract, for instance, for a new associate to sign. Afterwards, the pearls had to be retired to their pouch hidden in Helen's sleeve.

If she could not guess at her mother's features, Miss Williams knew quite affirmatively that Helen had to be pretty, if she was going to survive the kind of life her father was furnishing. This Miss Williams had figured bit by bit over the years of her life, particularly as she had to teach herself the ignominious business of salesmanship. Miss Williams had manuscripts, her credentials, and her qualifications to sell, but Helen had Mr. Williams, Eva's father, to peddle to the world. Helen not only had to be pretty but fetching, conspicuous in how she mastered beauty's virtues and details. She might have had to bat an eyelash or apply a confident, supercilious stare, to either secure a scheme with her husband or take down a fool no longer so bewitched by her husband's deals.

But Miss Williams was no longer confident of the distinct color of her mother's hair beyond the requisite brown; whether it bore streaks of blonde and red, as the course of autumn foliage takes in its languorous exit; and as Eva's own hair appeared, under the proper angle of the sun. Was her mother's skin, before her illness, bright, or defeated and sallow as it was when she was dying? There were other changes, too, as Helen Conover Williams struggled with age and infirmity. The shapes that made up her face fell away. Was the almond of her eyes always drooping, the plane of her cheeks always collapsing in painfully minute measurements? Or was her mother beautiful in some other way that now she could not name because she lacked the terminology, the knowledge of those elements that completed her mother's face? In the bed where her mother laid, benumbed and deteriorating, at the sanitarium, Helen was wrapped in shawls and linens but segregated from her animating properties. Her mother's voice, high and thin, as if on the verge of disappearing from the horizon, was what Eva had managed to hold onto, and the stories it told as it went along in its own kind of determination.

The first story Miss Williams remembered was the tale of the mirrored knight. He began life as a poor boy who liked to collect shiny trifles as any boy does. From the street he could cull screws and nails, horseshoes, and the spokes of bicycles. From the tenements, he took hinges off doors, and gears from clocks. The local ragman helped him yank the toes off steel-toed boots. He pulled buttons from uniforms and the metal levers off telegraph keys. They were just bits and pieces, salvage or junk, and people did not notice. This was a time of great factories, men and women pouring into buildings of brick-and-mortar to manipulate great machines. There was so much metal seemingly living and breathing among the people, and the bellows, and steam, that we humans were becoming mechanical ourselves. But the boy was not interested in saving humanity.

His plan was to build a castle out of all this refuse, these crumbs and discards, because of how his family was forced to live, much as Eva's family had to on occasion. They crowded into a quarter of a windowless room with three other families, each family's space cordoned off with rope and furniture, and sheets worn thin as the walls that separated each apartment. They cooked and slept and suffered through fevers together in that room, and they had to relieve themselves in a pot all the families shared. Babies slept in old dresser drawers, and young boys cried facing the corner of the wall, if they were lucky and managed to chisel out any privacy.

Once he finished building his castle, he'd take whatever was left to make tools and sundries, and he and his family would grow food on their own land, and raise their own animals; construct forges and roads and dig a moat so deep that none could pass over it. The boy wanted nothing less than a world onto itself so finally his family would have no need of landlords and butchers, grocers and dairy men, coppers who shooed them away from the public steps or the City Hall; and he wanted to be rid of carriage drivers, nurses, and doctors too, and all those who demanded too much in return for performing their duties when the boy and his family had nothing to give.

So he kept on collecting his scraps and flotsam until it seemed to multiply against itself; it truly became worth something in its weight and height, a spectacle people would pay to see, if there was a place to show it. A wise man offered the boy a warehouse where he could store his treasure as he added to it; the man would charge visitors a penny a peek to look at this man-made wonder, a mountain of steel. The man promised to split the proceeds, a square fifty-fifty deal. The small civilization of forgotten brass, copper, silver plating, and nickel was transported to the warehouse, and placed behind a broad set of windowed doors. There it grew again from the axles and siding the boy wrenched off carriages and the roofs of railroad cars. From the blackened iron and steel of potbelly stoves, he harvested doors and drapers, and he took in old pots and pans, irons and bodies of sewing machines that had been dumped along the railroad routes out of town. From the rubbish of lost homes, he would build what would finally be his own; with the pennies that came in, he would have the money to furnish it.

But one day he went to the warehouse to find the broad windowed doors open and his treasure gone. The entire lock, stock, and barrel of it had disappeared, not even a curl or shaving. It was as if his majestic collection had only been a figment of his imagination. All of those nights he spent staring at his work, seeing the castle take shape as though it would materialize out of silver clouds organizing themselves in the sky; all those days of hammering and ripping, the more stubborn and sharp castings slicing into his hands when a piece refused to be removed from its body, all for naught, unless . . . unless he could exact a price. For he knew who had done this, and the kind of man he was; a man who could only love himself, and wanted only for himself, so much so that he could not stand to think of another man's riches or pleasures. The most selfish man of all could be brought down, though, by the thing he loved the most.

So the boy started a new collection, one that would not have to be as nearly as massive as his original, but surely just as fantastic. It would be composed solely of mirrors. Out of hideous superstitions and disastrous circumstances he'd strike against the man who wronged him, and regain his fortune. What a small dream his first ambition suddenly seemed, to seek mere sanctuary in material that bent only to fire. Now he would avenge his loss through a method that was flamboyant yet invisible. Nothing registered among his friends and acquaintances as his hunting grounds extended throughout the city, for the antecedents of mirrors are so small as to go unnoticed, and yet they grow into instruments of mighty strategy. He found broken mirrors to be salvaged in the collapsed homes of the most desperate tenement dwellers, and he found broken mirrors in the former salons and parlors of beauticians and barbers, in old theaters, decrepit water closets, in schools and factories and any location where humans gathered and needed to be reminded they were still individuals.

From the nuggets of glass that had once aspired to masquerade as gemstone, to swaths of windows he converted to mirrors by smearing one side with silver paint, he welded the world's first suit of mirrors, an armor that freed its wearer from carrying weapons. He put it on and resumed his search, not for simple objects, baubles or ball bearings, or any substance that might be manipulated into an illusion to dazzle or frighten, but for that dullest material of all, the human kind. He went to the closest city, where younger boys were known to scour through garbage in search of their destinies, and planted himself among the warehouses. Soon enough he was approached by other scavenging boys who had a familiar tale to tell him. They led him to the man amid his stores, the sweat and anguish of the impoverished transformed into precious menageries of all sorts of ornaments: colored glass and cameos, wooden spools and Christmas wrapping, shards of tin and rocks meant to be gold or jade.

As the boy approached the man, he needed to do no more than raise his arms and catch the light as it reflected off the buffed surfaces. The man might have attacked the boy, but all he saw was himself in the mirrored armor and so was unable to move—against himself, against the boy, against all the boys he had so blithely trifled with. The boys appeared from behind the mirrored knight and attacked the man, tearing off his clothes so he would have to watch the length and duration of his shame. The boys sorted through his wardrobe to extract its riches while the man was forced to study the horrific patterns and textures of his bareness. Then they each recovered the pile of goods that had been taken from them as the mirrored knight refused the man in all his efforts to avoid his cowering likeness. It was a gratifying conclusion to the humiliation that had badly stung the first scavenger, who had now grown into a heroic man and found it more satisfying than the discovery of his own treasure.

Often it was difficult to separate her mother's stories

from the meter the railroad tracks and train cars exacted, as Helen saved her most hypnotic sagas for the long journey they undertook once Eva's father had left them—for the war, her mother reminded her. Her reminders were constant at first, but then they subsided as the journey slowed, as if calcifying, being made into a permanent condition. For if Miss Williams were ever pressed for when this journey began, the time she spent on trains and in train stations, coaches and carriages, and waiting in boarding houses, she would be unable to account for either a date or length. As far as she could place it, everything began with the word "confidence," and progressed into other vocabulary, most of which Eva could not pronounce: the names of laws, diseases, and methods for assuaging both, if not the outright banishing of their effects. Eva and her mother were trying to outrun them, sepsis and coppers, and an unlawful termination of some kind. They were going to have to run a very long way to avoid the disgruntled customers of her father's investment house—into the territories, where everything would be different, from the land they would walk on to the sun over their heads.

On the train was when the robustness of her mother's skin must have declined, as they were always inside a train car, or a room where the air was too close, or holed up in a station where the exhaust of men's cigars, women's perfumes, and the unrelenting distress of fidgety children steamed up the walls. Weak and fallow, her mother's skin turned, like the pages of a book that has been abandoned. Not pages from storybooks or the slick and shiny magazine print from which her mother occasionally made tales based on the illustrations—Eva instead pictured the lined and divided charts her father kept in a folder, without proper binding, where he was incessantly recording names and numbers. The yellowed pages fell out and he crammed them back in again, without regard for any order they might have had. But Eva was forbidden to touch them, so delicate was the writing there. Her mother was suffering just as the pages might have, as her usual warmth and glow were dispatched in favor of an off-blankness—something curdling under her surface, as if burnt or newly fragile.

"Now 'confidence' could mean many things," her mother said at the start of their journey, as if to explain why it had begun. "It might be a quality that is important for men to have. Or a feeling you have about someone or something. Or if someone tells you a secret, that person takes you into his confidence, because that person knows he can trust you not to tell and spoil it."

"Why does one word get to say three things?" Eva asked.

"I don't know," her mother conceded. Helen fell silent then, as though she considered supplying an answer, but knew the search would be too taxing.

"It isn't fair, for one word to say so much," Eva decided, "and for other words to say nothing."

"What words?" Helen asked.

"The words some men give," Eva said, "so when Daddy says, 'His word ain't worth a plug nickel.'" Eva was proud of herself for having answered so efficiently and in the voice and dialect of her father. "Sometimes he says, 'His word ain't worth the paper it's printed on,' and 'Anybody worth their two cents knows that guy's bogus, he's for doing a sucker's business.'"

"Ah-ha," her mother said, and to Eva she seemed to draw more heavily on her next breath, out of a sense of fatigue and surrender. "I think your father was speaking of what men in his business call 'terms of art.'" Helen tried to speak lightly, though Eva detected a rougher strain entering her mother's voice, along with an odd restoration of color to her cheeks and neck.

"What is 'term of art'?" Eva persisted.

"It is how business is conducted," her mother said. "Certainly your father did not wish for you to repeat any of this, not if you intend on becoming a proper young woman."

"Will Daddy come to meet us if I am proper?"

"If he can find a way, he will. But he has so much to do and it is all so far away," Helen said, and then her mother hesitated. Eva sensed it in how her mother's breathing quickened, as if willing herself not to talk when she must have had too much to say. But before Eva could form her next question, Helen said gravely, "Your father has a duty to his country, and he is going to perform his service."

Eva did not have a perfect grip on what "service" and "duty" meant but had already been instructed her father could accomplish these tasks only across the ocean, on an island whose name she could not sort out. It took too much expended breath in the middle of the word, after a balancing act of the tongue she had yet to perfect; when she tried, only the final syllable made it past her lips. She wanted to ask her mother to say the name again; if she heard it enough, she might say it without the embarrassment. Yet her mother appeared so diminished in posture, suddenly vacant and pale where seconds earlier she was irritated and flushed. Eva dared not to force her mother into another configuration of tone, standing, and breath.

Helen swayed as the passengers surrounding them on the benches were forced to adapt to the bursts and hesitations of the locomotive. Eva took her mother's hand, cold as if becoming bloodless, but Eva was relieved it was able to squeeze hers back. Her mother's hand would rest in Eva's lap as they fell asleep in their clothes, as they did every night of their journey, amid the dreams and mutterings of other passengers. At daylight, they rose to take their turn in one of the water closets, as they would every morning; they would change undergarments and wash the previous day's shifts and drawers as best they could. Helen was frequently restored in the morning; with an appetite she'd greet other passengers, the porters, and engineers. She'd make appointments with other women to read or play cards, and to the porters she'd pass in the narrow passageways, she'd invite them to smell the special perfume she had mixed in an atomizer. Helen said it was nothing more than rubbing alcohol brightened with citrus oils, though it smelled taut and fortifying, how the out-of-doors would be in the territory after their stifling city existence.

For a spray to their cheeks, the porters would agree to carry word of her services throughout the train: hair styling or freshening. Helen had been forced to part with her most important equipment, what she used to give her husband new identities: razors and moustache brushes, the barbering scissors and curling tongs. The beads and ribbons for ladies' hair were also left behind in the mad preparations they made; there was an urgency Eva did not quite understand, having to do with her father's shipping out to his regiment. But Helen could improvise so long as she had paper bags or newsprint, and her last bottle of Macassar oil. She had to stretch it, though, with her spit that she dabbed into the palm of her hand. This she reserved for the wealthier ladies, those in their private passenger compartments.

Eva witnessed her mother mixing a spate of oil in this manner as she posed as Helen's assistant. Eva was told not only to remain silent, but not betray any relations between herself and Helen, lest they appear as itinerants, permanently on board the train without a legitimate destination. Helen was to be a lady stylist, headed west where the ingredients for her potions were plentiful; a lady stylist with an apprentice, trusted by the authorities to educate and train a young ward of the state. A lady stylist was a woman certified for respect, to be treated with fairness. So Eva handed her mother strips of paper that would be wound around hair for a crimp or a curl, and was careful to address her mother as Mrs. Conover-Williams, for stating one's pedigree in such a public way was assurance that such a pedigree existed in the first place. Her mother did not speak to her during these charades unless to call her "Miss" or "Missy," or click her heels to summon Eva to a task.

For the wealthy ladies, Mrs. Conover-Williams demonstrated how they might collect their own hair to weave hairpieces. It was Eva's most important task to demonstrate how to best maintain one's hairbrush, so that it would not aggravate the scalp, or further damage the hair it collected. This involved removing the hair from the thistles, teeth, or tines in an assiduous manner so that the mass of tangles and knots could be used for the hairpieces, and then sprinkling a flowery concoction over the brush to rejuvenate it. The liquid might have been nothing more than the spray her mother graced the porters with, but Mrs. Conover-Williams promised, after previewing its scent for her lady customers, that it would strengthen and resolve the bite and pull of the brush as though the implement were a living creature. And it would do so "just enough to preserve the gentleness needed for gentle ladies." Eva tried using the same nonchalance and melody her mother employed when using this line, though remembering the words and when they should be said was too much for Eva at times. When she recalled their timing and content, it was all she could do to recite them, without her mother's proper, but casual, authority.

"And these women do not want rodents in their hair," Helen said sternly, since in the trade hairpieces women made for themselves were called "rats." "Our clientele are not French royalty," Helen reminded her, "and this is not an Imperial realm. Yet."

Lifting the balls of hair from the brush felt like morbid work to Eva. She might as well have been removing souls from bodies, for the amount of time it took, and the care she had to apply to it. Her mother would sometimes admonish her in front of the customers that no one should hear a snap when the hair was separated from the brush; nor should they detect a raking noise, almost like an ascending musical scale, when detaching hair from a comb. It was a wonder to watch her mother do these things, the flare and power in Helen's fingers, as though she were attending plants, beseeching them into a delicate growth. As she stitched and knitted up these impromptu hairpieces, she carried on conversations with these women, always fretful on some issue. They were very worried

someone should find out something or think in some way
that they were being taught a skill they should have mastered
long ago; that they were paying for a service they shouldn't
have to pay for; that they should appear too well coiffed upon
disembarking from the train, disproving that train travel is
the burden that it is; or that they might come off as haggard,
neglectful of their grooming upon arrival. Mrs. Conover-Williams pledged to provide them with a look from the golden
mean, and never to spill their secrets.

The poorer women had no such reservations about hiring
the stylist and her apprentice, and tipped Mrs. Conover-Williams more graciously. Helen did not use her spit-and-oil
treatment on them. She plaited their hair and twisted their
locks, securing these alterations with her own hairpins, and
returned the following day to the benches where her poorer
clients had been seated by the railroad. For these ladies she
released their tresses to pile them atop their heads so they
would appear as Charles Dana Gibson's girls did. On these
occasions Eva was encouraged to hold a small mirror to the
woman's face as proof of her mother's handiwork. They used
their fingers to smudge out the dirt the train had compiled
on their faces and declared their reflection to be nowhere as
beautiful as the girl apprentice displaying it to them.

The coins her mother earned were secreted into pockets
Helen had sewn into her corset. When her mother coughed,
or "had difficulty seeking air," as she put it, Eva imagined the
coins cutting past Helen's skin, into her ribs as they ploughed
through to her lungs and heart. Her mother would drown in
money, because they never had enough, or they had too much.
"The poor are so often denied the luxury of a quick death," her

mother said once, though Miss Williams could not precisely place when Helen had made that statement. On the train, time was compressed into three states: morning, afternoon, and night. But there were no days or dates on the calendar, only the roiling present. As the coins accumulated in Helen's corset, her mother found difficulty in making any movement, as though muscle and bone were hardening under the force of so much pressure.

"I've decided I don't like being an apprentice," Eva announced at the conclusion of one styling session; they had freshened the hair of five sisters bound for Chicago. The youngest, a year or two older than Eva, was blonde; the other four became darker in color as they aged, until the oldest, the chaperone, was a wan brunette, and she seemed bitter for having lost her youth in such a public fashion. She demanded to be attended to first, as the most senior member of the family, and referred to Eva as "you," clapping her hands when she needed something: a glass of water, the mirror, powder for her neck; it was infernal, even in first class accommodations, she said. The woman's dishpan hair had a sour odor of dross and chalk; the chalk was meant to conceal what came from the rest of her. "How long has this thing been your apprentice?" she asked as Eva tugged on her scalp, which she accused Eva of doing too enthusiastically. Helen had pins in her mouth and so merely smiled, as though engrossed in her task to the point of enforced silence.

"But it's just an act," Eva's mother said.

"But why do we have to act it?" Eva asked.

"Because it provides the proper illusion," Helen said.

"What does that mean?"

"It means we affirm their belief that there is an order in their world, and they are at the top of it," Helen said. "That is what they are truly paying for, to be fussed over and complimented, when if they had any sense they could just as easily do this for themselves."

"Why don't they do it themselves?" Eva asked, not because she did not understand, but because she sensed her mother's strength flagging. If she could not keep her mother engaged in conversation, Helen would drift off, leaving Eva to her own devices. Eva could watch the other passengers or the landscape: dark, mostly, with neither people nor animals for her to study. At night the train accelerated with tremendous force; it became more difficult to walk or maintain one's posture sitting on those benches, and yet the minutes while her mother nodded and muttered passed by stubbornly, as though they required a push, shove, and then some to lead them off the clock. Eva wondered if her parents truly loved her or if her mother would have preferred a different type of girl for a daughter—one who was older, more agile and adept at following orders.

Eva knew she was not an orphan, but she had to consider whether this was how an orphan felt, and whether she was anywhere close, in her estimations. It was not a pleasurable feeling in any sense, but it held an attraction much like moths are attracted to flame. They navigate by finding light, Helen had told her, so it was no surprise that they would seek out fire when the moon was new and light was unavailable. But like any living creature, moths identify warmth and beauty first from a distance, and are unprepared when their source is revealed to be dangerous.

"I will explain when you are older, although you are likely clever enough to sort it out for yourself, long before then," Helen said.

"Will you still tell me then, when I'm older? To make sure I've got it right?"

"If need be, my dear," Helen said. "You know, you are a dear. And you will be a fine young lady when you grow up. I just know it."

"How? How do you know that?" Eva asked, but it was too late; her mother had blinked. As the moment lagged and the train hastened its pace, Helen's eyelids succumbed to the weight of the nightfall outside, and she was asleep.

Through observation and error, Eva learned that her mother's voice and body could better withstand the darkness if Eva could lure her into a story. This could be accomplished only by leading her mother into considering some pedestrian item: mirrors and feathers, bottles and coins. One feather was fine for a quill, but a collection of feathers only God could use, and the murmurations of starlings were God's way of writing in the sky His messages to the world. The bottles the railroad porters hauled through the cabins were mere rubbish in their eyes. But to a smart boy, the neck of a bottle might be a telescope, and the glass bottom a magical lens. A young man she once knew used a bottle's secret qualities to look over his enemies, and found the bully who had been menacing him was not so much of a giant. Because the lens could sort out fact from exaggeration and provide perspective as it set people and objects against the curvature of the earth, that bully became a compressed miniature of a man, who could barely tackle an upward slope. The tall men who were always so intimidating were squeezed to their rightful size through the lens, and the little people—the short, poor, or thin—were stretched into towers of courage and masculinity, Helen said.

By far, Eva was most intrigued by the tale of the penny emperor, though it was not necessarily her favorite. Her mother began this story as she was sewing pockets in Eva's clothes. Helen could no longer carry all their coins in her corset. Their weight and rustling intruded not just on her waking moments but also her rest, her ability to dream. A pocket in Eva's cap would be an ideal place for storing coins, she said, since Eva could then become an empress of copper. She was, after all, heir to the penny emperor of Baltimore. On this train she was directing her first voyage of conquest, extending the empire's holdings across the continent, to the territories where they were headed. To Arizona, it was, and then who knows? Onto California, where she would challenge gold's supremacy. But first she needed a crown befitting her position, and a lesson in the origins of her sovereign.

The penny emperor did not begin life as a prince, but as a fatherless boy. While he fed and slept in his mother's warm belly, his father was killed in a most egregious accident. His father worked at the tallest building in all of America, the Shot Tower, where it had been his job to wait at the bottom as men at the top poured hot lead through a sieve. The lead stretched like quicksilver over the sieve's perforations, and then plunged as individual droplets into a vat of cold water. His father rescued this newly minted shot, or ammunition, from the vat, so it could be polished and packaged, then bought and loaded into guns wielded by hunters and soldiers.

One ordinary day, however, the sequence of locks and

pulleys that held the molten lead in place failed. The tumblers in the locks seized, the pulleys snapped, and the hot lead was sent tumbling out of the cauldron without the sieve in place. The air chiseled the rushing metal into a fine a point as an arrow, and the force, volume and stink of this freshly hewn weapon lanced right through his father. He was cleaved in two, but one side could not live without the other, just as a shadow cannot move without action, and a mirror cannot thrive without reflection.

And so he perished.

The workers at the Shot Tower fetched the penny emperor's pregnant mother from her home so she could be brought to the foreman's office, and the foreman would explain. He spoke of the locks and pulleys and added a treatise on how the gears in the tower also might be to blame. But this did not assuage the new widow. She called the accident murder, and was then roughly escorted out of the foreman's office. The workers saw to it that she got home safely, but the next day she was back. She demanded a more truthful narration. That was never to come, so each day she ventured to the Shot Tower in her mourning clothes and black veil and knocked on the door. She was denied entry and went home, but came back the next day. In her black dress and veil, politely requesting entry. This she also was denied, so she took to simply standing across from the entrance, fixing her widow's glare on the place. People said she was cursing the tower, though there were no more accidents like the one that took her husband—at least none that anyone heard tell.

Day after day, and all of the days afterward, she stood out there, hating, except when she gave birth to the penny emperor. Thereafter she brought the babe with her, on the chance her dead husband's companions might cross the street to admire the newborn, and the foreman might remember how this young son was practically orphaned. This was before the babe was known to be the penny emperor, of course, so she and the baby were largely ignored. He grew from infancy to boyhood rather anonymously, except in his own family. His little girl cousins adored the boy, called him "Sweetie cake," "Jimmy-bean," and "Junior-jam," as James was his name, being named for his father, James William Grabowski. The girls taught Jimmy-bean how to play five stones, run races, and use a stick to push a hoop forward on the cobblestones. James and his mother moved in with them, as she was no longer able to fend for herself. In their room, they were given a bed to share, and James was never in want of playmates.

His uncles groomed young James for great things. They taught him how to memorize sequences of numbers, how to use his voice to reach a great many people, and they bought him a matching cap and knickers so he'd be dressed properly. James's uncles hired newsboys who sold the papers by shouting headlines on the street corners. A penny apiece, each paper cost.

"Could you guess what happened next?" Eva's mother would interrupt herself.

"But you're the storyteller," Eva would reply. "You have to say."

"Did he become a baker when he grew up?"

"No," Eva answered.

"A circus performer; maybe he trained the elephants?"

"No," she sighed, dutifully.

"Maybe he studied to become a painter," Helen guessed. "Or an artist of some sort."

"No!" Eva always insisted. "He became the penny emperor!"

Indeed he did. When he was old enough to be left on his own, he was given a raft of papers to put on his arm, and told to shout out the headlines. The papers went flying off his arm as though they were snowdrifts in a high wind. And he'd collect pennies, which he passed onto his uncles. They regarded him as their most efficient newsboy, and their most honest. They showed him how they kept track of all the papers the boys sold, on lined green paper with boxes for all their calculations.

They had a lovely existence, this family, in a row house with bay windows. Each week the uncles brought home something plump and tender from the butcher's, and on Sundays there was turkey and all the trimmings. The aunts baked potpies and stews for the girls' lunches, and meat pies for James to eat on his street corner. On the brick range, a pot of water was always heated, for a bath, a cup of tea, or the washing. When the girl cousins played school, the young emperor was usually the only pupil, so the girls took turns placing their hands upon his as he held a pen. In this way he was initiated into the alphabet and cursive writing.

All was well, except for his mother. On the bed mother and son shared in the girl cousins' room, she rocked herself or muttered incessantly until she was exhausted. She still walked each day to the site of her husband's last day in this life, but the foreman and the tower's owner succeeded in having her moved farther and farther away from the tower; so far that the last bit of her husband remaining on earth—the last place he had been before he was evaporated up to heaven—may have appeared as no more than a crease in her vision. She did not care to see the pennies the young emperor accumulated, though he told her he would buy for her anything she wished. A team of horses, he thought, and a fine carriage, to carry her to the Shot Tower and finally say goodbye to his father in the proper fashion.

James shot up tall and lean as a tree, and as handsome as befits an emperor. But his form and copper riches attracted the wrong kind of attention. The hooligans of the neighborhood knew what he was carrying, and began to attack him. The uncles taught James how to place the pennies in his gloves, on his knuckles, if possible, in winter. In summer, he carried extra socks to hold the pennies, and he figured, on his own, how to swing a penny-laden sock as if it were a yo-yo, or a mace fit for a king. Anyone who dared to challenge the penny emperor on his rounds would wear telltale blue half- and quarter-moons, like new mountains and gullies, on his face the following day.

The penny emperor became a recognizable, dependable bearer of news and currency, so the men he sold papers to, in their frock coats and top hats, enlisted him in their businesses and political campaigns. Sometimes these men would entreat James to memorize a long, difficult number. The numbers came in bunches, in twos, sometimes threes, on scraps of blank newsprint that had to be disposed of immediately. Nothing was to be committed permanently to print or handwriting. There was barely enough time to get them all in his head, and sometimes the numbers were as long as the Shot Tower was tall! And then he was to accompany another set of men—the "policy men," they were called—from house to house, across town where the freedmen and fugitive slaves lived. Those numbers were their only hope for a better life and as James performed his recitation they would clasp their hands together as if in prayer. Finally the policy men would wrest him away from the doors and porches where the downtrodden would inevitably cry, or shout, or plead. James could hear it in their voices, their contrition and their begging, and it frightened him, to think his voice commanded such power and numbers held that kind of meaning. But the penny emperor's palm was met with real paper money, real legal tender, by the end of each day. He could not turn his back on it.

James much preferred working for the rich men on Election Day. At least it seemed more honest, working with a list of names printed on handbills that were not to be junked; people kept them, in fact, as souvenirs of their fidelities and dignity. The men would give James a stack of handbills to press into the pockets of voters as they lined up at the polling places. He had to do this delicately, artfully, without drawing the notice of policemen or operatives with their own handbills, with an entirely different set of names on them. Otherwise they might cry "Foul!" should they discover the small bottle of spirits wrapped within each of the handbills.

"Spirits?" Eva questioned, for she knew what a spirit was, although it was difficult to know just what a spirit in a bottle might do for someone waiting at a balloting station. Helen had read her stories of spirits from bottles that could be vengeful or generous, given the nature of the person in possession of the bottle. As the penny emperor, James must have known which type of spirit to assign to each person. People said her father had a nasty spirit, if his patience was tested. But was this how spirits came to be distributed throughout the population, on Election Day? What about the spirits of children, and women, who were not permitted at the polls? How were those spirits obtained?

"You are an astute listener," Helen said, though now the story was faltering. For the penny emperor no longer had need of his coins, with all of the rich man's currency— paper money—filling his pockets. He had volumes, as thick as Bibles, and he strung the legal tender as if it were fabric, and he meant to make for himself a cloak of all the denominations. While this cloak served as his credentials, it also made him more of a target. Anyone could steal the cloak and thereby defrock him of his status, but they would just as soon have themselves and their crime found out.

So her mother would abandon this thread and seek to start again somewhere in the middle, with the hope that she would find the key to a better ending. In one version, the penny emperor learned his numbers only in the pursuit of sound business practices, and pennies continued to buy his meat even as his uncles moved toward a more criminal practice. From his aunts, he learned to sew his pennies into the sleeves, cuffs, pockets and collars of his shirts, and in the hems and knees of his trousers. He was creating a kind of invisible armor for when he'd finally be ready to avenge his father. But lead is a far stronger, far more resilient metal than copper, and Eva's mother knew this either as fact, or intuited it, and therefore could not account for how the penny emperor might have overcome the leaden forces at the Shot Tower.

Once she told of the fine carriage he had promised his
mother, how he brought it to life with a team of fresh copper
horses. They pulled the carriage through the streets, and
people saw a rush of fire, one lit to forge shields that would
make quick work of lead bullets, rendering the products of the
Shot Tower obsolete. Or perhaps people witnessed a second
sunrise as the carriage passed by, heralding a new day when
men such as James's father would be remembered, and their
widows rightfully compensated.

In most versions Helen attempted, her voice wavered,
falling deep into her throat, into the chest, where it nested
like an orphaned bird, comfortable but anxious. In this voice
the penny emperor would sometimes escape his dilemma for
a ship to Boston, which Eva understood to be her birthplace,
and therefore the site of her parents' marriage. Only when
her mother's voice managed to find an equilibrium between
her teeth and tongue would Eva be rewarded with a more
complete version, where the forces her mother had arrayed
against the penny emperor would at least be addressed, if not
dispatched and conquered. For no matter the height and stur-
diness of his stacks of his pennies, the ingenuity of his armor,
or the peevishness or evil of his enemies, he could not bring
back his father or extend the life of his mother.

In her final days, the mother of the penny emperor could
go no further than her own front door. The owners of the Shot
Tower had laid increasingly elaborate gauntlets to end her
vigils; outside they maintained a thriving parade of muggers
and pickpockets, dirty coppers and flimflam men, and finally
lawyers. James and his uncles tried to bring doctors into
the house so they might ease her discomfort in the disten-

tion in her hands and fingers, the swelling of her ankles, in her constant sweating, as if she were excreting the effort her husband failed to deliver upon succumbing to an arrow of lead and fire. But all refused to treat the widow, given the labyrinth they would have to conquer just to get at their patient. Of course the mother of the penny emperor died, for someone usually had to die in her mother's stories. Death was her mother's consummate arrangement for distinguishing an era, or ending a story.

If someone did not die in one of her mother's stories, someone would disappear, his talents or insights no longer relevant to the lesson she was imparting, the epoch she wished to illustrate. The penny emperor was from another time, she'd confess in the morning, following one of her more lavish iterations of the tale. He gave hope to orphans and a counter-argument to those who said a boy could not rise above his origins. But the country was changing; it was relentless in its need for change, and the old tricks—hard work, sweat, slaving and saving—would get a boy nowhere these days. Or perhaps it would land him in the clutches of the United States Army. For the tale of the penny emperor was nothing less than a gussied-up version of her father's story, Miss Williams came to understand once she was ensconced in a teacher's college abroad and assembling her own tales. She exchanged her father's pennies for her mother's pearls, and hatched what would be the first of her tales to gain notice, the story of the pearl palace.

To begin, she thought of a young boy, poor and restless, following a rainbow for its pot of gold. He was to be disappointed, of course, but by tracing the dregs of the colorful spectrum, he found a kind of light. It was austere, and inconceivable to anyone who thought of light in the common sense. One did not see it directly; this was light in its infancy, which is nearest in the senses to something that makes a sound. The boy did not hear this light as one might listen for the rustling of other animals in the undergrowth, or the pluck of an instrument. Rather, he closed his eyes and drew upon his promises, so that the sound entered him through other channels: his hair, nose, throat, and knees. From there, the strands traveled to his chest, and in his heart, they intersected. Then he could hear that sound light makes, if others could have understood it; the slow odyssey of the earth and its satellite.

The boy became possessed of such grand feelings, he thought himself capable of slaying dragons, rescuing princesses, raising the dead souls of those he had lost, commanding the spirits of those who wronged him. But how to carry this feeling with him forever? Despite its virtues neither the light nor its sound could feed or clothe him, nor provide shelter from the elements. He cupped his hands to his ears as if to trace the sound's direction, and heard in his heart what he should do next. At moonrise, in this very spot, he should dip his palms into the reflecting light, and from there hold it fast between his hands, and allow it to shape itself.

The boy waited, listening through his chest to the intricate forces of the universe: all the suns, stars, and planets. He waited for so long he heard the moon's tug on the oceans and flow of rivers. He waited until the moon was suitably high so its light accentuated each blade of grass, as the dew does some mornings, and then he opened his hands so his palms would catch every sound the moonbeams made, like a hum that warms insects beneath the soil. He opened his palms only once he was certain that all was silent against his skin, and found a stone, or truly a pebble, in each hand. Like light compressed, each layer gently stitched into the next, an incandescence that was the heart of fire in one moment, and a coverlet of ice in the next. Pearls, if we could call them something familiar to us. He would not trade them for anything: not stone or wood, pitch or metal. Instead he would put this raw material to practical use; he would build a palace of pearls.

For the rest of that night and all the nights when the moon made an appearance, the boy took light by the handful and doubled his strength with every grasp. In the daylight hours he aligned his pearls to mark the boundaries of his castle; then he stacked and sculpted towers, gates and wards. He sang as he worked, as if being led in a chorus, and in the highest places he carved out turrets for the pearl weaponry he'd have to make, to defend his creation. On nights of the new moon, when no light fell to him, he rubbed his hands together and found nacre, or mother-of-pearl, ghosting the curvature of his palms, and used it for windows and mirrors. Over the months and years, his citadel rose where the rainbow had failed him, a Tower of Babel without the repercussions. Here everyone would be welcome, for succor and shelter, from they who had faith in him, to they who had not the courage to follow his ascent to the more recognizable pearl landmarks.

People were amazed, astounded, and ran to see what might have blinded them if built with different intentions. The boy, now a man, invited them inside, and they looked for their homes through the mother-of-pearl windows. They were mesmerized by their reflections in the mother-of-pearl mirrors. But neither window nor mirror provided perfect views or decent likenesses. The outside world, whether from the ground level or the farthest reaches of the clouds, was softened in a way that left the people questioning whether it had ever been real. The mirrors had a similar effect on the faces that could not stop staring into them, melting away age and infirmities and offering only a fawning smear of the basic features.

Once in the castle, the people forgot their names, and the names of their loved ones, as they were drowned out in their memories by the sublime song of the pearls. They lost all sense of direction; they no longer knew the inside from the outside; the present from the past; up from down. They spent their days pacing in circles, some wider than others, depending on how long they had been there. At first they would avail themselves of the kitchens and dining halls, but as the past faded into the air they could not remember the routes to these facilities, and they would waste away, until they were skeletons. Wherever they dropped, they would be absorbed into the floors and walls, so the entire structure would be reinforced with human faults.

Only a very small few, those with the stoutest memories for faces and landscapes, were not seduced into this waking ignorance. When they deigned to look into a mirror, or out of a window, they couldn't help but see the old world that had brought them to this point: the mud and wrinkles, broken down shacks and scars. Yet they were also imprisoned in this arrangement, by order of the man, who had elevated himself above his benefactors by virtue of a throne of pearls. Those who could hold onto their memories of life before the pearl castle were quickly drafted by the boy into becoming navigators, for only they could pilot themselves and others to the exits, or lead newcomers safely past the entrances. One would have thought that the dazzle of the pearl palace would have held a firmer grip upon those who were so enraptured by it, but instead those who could withstand its charms found themselves in a more pervasive limbo brought on by their self-awareness.

The man was able to resist the lure of the trap he had inadvertently built. But it was his plight to look after his admirers, to follow them as they became befuddled and frustrated. He found himself turning cruel and impatient, as his creation threatened to master him through a different method. The navigators peeved him frequently, and, when they did, he would remove a pearl, and another, from the rooms where they slept until that room had dissipated into silence and nothingness. The navigators had begun refusing his demands to be escorted to the edge of the pearl civilization, where he might leap into heaven, or have a running start ahead of the other penitents. He longed to be released from his duties, but he too had been burdened with the indignities of age: growths on his face, the downturn of his grin, the loss of teeth. He saw this not in the mirrors but in the faces of his visitors as he approached, and derived from this that he would never return to live off dirt and grass, and the occasional flesh of an animal.

The navigators pushed back against the man's pleas to be taken to the top of his palace, for no one can be led to the afterlife; reaching it is, and must be, a far more subtle test of will and endurance than having the means of hiring a guide. The navigators also feared too many of the visitors would lock onto the man's idea and follow him as he was escorted to the rim of the final, tallest tower—to the last tangible surface on the earth's sphere. Would they ever be persuaded to go back? There could never be room enough at the top; this they would see, if not remember. Some might intuit that they had reached the apex of their lives without comprehending how they had landed at this point. They would strand themselves like some sort of lost species. Others would leave and discard the adventure, only to hold onto a nagging sense that they had missed something. They might torture themselves for a lifetime, even more so than the agony they put themselves through on the lower floors. Who knew that the entrance to the hereafter would be so fraught and dangerous?

The man and the navigators came to an impasse. The navigators were too much like the man, who had made himself king, believing they had bested the creator whose ingenuity had granted them, purposefully or not, status. The king and the navigators, and those visitors who had unknowingly consented to becoming victims, alternately chased or evaded one another, and the king pursued his project of dismantling the rooms where the navigators gathered. He undid entire flights of stairs, wings, and landings. Whole sections of the palace might have been lost forever, if not for the speechless human bone assimilated as the visitors succumbed to the hypnotic hold of the pearl material. The castle became an even more confounding structure, a scaffold that afforded views to the madness taking place within.

Finally, when all the starving visitors had collapsed, all of the pearls had been detached, the navigators cornered, and the king stranded at the very spot where that rainbow had ended, the bones that had been floors and walls fell on the pearls haphazardly strewn about, until the entire thing and all the people were crunched into a powder. It is the same kind of powder now used to tamp down the sound and scent of the most wretched among the dead. In paupers' graves, submerged beneath with the broken backs of people and pearls.

Ten

MR. SHEEHAN HAD also changed over the course of Miss Williams's convalescence, in manner if not in appearance. He remained steadfastly quiet but less silent, in the language he must have developed between himself and the authorities. He acknowledged the doctor and nurses with nods of his head, and offered his hand in greeting to male visitors, including the reverend and the president of the historical society. To women, such as Miss Williams's colleagues, he bowed. His yellow eyes kept watch on every movement in the room and on her bed, Miss Williams noticed, but with less of the varnish that had once made its stare so threatening. He was a constant presence, and yet when he took her on those painstaking walks down the floor of the infirmary, he was more distant than he ever had been.

When they had been together in the cottage, Miss Williams had tried to intuit the wanderings of Mr. Sheehan's mind. She had failed, and this was the punishment; in the infirmary he was as much of a puzzle to her as he had been at their first meeting. She could know only how easily he met her pace, as he escorted her through the halls to the college's gardens; he did not rush or risk the slightest hint of impatience. She could know only how carefully he held her hands, whether they were on one of their walks or she was laying on the cot, and he was seated beside her. She could know only the soreness and fatigue he must have bitten off to continue supporting her at that leaden pace. She could know only that whatever his own suffering during the war, it had been lobbed off, discarded for a while, to attend to her suffering because there was possibility in it. The possibility of recovering, which did not necessarily belong to his own trials.

Her deliberate gait, the effort she put into each footfall—no matter how difficult—Sheehan took joy in them, because he was convinced she would come back to herself. She would be restored in place and prominence. It was all that he wanted, even for himself, once he repatriated. After the handwritten letter from King George was thrust into his hands, his welcoming committee boiled down to a pair of functionaries, a major and his secretary from His Majesty's Army.

His debriefing lasted for days, it seemed, in the Dover barracks. In some ways the British officers were no different from the Germans in the beginning, with their emphasis on names: the enlisted and officers, those he encountered in the camps but at peacetime could not be accounted for among the dead and injured. Then the names of other Irish with whom he might have colluded. It was a fact that the Germans gave the Irish preferential treatment.

But those two men, the major and his secretary, knew the answers to the questions they put to him before they started: the succession of camps, whether there were other Irish, what the International Committee of the Red Cross had so scrupulously observed in each setting. The major and his secretary also had what the Germans documented, with their impressive single-mindedness: acts of insubordination carried out by English prisoners, himself included. But the Germans didn't keep records, the men said, of their murder and neglect. Sheehan did not answer, because in either case, they had all the information they could ever need. They wanted him to help them make sense of it.

They had at their fingertips the date and location of where he was taken prisoner; Sheehan was the only prisoner taken that day, behind the enemy lines at LaVentie, on the Franco-German border. What was lost on the major were the circumstances. Had Sheehan been separated from his unit? So far from any target or strategic point . . . But there the major stopped. No one wanted to make an accusation outright. He'd rather Sheehan simply confess it.

Sheehan again remained silent, because just what would he confess? The cold, watery meals he ate; the sleep that by turns never came or, on some nights, overwhelmed him; the damp and infested barracks and cells that sheltered him. He knew the major's inference: Sheehan spending the war in relief and luxury while other men were fighting in the trenches, sleeping on their feet, rummaging for scraps, shooting, bayoneting, getting shot at, bombed, being sewn back together only to be sent out there again, their bodies the fodder that would outlast the Germans. Men such as himself were shuttled about as if a baton, or, better yet, a stick in a bundle, unceremoniously passed from one cart to the next, until the wheels were worn down to their axles.

Sheehan watched in his silence as the major repeatedly fingered his Lord Kitchener moustache. The secretary, who had also adopted Lord Kitchener's squint, fiddled with his glasses. They did not want to hear about who refused to work in the camps, and so were hauled off to harsher conditions. They wanted to know who moped, who feared the possibilities awaiting him in solitary and so attempted nothing. They wanted to know who lapped up the perks the Germans offered the Irish in the camp: more blankets, private rooms in warm huts, real trestle beds, the chance to wear civilian clothing. Some even stayed in hotels and were given revolvers. Wasn't that for a brigade of Irish the Germans were recruiting?

Hadn't he been to the Limburg camp? Of course not; it said as much in his records. The major and his secretary seemed otherwise convinced. The major waved a piece of thin, almost transparent, paper in Sheehan's face; Sheehan's first instinct was to grab at it, at the thing that he knew to be words. But his hands would only leave greasy smears on the page, and the words, should he read them aloud, would come out as mere dregs and drivel of the maelstrom in his ears. To speak them; to give a definitive "No!" would be useless.

He did not respond, but the pair attempted to remain right regular chaps, jovial and welcoming. The major raised his voice, the better for Sheehan to hear him. But Sheehan knew better than to trust the mirth of the British; it was always followed by some brutal mischief, like the edge of a penny rubbed against the scalp. The major slowed his speech, asked if he'd like an ear trumpet. Was he deaf from the shelling? Or perhaps just a touch hard-of-hearing?

Sheehan shook his head, and the major graciously continued with his pestering. He needed to know how to evaluate Sheehan's situation, whether to provide him with a train ticket, or vouchers for food and shelter, a new suit of clothes. Where would he go? Back to Gloucester? On a boat to Dublin? He'd get a right bang up reception there, wouldn't he? Had to hand it to the balls on those Micks, undertaking treason just as the whole western world was collapsing. Gave us a good scare, the major and his secretary agreed. They wanted to know if he had any relatives close by, a mate or some fellows? Sheehan wondered if the major was simply looking for more Irish to prosecute, or if he was truly suggesting he call on family to help. Perhaps the major was suggesting one to accomplish the other.

The major asked him about work. Sheehan showed the men his hands, because with their files, they might have known what his hands meant. How early in the trenches, he practiced against his thighs, or blankets, the walls of the billets. He sometimes thought of when he would be reunited with his instrument. But once Sheehan's hearing was shot, he did not think as often on it. Once his hands took on the appearance of any other soldier's, scalded with rashes. There was nothing wrong with them time and a few ointments could not correct, the major suggested.

In that room with the major and his secretary, Sheehan

considered rising to the occasion, explaining the depth of the damage, how his hands felt as if they had been sheathed in a new kind of undergrowth, but instead of stems and leaves, it was composed of sand or glass. On his right hand, the index finger had lost all authority in its extension, and on his left, the ring finger jettisoned its obedience. Within the hide that had been substituted for flesh, his bones and muscles now worked according to their own agenda. In both his pinkies, there was not pain, but forgetfulness, and it traveled through his wrists, to his elbows, and finally his shoulders. His arms would have been paralyzed if not for the routine in the prison camp of grasping, throwing, and shoveling—the blood and blisters that had become part of the limbs' automatic responses.

But if he said anything, if he swept up the description of one of his symptoms into a single word or phrase, what would happen? The sounds would go on too long, as if they had been commandeered by the bells in his ears. Or a word might fail, before he could complete it, be diced by the high whine that was the continuous background to his intentions. To say anything was to invite more disorder, to lose whatever control he had over his own person. He opted to say nothing, again.

The major advised that he attempt keeping accounts, running a cash register—a clerical position, nothing too physically taxing. Any number of businesses would take him on, or he could try to return to his teaching, occasionally performing, if anyone would have such a taciturn fellow as a musician.

The major next offered him money—not real money, but vouchers—for a training course, new clothes, a different existence. Sheehan thought he had not been afraid during the war—all that was wanted then was his body. Now, at peace, there was so much more to sacrifice. The major and his secretary wondered between themselves whether he should see a doctor; they might have even put the question to him directly. Finding a doctor for him, however, might lead to hospitalization, and hospitals were already overburdened, as one could easily imagine. There was nothing physically wrong with him, if he was not deaf. Obstinacy was not among the symptoms of shellshock or barbed wire psychosis, though perhaps they should be. But that was not their department, amending those regulations.

The secretary was cleaning his glasses with an Army-issued handkerchief and his own breath when he suggested that their subject might want to write about his experiences, if not speak. So they left him alone in a different room, at a desk, with several pieces of bright white paper, a pot of ink and a pen. Sheehan ran his hands over the paper repeatedly, as if it were the fine coat of an animal whose home—air, water, land—was not entirely clear. Because it was cold, as though it had clearly survived various travails, and almost wet, it soothed his finger pads to rest on it. His story must have been of some worth since the Home Office thought to expend such resources on it. But the only marks left there were those that his skin had impressed upon the page. They were faint, like a relief upon a wall the elements are intent on erasing. Once placed into a folder, into a filing cabinet with other folders, the pressure on them to disappear would be too strong to resist. Sheehan counted on that occurring.

Sheehan wrote, "I am not able to recall the events you inquire after." He remained in the room until the secretary returned to retrieve him. He was taken to other rooms, the last being an improvised barber's shop in a hangar that had the terrible effect of redoubling every sound beneath its ceiling. The secretary motioned for him to take one of the barber's chairs, but he was adamant, shaking his head as he kept his hands on his ears. He was removed from the hangar as a cadre of similarly hirsute men filed in, bright and eager, apparently, for their shearing. Because of his refusals he was denied a full new uniform, with the honors he had earned replicated in ribbons and medals, in which to travel home. He was not given a voucher for new clothes, and the train ticket only took him home as far as where he enlisted.

In Gloucester, there was no one waiting for him at the station. A Salvation Army captain found him a wool suit to wear. The fabric had him twitching as if he had been infested again. He walked to the music school, a steady march over which he recognized the flat he had rented, the pub where he took his evening meal. Finally, the school itself, where he might have just as well lived, before the war. There was a letter waiting for him.

From his mother. Through the haze and clatter, he recognized her handwriting on the envelope. *Don't come back*, it said. *It's not safe. Between the police and the Republicans, there's no room for a turncoat soldier. If you turn up at Summer-hill, I'll chase you to Howth or Kingstown. At least there you might find a ship that'll bear you away. You are flesh of my flesh, blood of my blood, but I'll do it still. I must, I've got the good of your brothers and sisters to consider. And the neighbors, and for everyone you'd ever known or loved or laid your eyes upon. For the love of Mary and all the saints. Don't come back,* she had written.

He tried to imagine the words in his mother's voice, though it was difficult, with all the furor and commotion the shelling had put into his head. He wanted only in that moment to recollect it fully so he might better judge the urgency she had invested in her writing. People said Catherine Carey possessed but an ordinary voice, serviceable though rough for choir, uninterested in harmonizing. People did not approve of its depth in a woman, how content it was within its limits, though that was its strength, the foundation of its confidence. At home, in a session, Catherine's voice was gallant, as if it were a flag raised in battle, its shadings and range like the tension in the canvas. *Contralto* was the term he learned to apply to it, so rare in its fortitude. But the letter from her hand was unfamiliar to his memory, so reedy and weakened, slashes and tears rented in its fabric.

His father had been the one to spur him into enlisting. "You might as well go all in, King and country and the sun never setting," was how Edmund had Catherine put it in a letter, since Edmund had no sense for reading, and could barely put his own name to paper. Edmund knew the light that was made to always shine on the British empire, particularly its squalor. Edmund Sheehan of Summer-hill Dublin was one of the light's unwitting caretakers. Edmund Sheehan was a candlebox man, one who brought the dawn once night had spilled across the continent and over the islands.

From house to house he traveled, through blight and rubbish, as night struggled to gain a foothold. He seemed to require mere moments to climb up his ramshackle ladder to the box, ignite the wick, and speed back down, to admire the candlelight spreading like daybreak through the Georgian window. He said he gave eyes to those houses, or a procession of torches for drunkards, whatever was considered by the most people to be practical or reasonable. It was quite a satisfaction, he would often declaim, to turn on his heel and bear witness to the pageants he had kindled. The lights in their cradles seemed to hum in concert with the stars' assistance.

The older Sheehan boys fought over who might accompany Da, and perhaps be compensated with a farthing for all the trouble and disruption a candlebox man's rounds could inflict on his sons' sleep. Ma tried setting a schedule for each in his turn, but Edmund decided it was best to have the boys settle it in their usual brilliant fashion. "They'll be fighting all their lives for a mite less," Edmund had reasoned, according to the stories that went back and forth like rags and twine improvised to provide a football. "No harm in getting them better acquainted with it."

Liam and Christopher, eleven months separating the dates of their birth, were said to wrestle not only between themselves but with the sticks and cushions that passed for the family's furniture to settle the question. Aidan, five years behind Christopher, and Patrick, two years behind Aidan, switched between throwing punches and bargaining with the older two, until Aidan took ill the year Easter came around late—too late, everyone said, for it was nearly May and the weather endeavored to foist summer before spring had a chance to flourish. Aidan was gone by the end of that week, and Patrick had joined him by August. There might have been an explanation, a malady they shared, but once Aidan had died, Catherine burned everything the boys had used in common, from their stockings to the straw that filled their mattress. It did no good and only made more to burn, once Patrick slipped away from them. By the time Michael could grasp that he had, through no fault of his own, lost two of his brothers, Aidan and Patrick were but the sunnier apparitions of the household. These ghosts did not all have names, and some had enjoyed too many days of this life while others starved or were worked to death in a poorhouse. Ma had preserved the fine linens that had belonged to her grandmother, and at Easter they were removed from their box to grace the table where they ate their Easter meal. Once, Sheehan could remember, a pair of baptismal cards fluttered out from the folds of the linens as they were being lifted from their cradle. Aidan and Patrick's, they were, his sisters immediately recognized them but said nothing until Ma had her back turned. The sound of those cards falling took up an almost infinite space in the tenement, like dried leaves receiving one of their species as it descends from twig and branch, to its final place of rest.

The competition to tag along with Da and witness his candle lighting prowess removed, Michael was invited to throw his arms around Edmund's neck and go at a far earlier age than his brothers. Catherine insisted that the boy be wrapped and attached to Da's back as if he were stowing away in a haversack, but no one knew the source of this fabric, and no one dare question its origin. In Dublin, the sun did not entertain closing its business until the hours of the following morning were near to beginning, and the sky clutched onto its streaks of pink beyond the dusk. Edmund hitched Michael to his back as the grip of those pink streaks was undercut by the darkness, the stars having yet to claim the night territory. Being that it was late, when a boy should be sleeping, Edmund was prepared for the boy to fuss, cry out for his mother, or for something to chew, a biscuit or soda bread or the carrots they tried to grow behind the tenement building. So Edmund tried singing a tune, and he carried some treats for Michael in his pocket for when the boy began twisting in the haversack as a lamb might, squeezed between ewes and rams at the feed trough. Edmund would halt his marching, and ask his son, "Would you rather walk then, little soldier?" before he launched into his tunes, the one about the shadows, ash, and silences ending once the sun had risen. The sound of his father's voice was not so much soothing as it was a distraction, a trinket with a reflection constantly changing, according to the wind and light, though Michael learned eventually how to follow Da's voice, from its natural lows to its dizzying heights.

From a distance, what his brothers must have seen as they watched from the street, their father's task of lighting the candleboxes appeared simple. A stroll up the ladder Da carried, a flash at the top, a jaunt down, and it was over until the next address. There, the process was repeated, until his father had ignited a procession of flame that pressed against the night. "Please, say nothing of the fairies," Edmund had intoned to the boys. He said this also to Michael, as Michael grew older and could better understand what his father meant from the tales his mother and sisters told him. "If the fairies could do this," Edmund often mused, "I wouldn't be so afraid of electricity. But there it is, a man's fears laid bare by candlelight. It should be good enough."

But because he was so secured to his father's back, and

because the weight did not seem to hamper Edmund as he gamboled up and down his ramshackle ladder, Michael was treated to glimpses of the light that his brothers never witnessed, from its apprehensions, to its acrobatics in the candlebox, and finally to its silence, when the morning struck. From behind his father's shoulders, Michael traced the progress of a gas lamp his father carried, the tapers Da lit before together they ascended up to the box, and the moment of contact—a distinct sound it had, of fire and falling just as the flame was caught and given a second chance. There were times when the box had been tampered with, and Edmund could not see properly into it, so he would have to intuit how deep the taper had to be placed inside, and how to steer it toward the candle. In this way, lighting a candlebox was much like the work of a fisherman, who must read the surface of the water to discern where the fish were gathering or survey the riverbank for which vantage would afford the most prosperous launching. But a successful catch was something one felt with his hands, a tug of resistance, and the flame caught by the candlewick was something Michael could hear, the temporary displacement of air, like breath, as the candle recovered the spark of the taper. It was this action, this momentary drop and restoration, that Michael found the most arresting of his father's errands: a sound with its own moments, the anticipation between them; as if time could be held, pulled apart, gently, and its power and logic observed and appreciated.

Once the candle was lit, his father rapped his knuckles against the glass above the door, and they returned to the street. From there Michael watched the light stretch through the Georgian windows overhead, half a sunrise, the curve of the world contained in the

plates of glass. Forty, sixty, hundreds of sunrises he could attest
to seeing, at the command of his father's arms and hands; only
later, as he progressed through his studies, could he understand
how his father conducted light and sound as though his taper
was a baton to be rattled before an orchestra; how he summoned
one out of the other, sound out of light, a 1-2 with the instance
between acts, between beats, between movements of the hands
and minds and the music they made together and, simultaneously,
all through such modest materials, a bit of pressure, and grace.

It was after his father had minded all the boxes and brought
Michael to the pub and treated himself that Edmund sat the boy
on the piano bench, and together they explored the instrument.
With his right hand Edmund tapped out the melodies he sang,
and then asked Michael to play it back to him. He couldn't, of
course, though his fingers could ascend and descend the scales
as nimbly as Edmund danced on the ladder. "What have you
got to run from?" Edmund admonished his son. "No need to
be so fast, laddie," he went on, because only by slowing down
could one detect the possibility of a pattern, a D-E-rest-F-F-
F-rest-E-F-A that made the song emerge from scales. "Take a
few steps back now," Edmund would often say. "Take a listen to
what you've done." From these variations, flashes of repose and
movement, Edmund demonstrated how music is assembled, a
quiet drawing together. "Listen," Da urged him, "not just to what
you bang out. Not just the notes, but how they go long or soft,
not all the same at once."

It was his father who taught him to play, who urged him
into University in Manchester, for there never was an Irishman
worth his heritage who did not aspire to escape the land and
start afresh. Edmund would have done as much himself, if he

hadn't met Catherine once she had lost all her siblings to famine, and then her mother gone too; she could not be coaxed far from their graves. Someone had to attend to them. And it was Sheehan's father, of course, who put it into his head what enlisting might do for him: coming back a hero and never wanting for work or kind favors again. The only man on Summer-hill who agreed to paint his door black when Queen Victoria died, as the English demanded; Edmund said he had no problem as long as he could take the door down, and dance on it for a session. By then there were no more candleboxes to tend; electricity had made good on its threats to flood the city from the high streets to the slums. Edmund was without work, though he still had the two girls and Ma at home. Michael had begun to display the prodigious nature of his talent such that music teachers from Belfast to London were paying him regular visits, with the hope of taking him under their tutlege. It was a deal with the devil to enlist, Edmund had said at the war's beginning. But Sheehan already met the devil halfway, living among the English as he had since anyone could remember, throwing his lot in with their teachers and patrons. He might as well go all in, for King and country, the royal family and Victoria's grandchildren too. Why not, when it would all be over by Christmas, and he might not see a lick of fighting. What did he have to lose?

SHEEHAN JAMMED THE letter his mother had written into his fist, and then he picked it apart, as if dressing a chicken. He threw the head and feathers in the gutter, clenched the rest of it by the neck. He might have swung the surviving body as if it were the band on a slingshot, aimed at himself. But there was nothing left to shoot at. He was a git, a feb, a bloody Brit, one of them now; they had said as much, his own parents.

Sheehan's fellows saw him on the street outside the school and gathered around him, to slap him on the back, sing "For He's a Jolly Good Fellow," and invite him back inside to play and discuss. He smiled and nodded, careful not to say anything. There were fewer of them now, their ranks diminished by the war or the flu. They led him into a rehearsal studio, where they sat him at an instrument. A colleague, sitting beside him, pantomimed on the keys one of the Satie pieces everyone knew Sheehan had loved. Furniture music, it was called, because of how it was meant to melt in into the wallpaper, settees, the Turkish carpets of a Paris salon. That it still stood out for its melancholy and yearning was not lost on the other instructors, though no one but Sheehan was as dedicated to the composer.

Sheehan placed his hands for the first major seventh chord and pressed; he found rearranging his hands for the subsequent chords simple enough, though the music did not come through to him in complete batches. He heard the shift in the pedals, the hammers that were required by his playing to avoid certain notes; he heard levers, mechanics, if not the notes he meant to sound, because of what had happened to his ears, his head.

To play Satie required a kind of stillness, a method of handling time that was not possible with his relative deafness. The pianist must pay as much attention to the beats between chords as the notes he must touch on, for it was the intervening silence that made the music so remarkable. For Sheehan there were no silences. There were hushed, quieter seconds, but always the persistence of tones that did not make sense, an intensity of noise with a needling persistence. Without the silences, the mazes of harmonics and dissonances in Satie's work were lost. He was playing over them, he knew; the emotion in the piece was unrequited. It was in these dark moments the audience compares what they have just heard with their own memories of love, longing, the heartbreak that was sweet because it was necessary. But no one, it seemed, wanted to remember such things; and no one said anything as he plumbed his way through the piece, and made such rough work of it.

When his performance was over, his colleagues applauded and then politely admitted they had no place for him. There were so many fewer students between their lot. So many had made economies that did not allow for musical instruction; some of their students had been orphaned by recent events. Still, they took up a collection so he could get what he needed: at least a pint to celebrate, a comfy room for a few nights, clothes, decent meals. They were well-meaning, his colleagues, and the headmaster wrote letters of introduction for him. He had for himself no expectations other than to survive, to start over, to live as he had not during the war, as a human.

He thought he could teach children. Their capacity for memory rested still and only in their muscles, and not yet where it would become debilitating, in their hearts. But the parents of his pupils complained that he did not give enough instruction; just a grunt here and there, and his repetition of the scales, or appropriate Hanon exercises. Sheehan told himself there was about as much talent in the north and midlands as there was income, and soon he was off to Bradford or Liverpool. Having failed there, he would gather his belongings under his arm—his clothes, the few notes he had managed to make, the scores and songbooks, and find his way to Newcastle or York. His travels must have worn a rut into the landscape. When he had the moments to consider where he had been, and where to go next, he thought he must be wearing the ground down to rock, boring new trenches for warding off the next enemy.

Sheehan dared not to ask his brothers for help; Liam and Christopher had become confirmed Republicans, from what he could gather through the rare correspondence he cherished from their younger sister, Lucy. She offered assurances that their parents would be taken care of, even if it was now his responsibility as the only unattached one among them. If he came back, his prospects outside the home were to be equally grim, regardless of his profession, as there was little money for music lessons and music teachers, and certainly there was no interest in tutorials from anyone who had made a traitor's bargain with the British. As Lucy's voice was completely lost to him, for she was barely a girl when he had left for school and time had since remade her into a mother and maid, he could not judge the underside of the things she said—that he should sell his soldier's uniform if he needed money, as there were plenty of Englishmen who might make use of it. They were marching all about Dublin in such dress, bashing the ribs of whomsoever's glance they found offensive.

He found one position transcribing the compositions of a self-made munitions baron in Birmingham. The man

fancied himself an autodidact and genius, and said he understood, even welcomed, Sheehan's reticence. Sheehan's task
was to listen as he rambled through the opus he had written
for his long late fiancée. He had imported from Hamburg a
baby grand Steinway for the project, as if looking to redeem
himself from the fortune he had secured through the deaths
of so many. The instrument was more than fine in all aspects;
Sheehan tested it himself. But as the hands of this Mr.
Havisham played, the piano's upper treble rang. The felt of its
hammers had worn clear to the wooden mechanism. Sheehan
was sacked when the maestro saw that the higher registers of
his masterwork were missing from the notations.

Soon enough his grooming became reason enough to
deny him the least daunting of any work: sweeping up classrooms and studios, stoking coal in furnaces. He thought of
returning to Manchester, seeking his professors from University. They did not think of him as a musical genius, but they
had been sympathetic, possibly encouraging. Hadn't he only
needed more time, some seasoning? He thought better of the
idea once he realized just what he would have to explain to
them, the words he would have to call upon. First and fore-
most, how his hands had come to be in such a state, cracked
to bleeding. In a shop window he saw the mask that dirt had
made of his face, the gravelly sheen stuck to his trousers. In
his condition there were fewer rooms to let, and, eventually, no
rooms at all. He kept to doorways and tunnels, deserted stalls
in the markets, dry walks beneath awnings. As long there was
some roof above his head, so he was not forced to confront the
sunlight, so he might not be assaulted by the brightness and
its disquieting symptoms, a bash and clamor that ploughed on

through the darkness. The worst was beneath the bridges of railroad trestles, where the sun barged through in the mornings.

But he was not hungry. And the longer he remained in this condition—the farther he traveled by foot, as his clothes and body, his beard and fingernails, accumulated soot and dust—the less need he had of food. For he could remember the hunger that was the ache of the prison camps, a low grinding murmur in the belly that could not be satisfied. Such was not the case now, though he did not have his three meals daily; on more days than not, he lacked all forms of nourishment. But he ate according to his own desires—if not the desire for a particular food, then his initiative to go find anything. The sticky remnants of jam or honey, cores and stones of fruit. Once the foam on a pub glass he found. Bread and cheeses his fingernails wrested from the attacks of mold. He ate from bins, from gutters, from the blooms and grasses he discovered in his wanderings. Bones he found most satisfying, a memory of stews and meats.

Milk from a pail at a dairy he took shelter in; it was fresh, and he drank too much. It made his stomach sour. He tried begging, on the steps of churches and the entrances of pubs, but hadn't the nerve for the touch that accompanied the crowns or shillings: a slap on the back, a squeeze of the shoulders. He had his routines, and he had his rules. As he walked, marched, stomped, waded through muck, he felt he was becoming large, massive. A halo of dust, lint, silt, and mire proceeded him, a darkened ring that people would not breach. The Mick from Ireland, he had been; now he was neither man nor animal, and whether he had succeeded in becoming something inbetween, he did not care.

Until he came upon Miss Williams, who gave him a bed, clothes, regular food, and, most importantly, a solid roof—a barrier between himself and the discordant clutches of the universe. If he walked with Miss Williams; if he remained with her every minute, to remember, to learn the construction of her every move and breath; if he did all that he could, what little it was, to bring back the life she had given to him, he might still not restore himself. There must have always been some aspect of himself meant for vagabonding, the pounding he allowed his hands to undertake, the freedom the rest of his body found in walking. Once he had volunteered to follow Miss Williams home—to read her books and care for her garden—he found that freedom wanting. It was as bereft as his critics had said his playing was, since it served nothing but his own sense of himself. That was how his senses worked, until Miss Williams. And now he had no need of them, except for his need of Miss Williams.

Eleven

WHEN CHRISTOPHER THORTON visited the infirmary, Mr. Sheehan stood so that Christopher might sit. But Mr. Sheehan did not relinquish his position over the bed, its patient, and her visitors. Christopher nodded rather than thank Mr. Sheehan formally, an acknowledgment of more than just the change of seating arrangements, but also of the measure of each man's importance.

Christopher began by presenting Miss Williams with gifts, which she struggled to open. Christopher was noticeably upset by the tremor in her hands; only after Mr. Sheehan laid his hands atop Miss Williams's fingers, guiding them through the boxes, ribbons, and tissues, was she able to reveal them.

"From my mother," Christopher said, as if explaining the women's bedclothes in scented boxes. The first box held a light blue nightgown. The second held a matching robe, made from a plush fabric, as if the function of the robe was to provide a retreat into a seedpod or a shell. Miss Williams promised to wear them, although she admitted she was having trouble keeping track of the days, and wondered, out loud, whether she might just save them for the first day of her autumn classes.

"You—you should be well enough to return in your regular wardrobe," Christopher said, although without his father present, he knew his statements sounded more like guesses. He was still wearing a summer suit, but he sensed that he must have looked as though he missed the season altogether. He had become gaunt over the past month and his skin translucent, as if the world could see his embarrassment.

"Perhaps," Miss Williams said. When fatigued, as now, each of her breaths sounded like sighs released from a heap of effort. If she spoke more than a few words, she sounded as though she was either full of woe or indecision. It pained Christopher to hear her speak this way—in short, almost curt, answers—as he had once enjoyed the bloom in her voice and language.

"We—my mother would have come herself, although my father . . . I don't think he would have allowed it," Christopher said.

"No," Miss Williams said. "I expect he would not."

"We—I almost did not come myself."

"Yes," Miss Williams said.

"But I—I wanted to apologize. I wanted—"

"There's no need."

"There is," Christopher asserted, but he let go of the

moment, allowed it to drop off and wilt, as if it was supported by a stem that had suddenly grown too hot for him to maintain his grip. "We—I was mistaken in placing my loyalties."

"With your father?" Miss Williams asked. "Please. That is to be expected."

"No," Christopher said. "I—I should have placed them in myself, my own judgment. And, I must admit, I was jealous."

"Please," Miss Williams said. "I don't understand—"

"He—your Mr. Sheehan," Christopher said. "He has proven his loyalty."

"Yes," Miss Williams agreed, and when she raised her gaze toward Mr. Sheehan, Christopher was forced to imagine the feeling of her blood, for so long dense and listless, now churning toward its normal pace and temperature. "He has been a godsend," she said, and Christopher noticed the man's gaze shift as well, although for reasons and details that he kept well hidden.

"I had hoped to be that kind of man," Christopher said, and his own words left him wondering what type of men were still out there—what kind of men were still alive to emulate? The war had deprived the nation of most of the types that he had aspired to be, and even those types whose lives he could never imagine and never desire. The regal, the self-possessed, the clever were picked off or blown to bits along with the derelicts; those who survived only did so in pieces, in portions, and in segments. This was Christopher's story, with his concave leg, twisted and atrophied. He did not know the precise anatomical damage, but he knew the utility of the instrument had been compromised to the point that surgeons had to remove too much of it to save whatever was worth the effort.

Christopher looked to Mr. Sheehan, another fragment of a man. In the weeks since he had learned that Mr. Sheehan had been living with Miss Williams, he had tried to fathom what the attraction was, from the baser physical characteristics to the spiritual, should that kind of attraction even exist. He still could not understand it, given that there was something obviously missing from Mr. Sheehan—if not a limb, then something just as essential: air in his chest or grease in his knees and shoulders. He still wore the clothes that Miss Williams had likely scavenged for him out of a charity bin, and his yellow eyes appeared as if they had originally been borne by separate persons. He was a man of discards sewn together, and Christopher wondered how it was that the village, his father, and even himself had managed to stretch such a small, improbable reliquary of self-doubt into a vast, frightening figure of half-man and half-monster.

They were both small people, Mr. Sheehan and Miss Williams, or so it seemed to Christopher. In physical stature and in impact: they would be forgotten as soon as they departed, the engraving of their names on their tombstones would fill in with dirt. What would become of the gifts to Miss Williams he was now making? Her possessions, like Mr. Sheehan's, would be scattered without regard to sentiment.

Christopher had once scoffed at such a fate, especially for himself, before the war. The trenches had changed that. The trenches—a subterranean existence, though not quite the underworld. He had lost weight in the trenches; he even lost his height once he was injured. He lost the ability to walk upright, and the men with whom he spent every minute, asleep or waking, had been similarly worn down by the fighting. Men with whom he had shivered and sweated, whose duty it was to die for him as his duty was to die for them. He had to ravage through their possessions, their very bodies, for rings, necklaces, a letter, or a photograph, so he might be their last witness. Should they be blown to bits, of course, he might write a letter home explaining what happened and why it mattered. And they were sworn to do him the same honor, no matter who they were or what their circumstances.

Who would be notified when Miss Williams died? Further still, when Mr. Sheehan dropped off the earth? He knew nothing about them; they were virtually anonymous people, as were the men he had served with. Seventy-four men were in the company at disembarkation for France, twenty-four, supposedly, by Armistice. As a captain, he knew each of their names, and he went over them in his head every day, preparing for the time when he would be called to account. Who were their parents, what trades had they apprenticed for, who were their tutors at University, who was headed for the House of Lords, who would make a girl into a widow? The right sloppy business that lost them a shin, then an entire leg, then their life. Historians will want to know how they contributed, if not about his own heroism, which he knew to be sorely lacking. He kept his head down when ordered and ripped the cap off grenades as the company's numbers had dwindled, but he was mostly smoothing out papers, finding typographical errors.

Early on in the war, Christopher had sustained a concussion that rattled his jaw and gave his mouth a taste not quite of metal and not quite of vomit. He still felt as though his upper teeth were wavering in their hold, and his bottom teeth had doubly braced their position in his gums. He was injured again when one of his tunnels collapsed; he had tried to be brave. Above him, the men were tearing through their rations at meals, through their dreams in their sleep, through their clothing as shots and shrapnel seared fabric to skin.

Captain Christopher Thorton shouted at his men to keep digging, though who could have heard? He was trembling under a mountain of dirt, his throat and lungs the only place for the soil to retreat whenever he opened his mouth. Between his teeth he tasted the bitterness of roots savaged, divorced from their purpose. Soon he would be another dungaree-colored, shut-eyed, grinning rictus, like the men on top of him. He was a British soldier first, and his individuality at that moment was unimportant. It did not matter if his name and education had gotten him a commission. It did not matter if he had a servant in the trenches. He swallowed and decided to keep still; it was best not to disturb what threatened to smother him.

Minutes later, or hours, or days—he did not know when— he was pulled out by his men. He told them he should have been left there, it would have been faster that way, buried already, but they said they couldn't lose an officer as good as he was. They got him an ambulance—an ambulance!—that took him to a base. Nothing was done for the small men who were like the pegs used to secure the tunnels; pegs that kept the ground above their heads, stopped the plywood from crumpling down, and held the floor beneath their feet.

"You still can be that kind of man," Miss Williams said, and the intake of Mr. Sheehan's breath turned audible at that instant.

A sound almost like speech, Christopher thought.

Miss Williams was trying to sit up. Immediately Christopher reached for her arm, as if to steady her, but Mr. Sheehan had already caught her by an elbow and a shoulder, and was lifting her into position.

"I need," she said, and then an edge of hesitation set in her voice, as if she was preparing to say something either very long or very ominous. "I need to sit up, for I must ask a favor from you, and I don't want to be lying down when I ask it."

"Yes, of course," Christopher said, and he felt as though he should be kneeling at her side, for his presence was more of a burden than any request she could put to him. "Please," he said. "Anything."

"I need to make arrangements for Mr. Sheehan," Miss Williams said.

"Arrangements?" Christopher asked, and again he looked to Mr. Sheehan, whether for an explanation or out of an apologetic sense, Christopher could not say. "Do you mean you will be leaving?" Christopher asked her directly. "Surely, that is no longer necessary. I can speak to my father—"

"No," Miss Williams said. "I want to set up a trust, an income, a place for him to live, in case—"

"In which case?" Christopher had to look away at that moment, but in the vast infirmary his eyes could only find the floor. The planks of wood were worn to yellow with black scratches from years of temporarily arranged furniture; the permanence of the infirmary's routine rubbing against the impermanence of its residents. When he could be sure the shock of what Miss Williams was saying had left his face, he righted himself and confronted the pair. Mr. Sheehan had also averted his eyes, but Miss Williams was sitting up, smiling. Whatever the future held, she was the only one prepared to meet it.

"I must meet with Lord Thorton, if Mr. Sheehan is to stay here, or anywhere, near Bridgetonne. Could you arrange it?" she asked, to which Christopher automatically nodded.

"I will go to him, if he cannot come here," Miss Williams said. She exhaled, then closed her eyes so that Christopher would know the visit had concluded.

"Of course, of course," Christopher said, although he realized she was likely no longer listening. "I—I will ask him. Good day, Miss Williams, Mr. Sheehan." Christopher rose and offered his hand to Mr. Sheehan. Once he left the infirmary, he read the piece of paper Mr. Sheehan had set in his palm.

Pvt., 5th Battalion, Gloucestershire Regiment

Christopher secured the paper in a pocket and had to stop himself from repeatedly rubbing his pocket to remind himself it was there. Otherwise all his remembering might erase the contents.

Twelve

CHRISTOPHER HAD NEVER considered himself to be in love with Miss Williams. To begin with, she was altogether too foreign. She spoke out of turn—not necessarily literally, for she was polite enough, and she often displayed a respectable sense of self-control. But the content of what she said, her tendency to disagree before she would agree, had been off-putting to Christopher, who had grown up amid conversations that always ended with a familiar resolution. And that resolution had been assumed from the beginning: who would win the argument, what the outcome would be, who was in charge, and who was meant to carry out the resulting orders. Miss Williams, naturally, was unaware of these conventions. Her voice, the gestures she used to make her mystical stories tangible and everyday, the tendency of her eyes to dart about as if they were the muscles in nervous, captured birds: all of this intrigued Christopher, but he was not in love with her because she believed too much, or wanted to believe too much, in possibilities that he could not imagine.

Yet she had to believe in such things, Christopher now realized, given her appearance and how she had been put together—not by a set of parents, but solely by herself. Neither was she traditionally beautiful; her skin, eyes, and hair were unremarkable in color and presentation, and the distribution of her features was off, uneven, as if there was too little space between the eyes and too much between the mouth and the chin.

In the infirmary, the qualities that had once intrigued him—for his interest was no doubt piqued by her, he could not help but acknowledge—had deserted Miss Williams. There had always been frailty to her voice, but he had been certain that, if he followed it, it would lead to a steely reserve. But in the infirmary, Christopher became convinced that all mettle within Miss Williams had dissolved, and there would be no reconstitution of it. It had been disbursed to bounds she could no longer reach, if any of it had endured. Similarly, she was so still, so motionless, on her cot in the infirmary. None of the protracted frenzy that he had come to expect from her body was in evidence. Before he had been introduced to Miss Williams, he had never thought it possible for someone to appear as if sitting, attentive and focused, and at the same time, be running frenetically through the gauze of one's own thoughts discovering new ideas, new worlds. But that, too, had been consumed by the illness. The sickness had decreased her.

But he was reminded of all that she was, and how little

she had become, as he now helped her out of the car in front of the house. Christopher had sent the car for her, and half-expected Mr. Sheehan to accompany her. She came alone. It was a strong possibility, though, that Mr. Sheehan had lifted her into the automobile. Christopher found himself wincing and regretful as he envisioned that man carrying Miss Williams as if she was his bride—if only for that one moment. He wondered how that man had reached beneath Miss Williams's back and legs to raise her up from her chair, and how he must have released her after installing her frame against the car's upholstery. He knew she had to have been carried, for she required the steadying influence of two men to exit the car: the driver and himself.

The driver gently pushed her to the edge of the seat before Christopher could lift her for himself. Once out in the open air on the drive, he had to unfold the hinges that had supplanted her once fluid joints. She could not take a step without resting her diminished weight against his arm and shoulder. To walk her to the front door, the atrium, and beyond, Christopher found that he had to use a good deal of his own resolve; she leaned upon him as if he were all that could keep her going. Her legs were antediluvian creatures.

They did not speak as they walked, as if it was enough that they were sharing the same silent, grim commentary on the task at hand. Not that Christopher did not wish to speak. There was her garden to ask after, or Mr. Sheehan's whereabouts, or her departure from the infirmary to be recounted, or even some token pleasantries that could be exchanged about her health. But once he saw how dearly she was concentrating on her steps, on her posture, on every facet of her person—the frailty and slowness of which confirmed her decay—he could not. The long sleeves of her dress against his arm felt far too thin. Although it was summer, she should have been outfitted in a heavier fabric; a cloak, woolens, or a rug should have been thrown about her. She wore a scarf, dark and floral, which had been elaborately arranged like a collar, as if it were meant to secure her neck to her shoulders, and her head to her neck.

Christopher thought of a story that his nurse may have told him, or perhaps another boy at school, or a girl cousin, or anyone who wanted to assert their authority over him when he was a child. It was a story of a pirate, who, with his riches in his retirement, attracted any number of luscious young girls. He collected them like coins, sovereigns that he could spin and flip and manipulate between his fingers. He rarely held them in his palms. One after the other, he married them, and each one eventually disappeared, sometimes as quickly as the dawn rose after the first night of wedded bliss. Those lucky enough to emerge from the marriage bed at all did so with a slick, red ribbon around their necks. They lasted until some young and meandering man chanced upon them, in the town square or in the market, and asked about the ribbon. The wives knew they must never touch the ribbon, not even to wash it. But those who were tempted did, and their heads collapsed into the laps of their curious and adulterous suitors.

Christopher knew the purpose of such stories, as they were told to frighten him, to make him dependent on the protection of those older and wiser than he. He had even seen some of this in Miss Williams's stories, with impossible powers assigned to animals and the spirits of nature, and to gods that her stories made visible, even though gods were never meant to be seen or addressed so directly. Her tales were really no different than the ones he and his fellow soldiers had told one another during the war, which were likely no more than rumors, of feats carried out by other soldiers—delusions they needed if they were to conquer a division, a regiment, an entire country when they were simply individuals, wet and hungry. These were stories about incredible men, half-human and half-wrought out of nature itself, the mud and the snow, the barricades and the unruly hides of forest mammals.

The monsters the soldiers created for one another were tall and wide, their faces just a formality, difficult to recall without the distinguishing features that mark one as German, or French, or even as an English gentleman. They were not born, but assembled out of the parts of lifeless men left to fester, to be kicked and picked over and forgotten; out of the animals that came to feast on those parts; out of anything and every-thing the weather and the landscape could add to the amal-gamation. Once alive and upright, these creations avoided the borders of foxholes and trenches. Once confronted with the radius of destruction the war made, they became so inflamed that they would take it into their own hands to end the fighting. They would pluck soldiers from both sides and throw them onto the open plains, to starve; to be shot at; to become the same compilation of misery and waste as they were; to make monsters legion, a new breed from the war's debris. To be caught by a monster and flung into No Man's Land was a far more dire fate than death, because it was tantamount to being left alone without the bodies and uniforms of other men to push one forward, to demand that one keep pressing without looking back, without the slightest form of consideration. This was the true, primary fear of all soldiers, Christopher included—individuals who were once certain they could distinguish themselves as heroes until they discovered they were equally as happy to endure as survivors.

This is what each man dreamed upon enlistment, the illusion that fed and inspired him: that he, a single man, might be writ large in history. It was not the same thing as wanting to be a hero. He simply aspired to be deemed so essential to the unfolding sequence of events that should any harm come to his person, some other soldier would be forced to come to his aid. He'd be dragged back by his fellows for medical attention; if he suffered loss of limb, a search party would be formed to find those lost pieces of his anatomy scattered on the battlefield. Other soldiers would be expected to lose their lives to rescue, and resuscitate, those integral bits. It was for far more lowly, and anonymous soldiers to be sent out to collect someone's elbows and fingers, ankles and knee caps. It was not his. Each man proclaimed himself worthy enough to be reassembled through surgery, so he might be the one who lived; so he might be celebrated and memorialized for his individual feats and courageousness. So he could appear whole though his brains had been liquefied by bullets, his heart lacerated by shrapnel, his intestines disrupted by explosives. So his family remained under the comforting belief that he died in an almost regular, coherent fashion, like a man dying in his bed, or in hospital, or one struck down at a job, or in the street. He did not want his family to know how he could be rendered into parts and sections, as cuts of beef or poultry are prepared, undifferentiated in the lives they led. Each man wanted his family to think he conquered this most primary of all soldiers' fears, that should his family be confronted with his death, they need not confront the cold, dripping violence of it. The stories that Christopher's men told themselves of the forest men were no more fanciful and unfortunate than these visions of death.

Christopher was lucky enough to have finished his service with both his limbs and wits about him, despite the fact that one of his legs was really more like a tail than a leg, which he could not wholly control and had to be dragged from place to place. Had he lost even more of himself, either on the battle-field or to a surgeon, he could have been replaced by another soldier, and in the history of the war, should it ever be written, he would be an unnamed soul, a body, a statistic. War made men famous, and it made them superfluous.

Entering the drawing room with Miss Williams, whose equilibrium was increasingly dependent upon his arm, Christopher was struck by how it took two men—himself and Mr. Sheehan—to replace what Miss Williams had been. It took two men to approximate her gait and carriage, to move her from one place to another. Even then, it was a shoddy imitation he and Mr. Sheehan would likely affect together, in no way similar to how she had once arrived in rooms and unaccountably made herself the center of every one.

"Miss Williams," Christopher's mother quietly proclaimed as they approached. Lady Margaret took Miss Williams by one hand and helped Christopher lead her to a couch with large pillows. "I was so sorry to hear of your illness."

"Thank you," Miss Williams said, as if she was relieved to have been able to manage this reply. She allowed Lady Margaret and Christopher to lower her onto the cushions. Lady Margaret arranged the pillows behind her back, so she might sit up without much exertion. "I look forward to being through with it," Miss Williams said with a sigh. "It cannot be soon enough."

"You look well," Lady Margaret offered.

"Thank you," Miss Williams said again. "And thank you for your gift. It truly lifted my spirits."

"Should we begin with a story?" Lord Thorton asked. He had just made his entrance. He was rubbing his hands together in an uncharacteristic fashion; Christopher thought it crass, if not insulting.

"Or perhaps we should call on your Rasputin to provide us with a musical prelude," continued Lord Thorton, and he smiled as though quite pleased with himself.

"I am sorry Mr. Sheehan could not accompany me, but I thought it best," Miss Williams said.

"I am sure you did," Lord Thorton said.

"And I have not been well enough to concoct a story," Miss Williams went on, "particularly one for you, for whom the story may not be enough, so it must be accompanied by a succinct explanation."

"One could spend a lifetime deciphering one of your tales," Lord Thorton said. "But I should like to tell you a story today."

"Please," Miss Williams responded with much resolution.

"It's about a woman—a girl, really—much like you," Lord Thorton began as he made himself comfortable on the couch opposite Miss Williams. "Her name was Emily Hobhouse.

"Having failed at marriage, she sought out something to occupy herself, and she became a—what do we call such crusaders?—ah, yes, a reformer," Lord Thorton continued.

As he added to his story, it occurred to Christopher why his father preferred to have others speak for him. The man could not contain himself, whether it was his malice or his ebullience, when exercising his cruelty. "I apologize, " Lord Thorton corrected himself. "She was not just like you. She was not a writer, professionally speaking.

"But she did manage to publish one story: a very fanciful, libelous story about the war in South Africa."

"Dear," Lady Margaret interjected. "Miss Williams must be well aware—"

"Is she?" Lord Thorton asked. "I offered to explain this all to her, but she never accepted my overtures."

"And for that I owe you an apology," Miss Williams acknowledged. "Please. Continue."

Lord Thorton nodded. "Once upon a time, Miss Hobhouse took it upon herself to rescue the women and children in South Africa, though their husbands, sons, and brothers were killing her own countrymen. She wanted to collect money, have her name in the newspapers, and all those things rootless girls want. So she concocted a scurrilous tale about starving women in the refugee camps, although there was plenty of food. I can attest to that. She said there were children dying in the camps, but their mothers were too backward to care for them properly. So the only good she accomplished—"

"I'm sure Miss Williams can guess at the rest," Lady Margaret said.

"I am certain I cannot," Miss Williams conceded, "as I am no longer at my peak strength and must preserve what little I have left these days, I regret."

Miss Williams delivered her last statement in the most pleasant register her voice could affect, but it sent everyone's eyes shifting around the room, and their hands fumbling for handkerchiefs or the tea service. Lord Thorton bandied his walking stick from palm to palm rather than break the silence, which he felt might bite back at him. Miss Williams leaned back against the pillows, and Christopher hoped they were cool against her back, restorative. The room's French windows had been opened to invite the last of the summer air from the lawns and gardens. Miss Williams shut her eyes for a moment, and Christopher could see the effort she put into each breath, her chest stalling at times, the tremors as she exhaled and prepared to begin the cycle over again.

"Which is why I trouble you now," Miss Williams said. "My circumstances have obviously changed, and I should like to return to the States." She paused and her chest rose again, although it did not appear to fall. "As soon as possible," she added.

"We are so sorry to have you leave us," Lady Margaret said.

"Yes, we—I am as well," Christopher agreed.

"Yes, yes, yes, we know all about it," Lord Thorton said, and he stood up as though he had been troubled enough by Miss Williams and her circumstances.

"Father," Christopher interceded. "We—I should like to hear what Miss Williams has to say."

"You already know what she has to say," Lord Thorton said, and he exhaled loudly, so everyone would know the precise degree of his irritation. "I assume you have tendered your resignation with the college," Lord Thorton said to Miss

Williams.

"Not yet," Miss Williams said. "I should like to discuss that with you first."

"As you wish," Lord Thorton said.

"What if I were to purchase the cottage?" Miss Williams asked, as quickly as she could expel the issue from her lips.

"Absolutely not," Lord Thorton said.

"If I provided an endowment, for him and the cottage—"

"No."

"I would of course pay you a fee—for administering the arrangement. Or I could make a donation to the college."

"You are mistaken if you think this is about as base a thing as money," Lord Thorton said.

Surely his voice extends, Christopher thought, beyond the drawing room and into the halls, the sitting rooms, the atrium, and downstairs into the kitchen and staff quarters.

"That thing, which you mistake for a man, needs to return to wherever it came from. He has no place in Bridgetonne or any place where I still have influence. If the Boer women went back to their farms and started over where they should have, there wouldn't have been a need to concentrate—"

"Arthur, dear," Lady Margaret pleaded.

"Very well then," Lord Thorton said. "I met my responsibility at every turn with regard to those women, and I am now meeting my responsibility at every turn in Bridgetonne. This lordship is the last bulwark against Bridgetonne being turned into an open camp of . . ." Lord Thorton paused, as if he dared not say what might most naturally follow in his speech. "Bridgetonne will not become another Bloemfontein, an open camp of the so-called lost to mewl over their supposed injuries. I offered you my expertise and you ignored it, so now—"

"But Father. Wouldn't this—if we—" Christopher knew he had to embark on a new line of reasoning. He had to, as he could no longer stand to see how pale, how absent of hope and blood, Miss Williams was becoming. He switched his eyes between his mother's and his father's faces, only to find himself caught between each parent's aspirations for him.

"But wouldn't the cottage—her purchasing it—wouldn't this contain the problem?" Christopher managed.

"Does he need containing?" Miss Williams asked.

"Mr. Sheehan does not require much," Christopher went on; it was imperative that the conversation keep moving. "We—I—could of course oversee whatever is set up for him. We—Miss Williams and I—think he only wants to be left in his silence."

"That, I doubt," Lord Thorton said. "For if you give him that much, he will desire so much more. And once those needs are satisfied, he will hunger for something else, until we—your mother and I, and you, Christopher, and this village, the entire countryside—will be under contract, like blackmail, to support all these malingerers, these—well, whatever they are calling themselves now. Perhaps the French will come up with a word for it, when they could just be peasants. And deserters—"

"A deserter," Christopher said, "does not volunteer his rank and regiment."

"And do we know anything of him beyond that? Is there a wife? Children? God help them. Why can he not properly present himself, explain his situation? Why must he go lunging about like some kind of monster, all to extract kindness? And why," Lord Thorton asked, now addressing Miss

Williams directly with the full force of his voice and oversized mannerisms, "why must you be so dedicated, so intoxicated by this, this *thing* that he is? I do not even know how to say it."

Miss Williams rose, without assistance but with great effort. Christopher thought everyone in the room, his father included, withheld their breath and watched Miss Williams as if she were a servant reassembling the contents of a china cabinet she had shattered.

"I brought him into this . . ." she hesitated, as if she had found herself in a dreadfully foreign place, unexpectedly, and there was no polite way to describe it. ". . . into these circumstances," she said. "And I am responsible for him. More so than you or your countrymen, obviously, who took him to war and abandoned him. Yet each of us has only our humanity to recommend us, and mine has been worn thin enough for one day."

She took a step away from the couch, and Christopher dove to her side, to catch her should she fall, then guided her through the gauntlet of his father's stare and the vacant furniture. She was cold in her hands, which he tried to take up in his own, but he could feel the fever that had begun at the crown of her head and was now bleeding past her hairline. Out of the corner of his eye, Christopher could see his mother rise in a show of respect, while his father turned on his heels and strode back to his library. He wanted badly to say something, to say anything—if not to apologize for his father's behavior, then for his own hubris for thinking his father was more of a man than he truly was.

They shared another silent walk through Lord Thorton's halls to the car waiting in the drive. Christopher knew each

table, every portrait, the framed medals, certificates, and proclamations on the walls, as well as the holes and cracks they
covered. But for Miss Williams, he imagined, all of it must
have seemed a maze of possessions, claptrap and pretension.
Everything was time and objects to his father; he must have
looked at the war this way, a clot of time that had not coughed
out people and heroics, but objects. Munitions, citations, maps
that would have to be redrawn . . . The men who were transformed by that war, the entire of Christopher's generation,
were the rubbish—the guts and skin made inconvenient in
the process. This must have been what his father saw in Mr.
Sheehan, and now, Christopher knew what his father had to
confront in his own son: the complications, the unintended
consequences that could not be uniformly buried or hidden
away, no matter the effort put into the project.

As they walked away from the drawing room, Christopher
could still hear the sounds of his parents' conversation—taut,
if not angry—and the sound of the servants scattering after
Lady Margaret and Lord Thorton. The clatter withdrew from
one room to flood into another. It was a bit humiliating, as
were the sounds of the kitchen downstairs: the collisions
of metal and wood, dustbins and coal boxes, pots and ovens,
cutting boards and floured hands. What was once seamless to
Christopher—or perhaps he never had occasion to pay it this
much attention—the estate that he would someday inherit,
now seemed a tottering, rusting machine that required so
much malice to maintain.

"Would you allow me to accompany you on the drive
back?" Christopher asked Miss Williams once they had
reached the drive.

"Yes, please," Miss Williams replied, and Christopher was heartened, although he knew it was her illness that was answering, and not any particular affection for him.

She was lighter to pick up now, easier to carry and deposit than just a few moments ago, although there was no reason for such a change. She was the same sick woman, but no illness could diminish one so quickly; at least no illness that Christopher could so easily name. Yet there was a new fluidity to her movements, the bending and adjusting, the intake of breath that she would not surrender until she was firmly nestled into the back seat of the car. She smoothed her hands down the dress so that the drape of the fabric was organized. Christopher asked her if she was comfortable, and she nodded. There was a dullness, a blank resignation, in her eyes. This is how vanishing begins, Christopher thought, not on the battlefield, but in the protracted fall of days and events.

Christopher signaled the driver to depart, and as the car proceeded, they watched the scenery outside of the window— the grounds of his father's estate: acreage cultivated by the tenant farmers; livestock roaming the pastures; fields of short, shaggy grasses, shorn for midsummer haying; hedgerows bursting with greenery—elms, hawthorns, gorse, and holly. There were stories here too, attached to the tree limbs Christopher and his sisters had jumped from; stone fences where they had tried to tie scarecrows; and amid the hay, rolled and baled, he and his sisters had tried planting their own seeds, or digging up roots for their own harvest. They played at being poor children, orphans from books that their parents and nurses would have been wise to have read to them, so they could be explained, set in the proper perspective. Instead, they usually read them to one another, and then, given the opportunity, they played at making their own versions of the plots. At the train station, they might count trains, as did children mysteriously deprived of their father in one story; in the house, they might invade a room reserved for the more pristine social events and use its furniture to build a city, as a jealous young boy did in another tale.

With the windows closed in the car, the air turned warm. Miss Williams removed the scarf, and Christopher caught himself, at that instant, delaying the next beat of his heart. Her neck revealed itself to be a vicious red, and in a lingering motion, Miss Williams used the scarf to whisk away the moisture that had formed at its back. Her neck was so much longer and thinner than he had imagined, and, although its slope and reach were not as graceful as he would have preferred, they were daunting, as if impossible on a woman.

"Is it too warm?" Christopher asked.

"Not necessarily," she said. She had trained her gaze on the scenery and did not wish to give up her concentration.

"I—we could open the windows," he suggested.

"No," she said. "No, thank you." She had moved herself forward on the seat, as if to be closer to the window, but she dared not draw herself beyond it.

"Do you think I should be buried with my parents?" she asked suddenly.

"Excuse me?"

"I suppose I should be," she answered, and she sat back from the window just as quickly, as if she had found something repellent in the landscape. "I have no idea where my father is buried. I barely knew him." Again she moved toward the window. "He died in the Philippines, during their revolution."

"We—I—did not know," Christopher offered in response. "I'm—I am sorry."

"Oh, you needn't be," Miss Williams said. "It was his sentence to serve, you know—to avoid prison." Her voice had taken on a lilt, as though it was not meant to produce words because words no longer mattered. It was the song of what she said, the tune and rhythm, that he would remember. She shifted her head back and forth, as if in wonderment, at the village coming into view. "He was a confidence man. Do you know what a confidence man is?" She did not give Christopher a chance to answer. "I have always thought it is something like I do—telling stories—although the confidence man has to be far more persuasive. My mother always said he was charming."

"Your mother?"

"She was buried in the desert. Arizona. We had been told to go there. She was a consumptive," Miss Williams continued. Christopher knew nothing of the desert, of the kind of air that could milk the illness out of one's lungs. He knew only that the pattern of her voice had changed, and he needed to memorize it, before it became like birdsong, and the wind made its source invisible. "I suppose the doctors will make the same recommendation in my case."

"If you—if you took him with you, he could—" Christopher ventured.

"I don't think he could stand it," she interrupted. "There'd be nothing familiar. It would all be confusion to him."

"Then you should remain here," Christopher said, as if he

alone could resolve the situation. "If not in Bridgetonne, then away but still in England. We—I—my mother and I, we could find you a place at St. Thomas's—"

"If the only place I can go to live in this country is a hospital," Miss Williams said, "then I might as well drop dead. And that I would prefer to do in my own country."

Christopher was accustomed to the idea of Miss Williams flitting about as she spoke. Even though her hands and arms, her whole body, could no longer produce such restlessness, her voice suddenly veering into unknown directions made him uneasy, apprehensive.

"I'm sorry," she said, as if she had heard herself too closely. "I shouldn't speak this way, I know. But the closer it draws, the less elegant it appears."

"You are not afraid of dying," Christopher said.

"I tell myself I am not afraid," she said, and she took hold of another breath; this one she did not let end naturally. She held it as if she meant it to stretch it into the words she needed at that moment, but they did not seem to materialize. "But I am sorry," she said. "Sorry everything is so unfinished."

Her eyes did not know, at that second, just where they should hide their discomfort. They flashed about the car's interior, searching for some previously undisclosed spot where her thoughts might appear opaque or ambiguous. But there was a gleam, a burnishing, that betrayed their interest; something like tears had begun to overtake them.

"You—we should marry," Christopher found himself saying. "We should have you marry him, I mean. Mr. Sheehan. He would be your heir, then. He would be assured of receiving whatever . . ." Christopher also found he could not finish.

Miss Williams nodded close enough to Christopher's shoulder that he might have imagined she was about to rest her cheek there. But, just as quickly, she was sitting up and firmly declaring her approval of his idea. Her eyes still and resolute, she studied his face, as if to judge how serious he had been. She shifted forward, eagerly, as if to hurry the car and the time it traversed the road. She might have made other gestures to Christopher's thinking, and he hoped that as her hands moved she might rest them upon his own hands, where they sat folded on his knees. But this show of strength on her part fled in the next moment; her tremors reappeared as if they had proliferated through her arms and reached for her wrists and fingers. Christopher took her hands into his own to press the unevenness out of them.

Thirteen

THE WORLD PRESSED into the small cottage in the days
that followed. There came acquaintances and associates of
Christopher's: solicitors and clerks from the registry. They
made the days go by faster, and last longer, as they gathered at the small table in the kitchen to work. Mr. Sheehan
brought to them messages that Miss Williams wrote from
her bed. Lady Margaret was also a regular visitor, leading
tours of bakers and cooks, tailors and seamstresses, florists and
photographers, through what vegetation had managed to hold
through the last of the summer in the cottage's front garden.

At each visit they were met by Mr. Sheehan, who
appeared serene and ever more close to handsome than Lady
Margaret thought possible. She offered him her hand, but he
would not take it, although he nodded respectfully both to

her and her entourage. And just as quickly, he would shake his head and shut the door, so the tour would be restricted to the gardens. The bakers and cooks, tailors and seamstresses, florists and photographers, all insisted to Lady Margaret that they had yet to lose their resolve in the endeavor of making a proper wedding for the village curiosity and her mute idiot. But after each of their unsuccessful encounters with Mr. Sheehan, Lady Margaret found it more difficult to boost their spirits and enthusiasm. Finally, when Mr. Sheehan refused to answer the door at all, they tendered their regrets, declining to offer their services for the wedding.

The minister, who had so often been a guest at the Thorton estate and publicly enjoyed Miss Williams's story-telling there, was not permitted to as so much as enter the grounds. Mr. Sheehan saw to that. The reverend had appeared at the front gate several times, unbidden, only to find himself confronted with The Hawkman. Mr. Sheehan would put a hand up, shake his head, and place a hold on the gate's swinging entrance that must have been convincing. The reverend, unable to lodge any protest, would nod and then depart with the small package he had brought—a Bible, no doubt—tucked under his arm, as if to shield it from offense.

Christopher was the sole witness to the reverend's last unsuccessful attempt to gain access to the cottage. It was just two days before the wedding, and Christopher had taken a break from combing through documents and signatures when he looked through the window of Miss Williams's library and saw the reverend in the distance. The reverend must have finally learned that any approach through the front was impossible, and he took to the college grounds to slip through the back garden. Mr. Sheehan was bent over a bush or a furrow of dirt, his hair beneath the straw hat Miss Williams had given him. Yet he still appeared intimidating, as if he might pop out of the hat—his clothes and boots too—and shower anyone who disturbed him with his squalidness.

Mr. Sheehan spotted the reverend and rose to meet him. Mr. Sheehan raised both hands, though not to surrender; there was a resoluteness in the way he now stood that had been largely absent from his comportment. Perhaps the nonthreatening churchman may have inspired it.

Christopher had become familiar with Mr. Sheehan's methods for communicating: beyond the obvious nod for agreement, there was the raised chin for what he was not immediately amenable to; the slow blink of his eyelids when he relented; his hands clenched together, near to a position of prayer, when he hoped his assent would be acceptable. But in this conversation, Mr. Sheehan employed no such signals, at least none that Christopher could discern from his standpoint. He did not seem to even shake his head. Instead, he stood there in a kind of perfect concentration, as a soldier withstanding a dressing down might do, if the reverend had the presence of mind to give one. This only prompted the reverend to make ridiculous gestures of his own, unreadable except for their agitation. To which Mr. Sheehan remained as still and polished in his impassivity as he had been during the man's previous visits; the two men stood there, the silent beggar and the reverend, who was silenced by the prospect of a man such as Mr. Sheehan truly living and breathing before him.

Christopher watched Mr. Sheehan take several steps forward with a quickness and determination uncharacteristic

of his movements; the reverend found himself pacing backward. Mr. Sheehan managed to escort the reverend to the
tree line that formally delineated the college grounds, but the
reverend stepped to the side, as if to lead Mr. Sheehan back
to the garden, the cottage, to Miss Williams, or whoever he
so frantically needed to meet with. But Mr. Sheehan would
not be bypassed by such a circuitous method. He stopped
suddenly, raised his hands again, and then pressed them to his
chest, as if making a pledge. Then Mr. Sheehan bowed slightly
to the reverend before bowing deeply in the direction of the
cottage.

Now it was the reverend who could not speak. He shuffled, wiped at his forehead with a handkerchief he found in a
back pocket, and searched for ways he might avert his glance
away from the confrontation. The reverend was forced to
speak Mr. Sheehan's language—signs and signals that, without
context, appeared to be insanity. The reverend concluded
his pantomime by offering his hand to Mr. Sheehan. But
Mr. Sheehan kept his hands over his heart. It was the most
detailed communication Christopher had seen him complete.

The reverend was waiting that evening for Christopher up
the road as if he were a cat determined to collar something for
the day, though frightened by animals larger than itself. "Sir
Christopher," the reverend called.

"How would my father feel," Christopher asked, "to hear
you address me as if he were dead?"

"I'm sorry, sir, but I must—" the reverend began excitedly.

"You must what?" Christopher asked impatiently.

"I must know," the reverend said, and he began to pace—
to finish formulating his thoughts, Christopher guessed.

"You must know what?"

"For her sake," the reverend began again, and what followed was a speech, both tentative and frantic. "I must know. Whether he is capable. Signing his name, nodding, shaking his head, of course, all fine and well. But refusing to speak? At the registry? In a church? How could he, in any legitimate sense, make a pledge—"

"For God's sake," Christopher interrupted.

"I mean, it could affect the marriage," the reverend said. "In a spiritual sense." The reverend was pacing now and failing to look at Christopher directly, as if he did not have faith in his own message. "I've spoken with Lady Margaret about this, and she promised—"

"I hope she didn't promise you anything," Christopher said, "because she's not in a position to give it. No one is."

The reverend placed his hands behind his back and glanced about him as though he was about to impart some gossip. "She said she would speak to Miss Williams about it. But I haven't heard a word."

"And you won't, I expect," Christopher said.

"Then how—?" the reverend started in, but Christopher began to walk away, trying not to smirk. He could be too much like his father; Christopher knew this about himself. But, at times such as this one, it paid to be Lord Thorton's son, for Christopher had come to understand that there was no reasonable way in the reverend's philosophy to ever satisfy him.

THE COTTAGE SEEMED ablaze with activity in the last

days: the composing of telegrams, witnessing of affidavits, attempts through messengers and telephone calls to obtain the language of publishing contracts Miss Williams had signed at one point or another. But such legal papers were not accessible within such short notice. And the bride could not be inter- rogated. She remained shut away, Mr. Sheehan her veritable sentry. He had moved her from her upstairs bedroom to the downstairs nursery, where she could be kept in her own bed and still he could sleep beside her, on the other. Though he did not sleep; he did not so much as rest his head. He watched Miss Williams through the night, as if to catch the moments of her transformation.

Each morning she appeared different to him: smaller, thinner, and yet her frame elongated, as though she had spent the night preening—indeed, stretching—whatever the disease had left behind in her. To measure these changes, Sheehan tried any number of tactics: he propped her up carefully on the pillows to ease her breathing and weigh how much lighter and lithe she had become. He attempted to remember what kind of impact she had made on his arms, his muscles, the day before, but the change may have been too slight. He wanted to envision her face from an earlier time, how her limbs had moved in their small ways, but he could not. Each new permutation of her form edged her closer to a kind of perfec- tion, and all prior iterations of her visage melted. He studied the twitches and ripples that fluttered beneath her skin as she slept; he made mental notations as to the frequency of tremors that overtook her in her dreams, the restlessness that he was certain would drive her awake, but never quite did. And in the morning, he was confronted with Miss Williams just a bit paler yet with a tentative vibrancy in her cheeks and forehead, her arms and fingers hanging onto whatever grace the disease spared.

If there had been an official diagnosis, it had never been shared with Sheehan. From what he knew of pneumonia and tuberculosis, neither seemed to fit her symptoms. Pneumonia galloped through its victims, trampling and breaking them, while tuberculosis was a kind of drowning. He had seen that happen too many times to children and adults: a body pulled under a current without ripples or eddies to soften its effects, so that everyone could see how a stricken body seethed when bloated with illness. By then, the soul within would be overwhelmed with water, its weight and minerals, and it would draw away as if retreating to the bottom. But Miss Williams was not drawing away from anything—not from him or her many visitors. She had lost the quickness, the acuity of her habits, and yet her being still darted about—if not in happiness, then in a comforting tranquility. More than the water that threatened to overwhelm her, a wind buoyed her, buoyed them both, when they were alone in the cottage.

Just as she had once sat up nights with him so that she could safeguard his sleep from dreams, he sat up with her now. He knew he was losing her as she ruffled and fluttered, as the illness redefined her. Her death would be like no other he had experienced. The others had made some kind of sense, whether they were from war, or the dampness that was life in his own country, as well as the country he had gone off to save in trenches of waste and mud. To save the Britons, he had given up every measure that made sense to him, from his fingers to his imagination.

There was always something to do during the war, if not for the fellow who was dying, then for the next one marked for death. Stopper up the works, for instance, by harrying the enemy: lob more shots, demolish his roads and bridges, blight his food, and poison his men against him. That was part of the training, part of the desperate struggle for survival—always find another way to be ingenious. In war there are so many things to hate; Sheehan did not have a moment, in the trenches, when he could rank them. But if one kept shooting, or left a man to die in No Man's Land, or cracked the enemy on the neck while he was not looking, one would also miss the moment another man—his mate, his fellow, his superior officer, or underling servant—met his end. One could lose this moment of witness.

Miss Williams was dying, and there was something he could do about it. He could behold as many moments of it as nature granted. He did not mean for her to collapse in one minute only to be found, evaporated, in the next. She would not die in her sleep for him to discover the following morning, for him to step into a wholly changed universe, desiccated and shrunken, as if she had never existed. Already the world that she had given him was dwindling, as she was no longer able to speak to him as she once had, in the voice she could not quite control. It was a voice that raced and sometimes ran over itself, so eager was it to come to the point, even if she could not capture it. He wanted to see her walk, and gesture, and even rest as she had once tried to rest, for she had never been able to maintain the kind of stillness expected of women. She was more of a wing, a chime, a vane, than she was a person alert and attuned to the changing discipline of the wind. So he would have to watch carefully for what breath might transpire. For every twitch and every drop of sweat.

If he fell asleep while she struggled through the night, he might find her as he had found so many of his fellows, as he found his own hands, his family, his own state of mind. So he watched her move off the pillows he had arranged to help her breathing, and by morning, he would have to reorganize them again. It was a trial to leave her afterward, if only to get her tea and whatever breakfast she could stomach, for that task took moments too—entire interludes when she was unattended, and she might very well slip away into the dew outside, and the daylight that made quick work of it. He was relieved to watch her eat then, once he brought her the meal. To keep her engaged he would try to describe whom they might expect that morning, or the look and feel of the garden through the window as it receded into the autumn. Then he helped her out of bed and into the washroom, where she insisted she could be left alone. He had to wait outside the door and listen, for the water, the soap against her skin, the wash cloth—for sounds he knew existed, even if they had gone beyond his hearing. He did not for a second consider making any up. That was what he had once done, teaching, performing, and composing. Filling in blanks and breaths was possible, expected, before the war; after the war, he could not forget how they could be erased altogether, and no act of will or imagination could ever bring them back.

Once she had emerged, he would escort her back into the bed, so she might rest comfortably, a notebook in her hands in which to put down her own words. Because eventually he would have to leave her again to fetch another meal or answer the door or tend to some business just outside in the gardens, and he could only do so knowing she had ink and paper to record the seconds he had missed. She would have to account for them when he could not. She would have to account for them, because he could not.

When she was rested enough, Miss Williams worked on a story. She did not want to tell herself it would be her last story, and instead thought it would make an appropriate wedding gift for Mr. Sheehan. What he would need most, in the coming days, was her money, and whatever measure of stability it might purchase would be coming to him, she was assured, with this marriage. What he truly needed, an explanation of, or apology for, all that had happened between them, she was less sure that she could supply. But a story was the only gift she had left to give him on this occasion.

She began, as she usually began, with an orphan, because that was how she imagined him; it was how she imagined everyone to a degree. Everyone becomes an orphan at some point, regardless of whether or how well or long their parents survive. Miss Williams had been an orphan for as long as she could remember, with her father's absence and her mother's illness framing her days, her fantasies, her adventures and education. The war had likely made an orphan out of Mr. Sheehan, but unlike others, he was still fighting the separation from his people and places. Instead of running away as orphans do, he was hovering, as if waiting for that missing part of himself to be, with the rest of him, reunited. Whoever Mr. Sheehan was before the war—confident, possibly; handsome, conventionally; successful, most likely, either in music or love or even banking—was the true prey of The Hawkman, a predator who knew how to bide his time.

So she began with an orphan, and an orphan who would, one day, fly. But how this orphan would meet this goal was not entirely clear to Miss Williams, whose simple, human powers were quickly diminishing. Her illness had been explained to her, but she still did not wholly understand the nature of it, since it was so different than what her mother had endured, in her bouts and convalescences. Finally, all Miss Williams could deduce was that like her mother, she would perish from something rooted in her lungs, and the pain that originated there before it fanned out from her chest as if it were the circumference that a bird's wings suggest in full flight. For fever begins in birds, beneath the follicles and feathers, in the pressures birds juggle, between the air they breathe and the air that supports them.

Her own breathing was difficult and would soon be nearly impossible; with each intake of air, Miss Williams felt as though there was a scraping among her tissues, as if those feathers at her center had become bold, sharpened, and set to whittling, prodding, poking their way out. And yet there was no blood in all this scraping and puncturing, no coughing, as her mother had been sentenced to; she had none of the grizzly liquids her mother expelled first from her throat, and ultimately her nose, and her skin; the lot of her mother was all but skeleton at the very end; there was no flesh left once the disease had finished consuming her. Miss Williams was spared most of the body's rude dramatics. Instead there was, with each breath completed, the sensation of down and layers, heavier each moment, an uncanny smothering. There were even moments when there was no pain, no awareness, a numbness that was a welcome alternative, although Miss Williams well knew what it meant: the severing of one more connection between her mind and her breath, the mechanism that kept her heart beating and informed her consciousness.

The orphan was given an illness—or, more suspensefully, Miss Williams thought, a deformity—whose cause and cure eluded the doctors assigned to treat it. What the orphan in Miss Williams's final story had, precisely, were a pair of humps on her back. Almost at her shoulders, symmetrical and oval in form—almost egg-like—they comprised a gentle rise and slide in the conformation of an otherwise delightful child. The nurses who rescued the girl infant from the steps of a foundling hospital assumed them to a temporary phenomenon she would outgrow with the simple collection of height, muscle, and time. In the intervening years, they were easily hidden beneath her blouses or her bedclothes. Still they ached on the poor girl, as if they were growing along with her, and the limbs and digits of the hospital's other charges.

As the girl grew older, the humps increased in size. But so did her beauty, in the vivacious green-gold color of her eyes; the resilience and calm of the skin on her cheeks and forehead; in her hair, which grew thick and long, in brown and lighter hues—blonde and strawberry—that fluttered as the light passed through the strands. Her face, her voice, her soul offered a suitable contrast to what continued to amass and distend on her back; as she neared the onset of her womanhood, the humps began to appear stone-like, the skin concealing them suddenly grayer and less elastic than the rest of her vivid, soothing flesh. It was important to Miss Williams that despite the orphan's disfigurement, she appear ever lovelier than any person or creature in history, for she herself had always wished for such beauty, to distract people from her own flaws—her impatience and neediness.

Like all the foundlings in the hospital, which Miss Williams had decided to place in a famous brownstone building in New York City, this orphan was properly schooled, and then trained for a profession, so neither she nor her compatriots would remain a burden to society. Whether they found happiness in domesticity or other suitable arrangements was not the concern of the nurses or the hospital trustees. Yet for this girl, special pains had to be taken; the humps were making her unsuitable for factory work, for work as a seam-stress, as a teacher, a charity worker, or any other occupation in which she would have to appear publicly. For while her beauty never ceased to grow richer and deeper, the humps also asserted their presence in weight and menace. They forced her posture into a terminal hunch, so much so that she was forced to walk on a horrible slant that brought pain to the rest of her body. Her smile, naturally, sagged at the same terrible angle, to the point that it might slide off her face and be trampled by her beastly gait.

So the nurses decided to make her one of their own, a nurse who would be surrounded by other disgraced figures: the boarder patients—crippled, blind, or silent—and wards of the state. In other words, they were orphans who never grew out of their original condition. To see one of their own, this hump-backed orphan of a nurse, would be comforting, the nurses thought; she would be equally as comforted, knowing she could serve others. She had always been generous in her spirit and in the friendships she formed, first with the hospital staff; then her teachers; the adults she met on errands at the grocer's, the post office, and the butcher's; and most of all, with the trees outside the hospital, and the dusty sparrows and squirrels which ferried leaves and nuts between branches and roots. She was never friendly with the other orphans—they shunned her, as if those humps were a mark, a sentence, a sign of why she had been abandoned and could never be made into a real girl, a real daughter.

Miss Williams could write about the innovations the nurses created in the clothes they made for her, or the perfidy of the skin that both gave rise and protected those humps on her back: how it resembled the schist of cliff faces found along the Hudson, or how, in its restless moments, it cracked and burned like the formation of new rock. But she could not decide on the precise contents of those humps, and how they would be shed, or molt, or implode on themselves, so that they might reveal the essential nature of the girl, now an adult, now an old woman. She considered medicines, and magic potions, charms like enchanted gowns and necklaces. Miss Williams even thought of love as a cure, or a purgative, for what sickened the heroine, but she could not find a man who might administer it. How could anyone offer her anything, now that two humps had fused together into a shell over the woman, and she could live with neither her body or face above ground level. No story is a failure, Miss Williams reasoned, but how this tale came to frustrate her, just as her breathing, eating, and speaking did. The only function which did not frustrate was her dreaming.

Fourteen

ONCE TAKEN PRISONER, Sheehan was disarmed and marched out of the church and alongside an odd formation of Jerrys. Five men—four recruits or conscripts and one officer, by the way that they marched. Their packs were heavy with spoils Sheehan should have been bringing back to his units: canned goods, ribbons of some metal, and slats and plywood stripped from somewhere. Their superior officer carried nothing, of course, as the sergeant—he guessed—brayed out orders. The conscripts followed suit, repeating the words, move it, get along, faster, *schnell schnell*, playing out the action.

He knew what this show of discipline was meant to communicate, and told himself it was evidence that each Jerry was held in his own secret terror. This was what he and his compatriots were fighting against, or so he had been reminded all during his training; what his parents and students and everyone he had ever known or loved in his life might face, should Germany and her allies be permitted to have their way with Europe. These were the men whose brothers had plunged Belgium into atrocity and chaos, and yet they appeared just as human as he was, particularly in the flaws their discipline exacted upon them.

He was the only prisoner this patrol had netted; for moments, it seemed they didn't know what to do with him. They swore at one another—or their dialogue sounded like swearing to Sheehan—over their next move. Kill him now, do it! Don't be a coward, *schwach, schwach*, he could imagine them saying in words which they spit like darts at one another. It's always, *immer,* like this with you, it's not worth it, the waste in ammunition. *Du, du,* you do it. Leave him for the rats to eat. *Nein*, that is against regulations. In the halves and quarters of seconds that careered around him, they apparently decided to keep him as a prisoner, and for that he was grateful.

But how not to show it—that became his next task. He looked downward, and if he could keep his wits about him, in this singular way, in single moments and instances, he might survive with some poise, or at least self-respect. But he was relieved as his feet followed the cadence of the enemy; but that relief was unaccompanied by warmth or release. Instead there was an awareness, a familiar tension he was still capable of affecting; his hands could be made into fists. They were still his hands even though he had been stupid, so very stupid. He could feel his fingernails grating into his palms and knew he was to immediately begin planning his escape as a bayonet urged him forward. He had to comply, in this instance, lest the bayonet find its way through his ribs. But his thoughts did not have to follow. They would remain on escape. They remained on observation, forgetting nothing, because some day he would have to report everything he had seen. Some day soon, when he escaped, or was liberated.

In an improvised Jerry headquarters, he was set down in a chair where supplies were being ferried into the enemy trenches. Weapons and artillery. The inventory must have been reassuring to the men who unloaded it, who carried it and handed it over, one man to the next: they had enough to take them through Christmas, it appeared, and possibly beyond, even to celebrate the outcome with neutered versions of their explosives. The shooting was supposed to be over next month, he had been told; they all had been told, on both sides, this prediction. The Germans didn't have the industry, the capacity, to keep going at this rate, the English said. But the Jerrys apparently did not believe it.

Sheehan watched the assembly of men and their munitions with a dull realization of their strength and depth. In the next minute, he remembered not to allow the Jerrys to see him come to such a recognition. Otherwise the rain of fire and metal coming to his fellows would be unrelenting. He would be giving away all the Allied secrets. He told himself that all he saw to explain this flurry of productivity and discipline was an inspection of sorts. There was nothing more to all this unloading and assemblage. It was all a trick, he concluded, staged for his benefit. He couldn't fall for it.

He knew some German, primarily musical terms, but he did not know any of the words he needed now, "Red Cross" or "I know nothing." He thought he might catch on to the language if he listened intently, but he could not listen with his ears bawling and combative. The exchanges surrounding him instead were a kind of floating madness. The words he could identify slipped in their order and placement; the rest were like notes a musician might audition without finishing.

He could surmise, based on the flow of men and where they had erected parapets, how the Germans must have recently dug accordion-style warrens in some locations, as if there were now multiple fronts lined up, one after the other. He might have struggled out of the manacles they trussed him up in except for the sensation of his wrist bone bending each time he fidgeted, as if screws were being drilled, thread by thread, into his carpals. This was where he identified his weakness, how far he could go, when he would fold, although he had always known what it would be; it was obvious. He was obvious. What he could not sacrifice. His heart, his stomach, even his soul, yes. But not his hands. The lilt of his wrists, the tender connections between sinew and bone, every individual digit. His weakness, magnified by ten, by blood and hair and nails: his instruments. Where the excruciation had to end, if he was to live.

Then there were the two nervous Jerry recruits, new men who had not been on the patrol that had brought him in. Their faces were still clean and their eyes clear, or that freshness was actually the fear in them. They were just as afraid to stop watching him as he was at having been captured; in his own eyes he could feel, and in theirs he could see, a rising berm of shame. Because this is where the hunger began—for him as a prisoner, for the recruits as cogs in a vastly indifferent machine.

His captors offered him nothing to eat, and he dare not ask for anything. Then came some water, some bread, a potato that was meant to be consumed without cooking. As days wore on the lack of sustenance burred into his stomach, and crept into every fiber he could account for: his hands, heavy with their numbness, each finger indistinct in its lack of sensation. In his feet, as if tunneled out, and re-filled with sand. His legs like rubber. He fell asleep from hunger in chairs, on open fields, in billets that had been reconfigured into prisoners' barracks. He fell asleep from hunger or he assumed he had, because he was always wrenched out from sleep, ordered to decamp in the darkest pitch of night. He was marching again, marching and starving, and he could not make out what was in front of him.

Perhaps he was marching in place, although there was a growing column of men cuffed and shackled, added to the space around him. A regiment of debasement. A regiment of slave labor, of soldiers who were delinquent. No speaking. No signals. No looking—not at the next fellow, not over your shoulder. Keep to yourself. Keep to your place. These were the instructions, at the butt of a rifle, the point of a bayonet.

How he heard them, though; in a vocabulary that was meant to convey the exquisite: *am anfang, schnell, gehend, rasch, frisch frisch frisch.* There were examples made of prisoners who violated the rules, shared cigarettes, gestured to one another: beatings, starvation, summary execution. One gunshot he thought he heard from a distance, but he did not know which infraction had prompted it or where in the column it landed. The sounds of other gunshots crept closer to his position or their impact was embellished by commentary of his fellow prisoners, especially those trafficking in rumor. He did not count the losses to his line because of his hands, the needles in his palms, the fire in his fingers.

He felt as if they were being marched the entirety of the Franco-German border, and then the width of Germany, but of course he could neither firm it up in his own mind nor ask the fellows shackled on either side of him: both French, one limping terribly, something about his shin. Sheehan thought it might be gangrene, the way he wrapped and unwrapped a freckled cloth about it, how it wore a hideous purple sheen. The French soldier doused it with whatever he had; he begged for water, he begged for kerosene. The other one was taller, blond, and in far better condition than any of them, withstanding several butts of a rifle to his cheek because he had shifted his eyes in a particular direction. The Jerrys got rid of him quick, before crossing their own border. The speculation as to this soldier's fate droned through the line as if an electric prod was being put to each one of them.

A sameness poured over the days—not like acid, that would be too dramatic—a glaze that was cumulative. They awoke exposed, and were rousted and re-arranged into their formations. A day's rations, when available, were plopped into the cup of their hands and then they were told to move on, move on. Into the cauldrons of German towns they marched, to be spit on, shouted down, have bed pots and other unpleasant fluids fall on their heads and shoulders. At nightfall they slept where they fell, and a fresh set of conscripts was there to guard them.

The man with the limp succumbed, finally, at one of the hospital camps near Cologne. This was what the guard seemed to have said when the limping man was not there one morning. Sheehan was shackled to other prisoners; more and more Russians, the deeper they poured into German territory. The language the Germans heaved at them—*nein, nicht schleppen, staerker, viel*—was shrinking. There was another morning he awoke moments before the prisoners ahead of him in the column, but he did not lift his head. Instead he watched, terrified, as a set of guards, unfamiliar to him, slapped three prisoners awake. Before they could rise to their feet, the guards dropped all their biscuits and rinds, then poured water from the canteens on these rations. Just so they could see the prisoners claw and scrape and roll over one another to get at the food. For the chance to rescue something from the dirt. *Na-ja, sehr traurig, wie munter*, the Germans urged them on, in the language the Jerrys made coarse. He knew what was being demanded of him; what it portended, and so he forgot the words meant to ask for more subtlety in the timing, nuances in volume. Instead he learned the predation of the language.

THERE IS ONE hunk of bread for the five of you, one potato for the ten. There is coffee for those who don't step out of line, cigarettes for those who do not try to escape. You can count your sips of water on one hand. If the man in front of you should fall, slip up, find the yeast of his wound blurting out, forget it. He might only get you infected.

The green mold, he heard the other prisoners talk about; the green mold that overtakes a man's initiative when he's been in the camps as long as they have. When he forgets women, his family, his place at home, food. Although one never forgets whether he was Regular or New Army. Stay away from mold, from staying still, from growing anything, or anything that grows. It would be better to be reptile-skinned, cold-blooded, to shiver alone with one's sorrows than to be locked in the fortunes of others, one's fate tied up in his comrades'.

Upon arriving at Merseburg, they were stripped and sorted; the Jerrys were always sorting men, into sizes, abilities. Sheehan was taken to the commandant's office. In his own language, he was asked how he might make himself useful. The scent of the place, low and fetid, as bad as the trenches. He looked for a window, but he could see nothing, his eyes unable to adjust to the bright new circumstances. So how could he have been useful, in any way, shape, or form, the commandant asked again. *"Kannst du mich hören?"* the man asked; frustration had sent him back to his own language. He meant to take his hands out of his pockets, to show what they could do. But his hands were ruined.

"He'll adjust," he eventually heard in English. He was taken to a cot, given a blanket, and ordered to write to his family, to tell them what happened. He could ask them for food, clothing, more blankets, tobacco; if he didn't smoke, he could use it as currency. "I am safe," he wrote. "I am sorry." Now everyone would know: his parents, siblings, colleagues at the music school, perhaps even his students. His students had given him jams and tins of meat before he left, so he would not have it so bad. Now all they'd get for their good deeds was a tale of his rank foolishness.

His fellow prisoners asked him the same question again: how could he be put to use? He didn't want to be the only Paddy in the barracks. If he spoke, they'd hear his accent. He put his hands in his pockets and shrugged, said nothing, and followed them as they walked along another set of wires. Barbed and woven, separating the prisoners from the conscripts across a moat. The prisoners walked in twos, side by side, and he walked behind them. He might as well have been a mile away rather than just out of earshot. He walked in fear that they would find out. He would talk in his sleep. He would reenact the whole debacle. There weren't many English prisoners compared to the French and Russians. He was English to them; it wouldn't matter to them how he was captured.

There was an English lieutenant to command them in the camp. He seemed to be of a good sort, concerned with packages and morale. His name was Wilson. Perhaps he was from the south of England, from Dorset. He said to stay away from the *kommandos,* if possible, and the reprisal camps, although those camps were closest to Holland. They were all aiming for Holland. In the meantime, he could surely find something to do. Write letters for other men or put hammer to wood and nail.

He lifted his hands out of his pockets for Wilson, held them out as if he were a child, for inspection. "Piano. I played, a bit," he said.

"And where . . .?" the English lieutenant began, and perhaps he finished his question. Sheehan could only assume that he did.

"Gloucester," he said, and his own voice sounded strange, as if the ringing blocked out random letters. "Gloucester," he said with more force, to cut through the obstacle. "Manchester before then, sir. I trained there."

"I see," Wilson said. "I'm afraid you won't . . ."

"Yes, sir," he answered. He closed his eyes, hoping it would stop the clanging, but it went on like a beating, the landing of punches.

"You'll want for no lack . . . we'll see to it," Wilson said. The lieutenant picked up a clipboard. He was assigned to the kitchen.

There was no working with food. That was for the Jerrys. The prisoners might steal it. He washed dishes, mopped floors, hauled rubbish. The prisoners slept and ate with only their own kind, the better to reinforce the Jerrys' tactic of dividing and conquering. But the kitchen staff was international if it was to function. His supposed kind was not having him as he was, so he knew he'd have to throw in his lot with the French or the Russians.

The French ate whatever was put in front of them. Like dogs, so happy to get anything. They played pranks, stole light bulbs and utensils, sabotaged doorknobs with grease. But the Russians seized upon the potato in each day's consommé and threw it at their captors. They threw entire bowls at the Germans, or they smashed the potatoes with their feet at the evening's roll call in a fit of disrespect. They kept at this protest, even as they were jailed in solitary. They were indomitable, better equipped than the Europeans: solid caps, thicker, longer coats. This war would go on like a Russian winter, until every last soldier was peeled and boiled, thrown into a pot of nothingness, and wasted by the Russians.

"You, musician," one of his fellow dishwashers asked, in

discernible English. He was Russian, bearded, one eye a ruin of white with blue smearing. Sheehan ignored him.

"You play," the Russian continued as he approached Sheehan to leave behind a sink drowning in dishes. "What you play?" the Russian said, and his voice became louder, through the dint of language, Sheehan guessed. "You play what?"

Sheehan raised his hands and pantomimed the keys with his fingers. The Russian grabbed at his hands.

"Let me see," the Russian commanded. His breath was sour from starvation. He flipped Sheehan's hands, and his single eye searched them over.

"You play different instrument."

"No," Sheehan insisted. "Piano." He repeated the pantomime, much to the Russian's dissatisfaction.

"Different instrument," the Russian persisted.

He shrugged, and nodded.

"You come," the Russian said. "After dishes."

The Russians had to steal him into their bunk, and once he was installed within, they pushed a squeezebox into his hands, as though it was a contraband loaf of bread.

"You play different," his one-eyed friend instructed, and Sheehan took a moment to feel the weight of the thing, finger its buttons on its sides, the give in its bellows. As he tested its tones, he felt as though he was holding something small and important in his hands, a living thing amid all this mortification.

"I can teach you," Sheehan said, and he tapped out a scale. "I don't know yours but," he said as he tried a few notes of "God Save the King." The one-eyed Russian took the instrument away, and led him to the far side of the bunk. But there was nothing but a wall, until the men standing on either side raised it, as if it were a curtain. It was a false wall, to hide the hole the men had either dug or, possibly, inherited from the previous inmates.

The Russian's broken blue eye lolled as if he was trying to focus on something far away—the bottom of the hole, and the tunnel that led the way out underneath their feet.

"Do you play the big one?" the Russian asked, and he pantomimed with his fingers just as Sheehan had done earlier.

"Organ," another Russian said, although it sounded like two words when this man said it, as though he were pronouncing a specific man's name. When the word did not register on Sheehan's face, its speaker came closer, his blood-red eyes boring into his own. "Organ. Do you play it?" he said, and he clapped his hands in a wide motion. "We need air," he said, pointing to the hole. "Air," he repeated again with the exaggerated clapping. "Do you know air?" he asked.

Sheehan threw in his lot with the Russians.

IT MAY HAVE been early September, still temperate enough for an escape; the men wanted out before the first snowfall. That might be six, eight weeks away. After such time, the forests would be impassable, or starvation would be the only fate they held for men on the run. This Sheehan understood as the Russians explained through hand signals and their consonants. He had to listen carefully, so as not to get swept away by their stunning pronunciations, as if they were chiseling out each letter with their tongues. He nodded and made his own signals for the material he'd need.

Leather and wood was the sum of it. Wood of so many kinds, and door hinges, glue, tacks, screws, nails. They needed air, but he needed to make a device that was airless, airtight; he did not know if they understood this explanation, and he was tempted to write it down, make a list. He went for a pencil on one man's bunk, but the Russian who had introduced him grabbed his hand, shook it until the pencil dropped to the ground.

"*Nyet*," he said, and Sheehan understood.

He found the Russians to be a creative sort, as they would try anything—stealing, sewing, building, demolishing and rebuilding—to get their work done. They were neither competitive nor craftsmen, and the deadline set by the weather was the most salient influence on all of them. Sheehan marveled at their impossible speech, like pieces of green wood, wedged and latched into each other. They offered up their boots for the leather that would be the bellows, and their coats and jackets when their shoes could not provide enough. They'd run through the winter to keep warm, once they escaped, they promised. They brought him wire for thread, bits of fencing for the bellows' springs. The raw potatoes they stole were ground into flour and then water was added, when he asked for paste, to stiffen the bellows. They dug with spoons, the bowls they ate with, their hands and fingernails, and the excess dirt they could not nonchalantly plant in the yard went into their pockets, or the latrines. The Jerrys could not account for why the latrines at the Russian barracks filled up so much more quickly than the rest of the camp's, and took to ordering deeper holes dug in the unco-operative earth. In this way, they were able to get a hold of proper digging equipment.

⌘

THE RUSSIANS GAVE him the squeezebox, whether as payment or a model for study, he could not figure. It became clear fairly quickly that he did not know how to build a bellows, but together they improvised as they took apart the squee-zebox and fashioned it back together. When they pressed it into his hands the final time, the bellows secured over the hole, he shook his head, no, no, and told them to keep it; it gave him a plausible excuse to come back to their bunks, he said. God only knows the suspicions they had raised among the Jerrys, to say nothing of his own kind. Stashing the instrument with the Russians gave him excuse to visit them each evening.

Because it was a bellows designed for an organ—and then some—it was controlled by pedals. The Russians set him up on a stool as if he were to play at a pub, and he stepped on a beam at the base of the contraption. The bellows expanded in height but declined in width until he released the pedal, and then it descended as it expanded around the middle. Another man had to hold it in place and still another, with a pail of the potato-paste and a paintbrush, watched for leaks or any other slippage. But it worked.

The bellows worked as long as he could keep his foot going: toe on the pedal, then heel off, in 4/4 time. Its opera-tion was more akin to driving a car than it was to playing an instrument, he thought. Three men climbed into the tunnel, testing the premise the bellows was built to power. It had him think of his mother, at home, at her Singer, tapping out the stitches she made in his shirts and trousers. The sound was one of a window opening, the shade drawn over it, the wind jabbing to draw the shade back against the wooden frame. The looms he saw once at Tralee, what remained of his father's people. Warp and weft—a blanket, a shawl, sweater, and scarf.

The wall that was like a curtain: it rose up in silence. But he did not sense it. Instead he felt the immediate space around him enlarge, as if he were pumping air into the room, not down below it. He might have heard shuffling, friction in sawdust, but he could not be sure if it was a true sound, or leftover or anticipatory noise, the howl that would engulf the bunk once they'd escaped to Holland. Suddenly the room became awful with light, and he put his hands to his ears and shut his eyes. When he released his hands and opened his eyes, he saw that the Russians had withdrawn from his side, and opened up a clear path before him.

"Prisoner," the commandant was shouting. "Sheehan. *Achtung! Halten!*"

Sheehan drew on his breath.

"*Du kommst als erster,*" the commandant said, and the guard next to him motioned with his bayonet. "You go," the guard ordered, the rest of his instructions dropping off into the hole, now airless and fatal.

THEY FIRST WANTED the names. Then they didn't. His was not the only name they needed. Others didn't matter.

Everyone was guilty. Everyone would be punished. But if he gave them names, it would go easier for him. More food, more rest, more time outside: the offers were vague, and, in his hearing, unfinished. The names they wanted: first the Russians, then the English. The English must have been involved; otherwise how could he have spent so much time with the Russians? Just give us the names, and we will prove it.

But he did not have the names of the Russians. He could not say what they sounded like, the concluding syllables. He did not know the ranks, their honorifics—all fell outside the span of his hearing.

"What about their uniforms?" the interrogator asked. "You can still see, read, interpret military dress?"

Sheehan closed his eyes, as if to feign effort. He shook his head, and chose silence. For a method of lying, it was the least offensive.

In the background, behind the desk where the interrogator was sitting, a procession of administrators debated with their whispers, although all speech had long since begun to sound this way. He heard the word "English" quite crisply on many occasions, and more infrequently "Irish," but he could not confirm anything. There may have been a tussle going on over how he should be disciplined, but he could not say. Surely they were not worried over what protocol they might ignore, or the protestations of other governments, despite what it meant for their own prisoners in the custody of the Russians or English. But who would be held responsible for this lapse, whose head served to whom on a glittering platter?

The English lieutenant, Wilson, was brought to him. "You've done it now," the lieutenant said. Wilson was not angry with him, if jealousy is not anger; he was not affronted, if bewilderment is not indignance. "How do you propose . . .?" the lieutenant began, but Sheehan proposed nothing and kept to his reticence.

Someone turned on a light; it was devilishly loud, submerging all speech that challenged it. Gradually, Sheehan felt himself withdrawing from the situation—not a retreat, precisely, because that action was not an option, but a kind of drift overtook him. He became more reliant on his other senses, so the alarms and battering between his ears would not pitch at him so harshly. He watched, tried to feel the eyes of his commanding officer upon him. Scalding with a heat that splits the flesh, but tentative, remorseful, as though it knew what the soldier had already been subjected to.

Wilson was reading to him from a document. The man handed him the paper, and a pen to sign it. "I had warned you," the lieutenant said. The good of the unit. The morale of his fellows. A jangle of piano keys, as if a hand had slipped out of its proper positioning. Sheehan did not take the paper or the pen. He made no movement to sign it.

"Congratulations, man," Wilson said, although he might have said something else entirely. Sheehan was being lifted by his armpits, pushed out of the commandant's office. The yard, the barracks, the familiar settings were washed out suddenly by a roving searchlight, louder and more powerful than he had ever observed it; he heard in bunches about the harm he was causing others, the lot of good that he had done to the Russians, what awaited him, and the bets that were being taken on whether he would survive. At the end of the march, Sheehan and his escorts came to a row of cinderblock buildings. Inside it appeared divided into separate water closets. They opened the last door in the row and hurled him inside it. The light was switched on, and the blur of anarchy began in his head.

The noise that the light forged—Sheehan felt as though he had been placed within a piece of artillery. Soon it would be winced open, as if in a blast. Sheehan set his hands to his ears but that only made the constant drone more prominent. He fell to his knees, curled his head into his chest. He was taking cover against himself. It might have worked, if not for the vibrations of his heart and breathing. To hide away from the clamor was to invite another kind of disturbance, so that it would not be the Jerrys who would be administering torture. It would be his own soul and body.

Sheehan did not know how long he kept to that posture, as if he were a ball of sweat and limbs, huddled against the chastising silence. Trays of food were slid through a slot in the cell door, but he could not eat. He was choking on sound alone as it took residence in his stomach and throat, his lungs and sinuses. The light turned nights into days; it turned the days within the cell into nights in the trenches. If he screwed his eyes shut as tightly as he could manage, he could not block out the brightness. A red scrim tore through the underside of his eyelids while a line of white sparks bled through, as if to consume the darker color.

He may have slept for moments at a time; he may have broken down, sobbing out of the pain that was unremitting. Since he could not tell whether it was day or night; since the guards would not answer when he begged for the date, or the length of his incarceration, he tried counting the meals served to him. But he could not make sense of the numbers. There were either too few meals, or too many; they competed with the beat of his heart, the pummeling drill of recollection: the bombs. He tried to break down the sounds, hold them separate, to secure a room within himself; he knew he needed to listen for other prisoners, the comings and goings of the guards.

Sheehan listened, particularly after the tray was slid under his door. What would the footsteps of the guards sound like, through the cinderblock, beneath the light; the rubbing of the wooden trays as they were slid into other cells, wood catching against cement, a sound of quickened erosion. A simple noise, like a washboard. The hinges of the metal slot as it was opened, the oxygen that rushed out, the slap as it closed. He could imagine some of this, but could not hear it for himself, no matter his effort.

Banging on the walls with his fists; shouting until he could hear himself through the riot in his head; he wondered if it was possible to scar one's own throat, just as he was bloodying his fingers. No other prisoner seemed to answer his calls although he might not have been able to hear anyone, in his state. Two of his senses cleaved from his grip. He ate the food, the consommé and bread, to determine whether he still had the senses of smell and taste. For touch, he worried his hands over the door to his cell, the ridges in the wood, a mountain range at his fingertips. He pressed harder into the wood, to summon the hills to rise, to splinter, to drive themselves through his skin. Then he'd be assured that his sense of touch was still intact.

He did not know what day it was when he discovered

the area immediately outside his cell was not as bright and, therefore, not so loud and dispiriting. For an instant when the slot was open, the world on the other side was almost dark, as though the light had been switched off, or its strength after so much use was wavering. Once the tray had been retrieved, Sheehan contrived to open the slot. With a shoe, he was eventually able to rig it halfway, so that he could see the darkened floor if he positioned himself on his elbows, hands supporting his face, eyes locked downward. The guard found him sleeping in that position, perhaps the next day, perhaps at the next meal. The slot was nailed shut, in the rhythm of admonishment.

He was left with the light, what it soldered onto his mind's eye. He forced himself to look directly into it, as if the concentrated exposure would acclimate him, build calluses on his nerves and eardrums. The noise reeled on, but he sensed there was more to the light than a mere blaze, a prick of color, the more he studied it. He could see the birth of small, small creatures in it, transparent beings no bigger than a fingernail, and they swiveled and turned as if reacting to some larger force impinging on their territory.

If he could stay with the light, not take his eyes away, those simple insects might unite into a larger being, more complex. This thing did not swim, but floated in the juice either his eyes or the light made. It held itself aloft as it grew, as it compiled itself out of other things. It was a scavenger, waiting patiently as the less sophisticated formations came to it, and added the newcomer to its layers. As it grew, it became more animated; it developed a gait, fanciful though not particularly efficient, as a bird may walk. Arms sprouted, flapped, and a neck stretched out above the arms. A head was born, but without a mouth or nose clearly delineated. Sheehan put out his hand, as if he could stop the process, the incubation. His hand revealed nothing but air, a figment of the light. The light left brown spots darting about, then they drew themselves together.

Sheehan moved his attention away from the light, thinking it had burned through his eyes to create the hallu-cination. But the brown spots took on a shape he should have recognized; they became a shadow on the wall, then the ceiling, and then he saw it, a predator magnificent in wingspan and coloration. Spread as they were, so the beast might coast down onto him, the wings were more than half his height. It hovered to display to him its claws, the underside of its tail—red as the Clare sandstone. In the next moment, its beak dove into Sheehan's neck, at precisely the location of his Adam's apple, where all speech resided. The bird sunk in its talons. The animal waved its head back and forth, as if to wring out the neck from Sheehan's skin.

He wanted to fight the bird off, but its grasp was too expert. Sheehan twisted and wrestled but could get no hold on the creature other than its wings. Feathers and bone ran through his hands as if through sand. Next he attempted to kick it off, to make his body hurl itself from the ground, where the bird had secured it. Yet every move Sheehan made was matched by the bird. It flapped its wings not to take flight, but to bear down on him. Sheehan knew something of birds of prey, how they clenched and prodded, exhausted the mice and children they caught, so they might carry them off before devouring them. This bird seemed to want something different, though, as if it were extracting a vow of silence. And there was nowhere in the cell for either man or bird to go. Together they rolled, then smashed into the wall, bloodying Sheehan's forehead, then the knuckles of his human claws.

He might have screamed a call for help, in German as well as English. A guard would not look into the cell, as that would have required his opening the door. Though a guard could have taken a moment to listen to the prisoner in the throes of a rigorous nightmare; it was not uncommon among the subjects of solitary confinement.

Fifteen

THEY TRIED THEIR best to be a handsome couple, Mr. Sheehan in his rescued suit, and Miss Williams in a new dress. She did not wear white, as much as she might have deserved it, but a shade deeper, bordering on gray, like the bits of web and lint birds sometimes make their nests with. She chose it in a creamy fabric, velveteen, that she had seen in a village shop before her illness and mentioned to Lady Margaret in an unguarded moment. Lady Margaret then set out to secure it by sending her lady's maid. The maid reported that the material was more likely appropriate for gloves than an entire frock, but Lady Margaret told her to go through with it. It was lovely, once the bolts of material had been delivered, but it was all the seamstress could do to swaddle Miss Williams in it. Still, the color was both smooth and comforting on her, gently hypnotic.

When Christopher offered to buy Mr. Sheehan the requisite outfit, Sheehan bid him to come into the nursery. From beneath the bed Sheehan extracted a ball of clothes, encapsulated in dust. It appeared as a sac of eggs might, gossamer and compact, where a spider might nurture its young. From there he removed a jacket and trousers, and a day shirt with a club collar. Sheehan lay the clothes atop the bed as if making a case for their rehabilitation. From the jacket breast pocket he produced a handkerchief, monogrammed with his initials. Miss Williams had evidently had it made for him—had purchased all the clothes, which he discarded in a fit of pique. Having returned the handkerchief to its rightful place, Mr. Sheehan stepped aside, to allow Christopher to make his own assessment.

It was a perfectly adequate suit, though not for the occasion. A morning jacket was in order, though Christopher quickly realized Mr. Sheehan would not be able to withstand its restrictions, nor those of the waistcoat and double cuffed shirts. A simple, but thorough, washing would likely restore whatever he already had, Christopher told him. He would take the clothes to the estate and personally ensure that they were washed and pressed properly. As for the hat, the fraying straw one Mr. Sheehan used in the garden would not do. He must have a gentleman's homburg hat to wear to the registry. As he had already promised to stand up for Mr. Sheehan, Christopher said he would happily buy one for him.

For his part, Sheehan trimmed his beard and slicked his hair back into a ponytail, so that he now exhibited the features of an individual. His face was long but not gaunt, though the bones of his cheeks were clearly defined. His jawline was strong, and his eyes were small, although they revealed a gamut of colors, the stages of autumn. His forehead shone too, and promised intelligence.

Dressing Miss Williams that morning was a chore, one that the lady's maid could not handle on her own. The bride could barely sit up to help herself, nor remain upright long enough for underclothes to be chosen and laid out on the bed. Miss Williams's body had become unfathomably complex in the process of her illness. Her skin was pallid and shivering. Her limbs could not be controlled. Well, of course they could be, but they seemed to fold and unravel in so many confounding patterns. When they left her unattended, even for a moment, her arms began to squeeze around herself, or her shins disappeared under her legs. When she slept, Lady Margaret thought, she must have turned into a huddle of bones, as if she were an egg or a stone. She was almost silver in complexion.

Lady Margaret held her gently by the shoulders as the lady's maid knelt to begin putting on the stockings. A fine down, like that of a newborn chick, had begun to come into her skin, in patches. Together Lady Margaret and the maid could not properly fit Miss Williams's feet into the shoes; her feet were so narrow that the shoes slid down too quickly from the heel. When Miss Williams finally did stand up, she seemed to sink into the floor, and had to be gathered up again by the two women. Lady Margaret feared for the dress; she feared for Miss Williams's nakedness, for, when the dress was finally put on over the bride's head, it would just as quickly slither off, Lady Margaret was certain. It was nothing short of a miracle once Miss Williams found her way into the garment. It did not fit—nothing could, given Miss Williams's lack of resources—but it did not fall off. She was cosseted in the dress, as a moth is shielded before it comes alive again.

Miss Williams declined a veil and even a hat; she wanted to feel the sun and air on her face. Her hair she wanted on her shoulders. It showed sprigs of age that might have, in fact, always been there, but Lady Margaret had never noticed, for Miss Williams formerly had kept her hair tied back in buns and braids. Lady Margaret was struck by how the gray nettled through the loose and lank strands, as if to confound the darkness surrounding it. Around her neck and for her ears, Miss Williams asked for a matching set of a pearl necklace and earrings she said had belonged to her mother. Once secured around her neck and on her ears, the jewelery gave Miss Williams a strange, subdued radiance. She was too eager for Mr. Sheehan to see her, tradition be damned; Miss Williams made no secret that she was afraid the effect would wear off should she wait too long. She could only stand to be a lady for an instant.

Lady Margaret found herself having to allow it. Christopher was able to secure only one car from his father's garage, which meant there would be no concealing the bride from the groom before the ceremony. There were other obstacles to sequestering the two principals, given Miss Williams's immobility. It would be a day of tumult, for Miss Williams's physical condition, and for Lady Margaret's sense of etiquette.

Miss Williams insisted on walking "on her own power" out of the nursery, as if she had to convince everyone that she was a willing participant. If she was willing, then this wedding would not be a ruse, as Lord Thorton had said of it. Lord Thorton had said he was certain he could prove it was a ruse afterward. That it was his own son, Christopher, who was orchestrating "this little passion play"—another from the earl's cracking good terminology—seemed cruel to Lord Thorton. But Lady Margaret wished he could see the good in it. If the marriage took, and not necessarily in the way that her husband, or most other men, would think of it; if it took in the minds of the witnesses, in the hearts of those who had to sanction it, it would be a blessing, she reasoned. That was why the success of this production was so essential. Mr. Sheehan would be provided for; he would no longer pose a source of distress for the village—or her husband. He was never so dangerous, Lady Margaret decided as she glanced ahead of Miss Williams and spotted Mr. Sheehan waiting before her in the kitchen. He was focused, and therefore gallant, in his own fashion. The Hawkman required more protection from the village, it seemed, than it ever did from him.

Miss Williams had extended her arms on either side, as if for balance, as she tottered toward her groom. Lady Margaret and the maid trailed behind her, as if they held a net between them, or some other means of catching her. Miss Williams paused, just as she was crossing the threshold into the kitchen. Perhaps a cloud scattered away the sun, or a set of branches parted in a breeze, because at that moment the sunlight poured itself through the small kitchen so that it was suffused with the time and heat of the hour. The smiles of the bride and groom were faint as they were overwhelmed by the light's temporary exuberance. Christopher, whom Lady Margaret could not ignore, grinned through the loss he was bearing.

He was trying so hard, so much. In Miss Williams's posture and Mr. Sheehan's eyes, Lady Margaret next sensed a thrill, and then relief: they had not disappointed each other in their appearance. There would be so many more opportunities for disappointment later, Lady Margaret thought, no matter the duration of their marriage.

"Good morning, Miss Williams," Christopher said, and it was strange to hear him—to hear anyone—speak in the cottage, where the moments dropped off the clock so heavily, due to the silence.

"I hope it is a good morning," Miss Williams said. It had been a task for her just to utter that one sentence, Lady Margaret thought. Mr. Sheehan immediately stepped forward. He offered his hand, and then his arm, as support. Gladly Miss Williams took up the suggestion, and, for a moment, they stood in fascination of each other and their small accomplishments.

"It is a great morning," Lady Margaret volunteered, and it was a solace to have something to say, to be useful, in that atmosphere. It was a gift to have Miss Williams smile in agreement. For so many days, Lady Margaret felt she had been relegated to the marriage's symbolic details—cakes, bridesmaids, all of the accouterments she thought might make the wedding real in the eyes of the village, in the eyes of her husband—none of which would be on display today. They held no attraction for the couple. They were desperate only for sanction, not a celebration.

"Is it too early yet?" Christopher asked.

"Not at all," Lady Margaret volunteered, and she, in turn, reached for her son's arm, so that there might be two couples that morning. But Christopher took Miss Williams's other arm and helped lead her through the entryway and out the front door.

Still, Lady Margaret was proud of her son at that instant: proud of his patience, forbearance, and how he fearlessly confronted his own limits. She wondered if she could be responsible for any of this, or whether Lord Thorton's branch lay claim to it. Most likely it was neither, and it had something to do with some event or friendship she knew nothing of. Perhaps an incident at school, or in the war, influenced her son to make something of himself. It came from his respect for Mr. Sheehan, a fellow soldier, from his admiration for Miss Williams; as he held her arm, he walked slightly ahead of her, in careful steps, and waited as Mr. Sheehan gently pushed her ahead. On the worn floors of the cottage, their combined footsteps seemed a discomforting shuffle. Would that it be this way for the rest of his life, Lady Margaret wondered and lamented: the chains people, even her son, had to forge nowadays because of their crippled limbs, their injured faith. That was why she was so proud of him, she decided; because her son could admit as much.

Outside the cottage, Miss Williams's steps became even more delicate, as she navigated the stone walk to the front gate. She was not wavering or trying to delay, but she was testing something she had not felt for far too long—the air; it seemed as if it was too slack and thin to support her. She stopped, and Lady Margaret stopped to watch her take deep breaths. Lady Margaret noticed how Miss Williams closed her eyes and held her blind face to the sun, as if the combination of light and air might lift her, transport her, to what was above and beyond the strictures that illness had put on her. It was then Lady Margaret saw Miss Williams had left behind the bouquet she was meant to carry. Miss William had chosen white ranunculus for their many petals—their many layers and, therefore, many interpretations, Miss Williams had explained. Lady Margaret rushed to the bedroom to retrieve them, all the while realizing Miss Williams could probably not spare a free hand to hold them for the rest of the day.

They had just installed Miss Williams into the back seat of the car when they noticed she was not quite breathless; so Mr. Sheehan could wait on Lady Margaret and sit with her in the front.

No, no, no, Lady Margaret wanted to say to The Hawkman. Don't be ridiculous, sit with your darling; after all this, don't you deserve it? But her own voice, as she remembered it, would be too disruptive: belittling and filled with an intimacy that now seemed frivolous. It was better to join the silence and wait for Christopher to give her—or Mr. Sheehan—some sort of signal. "Mother, please," Christopher said, and she was grateful to hear him say it, despite the discomfort in his voice. He motioned for her to take the passenger seat beside him. She held onto the bouquet, for she assumed that the bride and groom would be more apt to take each other's hands on the drive to their life together.

"Is she all right?" Lady Margaret asked, turning in her seat to face Mr. Sheehan directly. He raised his chin and blinked slowly, as if to reassure Lady Margaret, and then he gripped the mound of fingers Miss Williams had created on her own lap. They sat so close together that Mr. Sheehan's face was within a wisp of pressing against Miss Williams's ear, as if he were finally to break his silence, if only to her. Lady Margaret turned away, freshly embarrassed. When she looked back on them again, once Christopher had started up the car, and they were on their way, she saw that Miss Williams had closed her eyes, not because she was fading but as if to concentrate on the scent of Mr. Sheehan.

Lady Margaret wished her husband could have seen the two. They were odd and ill-suited for Bridgetonne; unable to care for themselves, or for each other, they were ill-suited for any place in this age, Lady Margaret mused. The world had not necessarily changed since the war; people were still cruel, and careless, and hateful of what wasn't theirs. Except now, there were so many ways to hide that neglect; new charities, campaigns, and aid societies sprung up daily, in which one could conceal his false concern for the unfortunate. Had Lord Thorton listened to the dirge of Miss Williams's breathing and Mr. Sheehan's devotion to easing it, he might have seen that there was no need to hide from his responsibilities, and the opportunities he had missed to truly display them.

At the registry office, the clerks were polite enough to assume that Lady Margaret was the bride, given the bouquet she was carrying. They were sensible enough to offer Miss Williams a chair as they fumbled about their books and files. But that was where their manners, or perhaps their confidence, ended. Through Mr. Sheehan's silence, they struggled. He would only nod at the questions put to him. Christopher had brought the paper on which Mr. Sheehan had named his battalion, but the clerks refused that record as unofficial. When they demanded Mr. Sheehan speak, he walked back to where Miss Williams was seated and took up her hand, as if it contained the answers. He began and ended with her, and existed only so long that she was beside him. Lady Margaret asked if she, or Miss Williams, might attest to the facts of Mr. Sheehan's residence first, and if questions to Mr. Sheehan were still necessary, that they continue the interrogation in private. That was highly unusual, the clerks protested.

"For the love of God," Sir Christopher admonished, "will you not respect the urgency of their—our circumstances?"

"We are sorry, sir," one of the clerks offered. "But we have never dealt with such a—this—these kind of—departures from the protocol, sir."

"So you should feel free to make up a new protocol, then," Sir Christopher suggested, "as these circumstances require."

"Wouldn't that call for," the clerk stumbled, "for someone's approval?"

"You have mine," Christopher said. "Now get on with it."

"Yes. Yes, sir," the clerk agreed. "Yes, of course."

They were escorted into a room where the tableau the wedding party was preparing to make might be better addressed. Or contained, Lady Margaret thought. They were close to making a spectacle, and no one wanted that, surely. The room could have doubled for a chapel, with a dais at the front and center, but there were no accommodations for a congregation, only a single bench beside the entrance. Presumably the betrothed waited here for their betrothals. The room was dark, given its low ceiling, which appeared a hasty measure to hide the decay of the original roof, or a leak, or perhaps the squirrels and birds that had likely made nests in the rafters. The room smelled close, of dust baked on radiators.

Two clerks took over the dais with their ledgers and

stamps. Christopher placed himself between either man, and watched as they apparently pointed out the unconscionable blank spaces on the couple's application. Mr. Sheehan sat beside his bride, his arm supporting her back as it alternated between setting itself straight, and curving with exhaustion. Between the dais and the benches was too long a distance for Miss Williams to have to navigate in her condition, Lady Margaret thought, should Miss Williams and her groom be permitted to approach, swear their oaths, and seal them with their signatures.

"I am so sorry," Lady Margaret said to Miss Williams, as quietly as she could manage. "This was supposed to have been dealt with."

"Oh, it's quite all right," Miss Williams said. She inhaled, as if to have the strength to speak. "No one remembers the details of their weddings, or so they say."

"I thought it was only the groom who cannot remember his wedding day," Lady Margaret said, and she found herself trying to avoid Mr. Sheehan's reaction, as she feared to read his face, even in profile.

"No. In this, the bride and groom are apt to be equally forgetful," Miss Williams said. "It's why people never tell stories of their own weddings, only the others they've attended."

"I thought some of that was out of kindness—for the in-laws or for the sake of the marriage."

"Stories should not have to be cruel," Miss Williams said. Lady Margaret was not certain what she meant. Miss Williams had never said much about herself; Lady Margaret perhaps knew less about the bride than she knew of the man

Miss Williams was marrying. And yet, in those few words, Lady Margaret wondered if she might comprehend the mission Miss Williams had set out for herself; a mission she seemed on the verge of accomplishing.

"I am sorry for that story my husband tried to tell," Lady Margaret said. "That Emily Hobhouse—"

"Please," Miss Williams replied, as if the conversation had turned fatiguing. "There is no need."

"That business about South Africa, the refugee camps— Arthur takes that failure so personally." Lady Margaret could not stop herself. "Each time he sees or hears of a lost soul in our midst, he thinks of South Africa . . . well, you can imagine."

"No," Miss Williams said. "War is not for women to imagine. It is for us to weather its echoes and wrestle them into silence in our homes."

"And so we are engaged, with each generation," Lady Margaret assented.

"Then when we succeed, it is to the detriment of the next generation," Miss Williams said. "Don't you think?"

Again Lady Margaret was puzzled at Miss Williams's remark, for now she could not even be sure which topic— the failings of her husband, or of all men in general—they had been addressing. In pausing to consider how they had arrived at this conclusion, she could see how arduous it was for Miss Williams to carry on; perhaps it was the simple act of speaking, and not their conversation in particular, that the woman now found to be so tedious. So Lady Margaret nodded, gravely, as the subject seemed to demand such a response. Small beads of sweat, like clusters of seeds gingerly deposited, had arisen on Miss Williams's forehead. In his pocket Mr. Sheehan found the monogrammed handkerchief Miss Williams had given him, and carefully blotted those beads out. He lifted her hair away from her neck, and passed the handkerchief over the moisture there. Lady Margaret felt the tremble that suddenly gripped Miss Williams from her shoulders to her toes.

"I am so sorry for all this trouble," Miss Williams said.

"Oh, but it is an honor, really," Lady Margaret said, and she pushed the bouquet into Miss Williams's hands, so she might be reminded of something fresh and vital.

Lady Margaret heard a door open and shut somewhere behind her.

"We're ready for you now," Christopher said; he stood ready to lift the bride from the bench as Mr. Sheehan steadied her from the side. At the dais, one of the clerks was pacing, his concentration resolutely on his feet, it seemed. He could not lift his eyes to acknowledge them. He had donned a jacket, at least, and when he refrained from pacing, he patted down his hair on the sides and crown of his head.

"What did you do?" Lady Margaret whispered to her son.

"Nothing that Father cannot afford," Christopher said, if only an ounce too smugly.

But he deserved to be smug, Lady Margaret reasoned, and they marched, the four of them in a row, Lady Margaret on Miss Williams's arm, and her son on Mr. Sheehan's. They marched toward the clerk and the pair of candles he had lit. The flames competed with the electric lights above. They should have been in a church, with a high ceiling, stained glass, and darkness for candlelight to reach through. There should have been the scent of roses and the cold feel of new gold in the palm of the best man, Lady Margaret thought. She could remember how the ring first felt on her own finger, and she had assumed it would be the same for everyone. Now she did not know if Mr. Sheehan even had a ring for Miss Williams, or if Christopher might be carrying it. It was one detail she had allowed to escape her notice, for how impolitic would it have been to ask after something so expensive?

In a church, Lady Margaret thought, there would have been music and the proper awe. It was how she imagined her own wedding to Lord Thorton, for Miss Williams was right; not even a bride remembers her wedding, she only recreates it from all the plans she made before that day. As she entered the church for her own wedding, Lady Margaret was struck by the pearlish haze over the congregation, the shadow that was Lord Thorton in his morning jacket at the altar, and the clouds that buffeted the shortest walk of her life, the last obstacle out of her childhood. She had always been certain of what she saw at that moment, even if it was only tulle and blurs of the people she would soon no longer have time to know. Now that all seemed helplessly artificial when compared to the bright relief of this ceremony. It was clear, so clear, under the electricity and beside the noise of registry business, which could overpower any words Mr. Sheehan might dare to utter.

The clerk read from a piece of paper, an improvised service possibly—obviously, judging by the speed at which he read it. Indeed, he read so quickly that Lady Margaret forgot to look at her son as Miss Williams pledged her troth in her meager voice. The clerk slowed his speech when it came to Mr. Sheehan's portion of the service; the paper suddenly waved and sputtered in his hands, as though it refused to be read. The clerk struggled with familiar syllables. And then Mr. Sheehan withdrew something small from his pocket, a ring that stayed on Miss Williams finger only because she made a fist of her hand. Otherwise it would have disappeared: into her palm or onto the floor, where the thin band and slight stones might not have made enough of a sound for anyone to trace it. Miss Williams lifted her fist for Mr. Sheehan to see that the ring had reached its proper destination, and as the clerk read the words Mr. Sheehan was meant to repeat, Mr. Sheehan kissed his bride's hand, unbidden. And then he kissed her lips, before the clerk could sanction it, and they embraced. They did not release each other until Mr. Sheehan had finished whispering in his bride's ear. "I will, I will, I will," is how Lady Margaret thought she heard it, although she knew the truth of it rested solely in the bride's imagination.

Sixteen

As if to demonstrate that she had not been done in by the morning's events, the new Mrs. Sheehan would not allow her husband to carry her across the threshold. This was a disappointment to Lady Margaret, who had hoped to maintain at least this small tradition after the wedding. She had originally planned a luncheon party in honor of the bride and groom with champagne, garlands, and tea cakes rather than an unnecessary, towering confection that would feed far more than could be gathered for the event. But as the days piled on, Lady Margaret came to realize that any such arrangements would dangerously weaken the bride, whom she had come to admire for the manners she maintained in spite of her condition.

"It is time to leave, Christopher," Lady Margaret said,

and she put out her hand for her son to take, so she might be helped into the automobile.

"Yes," Christopher said. "Yes." Yet he did not immediately respond to his mother's touch, and kept his glance on the door of the cottage, now shut.

"Please," Lady Margaret said, and she grasped his shoulder. With that Christopher turned to see his mother smiling at him. It was neither a smile of joy nor awe, as she regularly gave him when he was a boy or even a young man, before the war. Now her mouth quivered, her eyes switched about, as if his mother was struggling to stave off the emotions that he too was confronting. He did not care to name them, with their contradictions and impolitic nature. But he also saw pride in his mother's face, in the dauntlessness of her expression, and he dipped his head and neck away, as that honor was so unexpected.

"You've done all that you could," Lady Margaret said. "Come on, then."

Sheehan felt a difference in the cottage before he could hear it: there was relief in its joints and beams and in the paint and floorboards. No more sounds of dithering, of footsteps and washcloths, soles and palms carrying out errands and bringing messages. The little house had exhaled, its organs gaining a reprieve. This was an unconfined silence, one that was ready for nature to fill. He felt himself leaving a mark on it as he drew the breath he needed, suddenly, to lift his bride and carry her into the heart of their new marriage.

He thought of the swans she had spoken of as she responded, resting her head into the nape of his neck. She had lost so much of herself to the sickness. She did not seem real this way, so much less substantial in bulk and weight. But her breath was at his skin, pattering and faint.

He thought of taking her into the nursery, to the separate beds. But her pulse flourished against him, as though she might turn to gusting wind and water, and she had wrapped her arms around his neck to secure her position. He slowly took to the stairs and heard nothing of the complaints the wood had made on those nights he paced and cowered. She warmed, it seemed to him, as he made his ascent, but in more than mere temperature. Her hair against his neck was thinner and softer, the skin of her face smoother, infinite in its responsive qualities. She may have been crying, with the wetness he sensed on his cheek. She may have been beaming a smile that chased away nightfall, the heat of her forehead against his ear and brow.

In the bedroom, the darkness of the afternoon was making its first foray. The sun must have been slowed behind the trees at the college. He thought she was hushing him as he set her down on the bed, but it was herself she was hushing, as if her body was ceramic—a temporary arrangement of sand, glass, and paint. She sighed but said nothing, except to take up one of his hands.

The room had not changed since before her illness, though now it felt immense. How far from her he stood, how distant from her hair, eyes, her face. "Come, come," she said, and she pulled at him, a slight gesture, and yet her strength at that moment was considerable, unavoidable. He sat beside her obediently.

"I will keep my eyes open, so you know I have not left," she said.

He put a finger to her lips so that she would not expend more than she had in sound and words, in breath and endurance—in everything she was and had been to him. He could see it receding in her, as if it were being drawn deeper into her body, somewhere inaccessible. Still, her neck and face remained flush as she looked at him. On the exposed skin of her arms and legs, she was pale, again, and shivered openly. They had agreed that morning to embark on a lifetime together, but in the glances they now shared, they realized that they had perhaps hours, or mere minutes, to accomplish it.

"I know," she whispered, and she hushed him this time, her hand upon his mouth. "Let me show you where to go," she said, and took his face into her palms. "Look. Into my eyes. First, my eyes," she directed him, and he could see the red rimming the irises within her eyes, as if her heart was beating just behind them. "See, see," she whispered as her eyes changed again, the redness seeping into the intricacies of the irises' coloration.

"Watch," she said, and her eyes began to lose all differentiation. It was as if she were bleeding there, where her heart had just been; Sheehan drew a breath as if in alarm and raised his hands as if to cover her eyes, to staunch the bleeding. But she shook her head, hushed him again, and held his hands tight, so he could not resort to hiding her, or hiding behind his hands.

"Just watch," she commanded, and the blood found its way into more of her sight, into the whites of her eyes, but he could see this was not bleeding, not as he had known it. There was nothing to be caught falling into mud; nothing to be swabbed away. There was no wound, only a richness, as her eyes swept over his face. Her eyes had enlarged, amplified themselves, as if to draw more heavily on the light and his visage.

"It's all right," she said. "It's all right."

She was breathing deeply, confidently, with more reserve than he had seen in weeks. Her lungs had been the source of her problems, the doctors had postulated. Sheehan imagined that what had sickened her lungs these weeks was moving to a new region—her eyes, her mind behind them—and this was what he was witnessing. Her lungs were free now, and she savored each draught she took: his wife, his love, suddenly repaired and infused with a different force, alluring but familiar.

"I tried to tell you," she said; her words mere vapors, he thought, as she released them into his ears. "But now, my hands," she said. "Look at my hands."

The long tendons from finger to wrist were suddenly so pronounced, as if to suggest crow's feet, the tracks they leave in wet soil after a night of scavenging. He ran his fingertips over the seemingly naked musculature of her hands, their skin-like shell, pale and endangered. "I tried—" she began, but he embraced her, whether to force the words out or prevent them from escaping, he could not say.

Against his palm, the back of her head was hot, but her hair was silken, like rain that divides the times of the day in Ireland. He had forgotten that kind of rain—from before the war—the softness that melded into skin, that kept his hands supple and ready for playing.

"My hair," she whispered. "You feel my hair now."

He moved the locks of her hair to reveal her eyes still open, still disquieted. He tried to confine his concentration to her eyes as his fingers teased through her hair, but he could not help himself. Her hair came to feel more complex in its individual strands. It had become more like a nest of feathers, shaft and stylus for each one—the system connecting keys to the strings of the piano. Each piece of a feather held its position in an array, and together feathers moved and reacted, moved and reacted, to lift a body, bank it against winds, glide it through clouds. He did not know about birds when he was a boy, but he did know the strings of the piano: their resolve and responses to the instrument's felted hammers.

"My skin," she said, and she sent his hands to her neck, her arms, the opening of her dress. He ran his hands just as she instructed, and for the first time in so long he found himself unafraid of touch, of his own touch. He ran his hands over the pores of her face, the follicles of the hair on her arms, and did not worry where he would leave the terrible impact of himself upon her. "My skin," she repeated as she opened more of her dress. "My skin," she said as she revealed her breasts, her stomach, her thighs, and then had him remove the dress completely, and she was revealed to him in full. In that instance the pallidity that was the dominant quality of her flesh changed, as though thickening like a mat of leaves on the pavement after the morning's first rainfall.

"My flesh," she said as she directed him to her arms again, her breasts, her thighs, and her back. He noticed a confusion to her skin now, as though she was coated in a slight down of something newly born—damp and roughened in parts, but smooth in others. Each touch of his hands changed her in some way, just as a feather never recovers its precise symmetry once it is scaled by the wind. With his touch, her skin rose to meet him, so that she flushed with color from the silken crown of her head to her torso and where her color ended in a different nest of hair.

"My flesh," she said, but he detected a presence growing in her shoulders: a rise in the bone, or a pair of rises, equidistant from where her back dipped, curved, and led outward toward her breasts. These rises, new appendages, felt sleek yet delicate, as though constructed out of soft, even hollowed material. He had anticipated such delicacies further down her body, where he feared his touch would become frightful and pitying to her. But not so here, so close to her lungs. His touch should not have so much meaning here, on her back; and yet, it was everything. She flushed deeply, so much more vividly than the simple moments previous.

"My bones," she said, and pressed her face to his. "My eyes," she said.

He could feel their blinking like palpitations, an exchange of commands and answers, or a pair of brushes rather than sticks against the drum of his chest.

"My bones," she murmured, and beneath his hands her back seemed to be splitting, separating, layer from layer, bone from organ, into two equal portions. Something was trying to escape from within. Something had an urgent need to stretch, to meet its full length and agility, and his touch could stop them. "My wings," she said, and she no longer felt tethered to him or the bed; she seemed to be floating. She threw her head back, as if to remind him of her eyes, but she did not say anything. Her eyes were slurred in a kind of flame.

"I tried to explain," she said, "but now, now, my love—" and the flesh that colored and ripened so flashed back to white again, glossy and hard, yet delicate. Throughout her body it had hardened, except for a glimpse of liquid running beneath it. "Now I am ready," she said, and he entered her.

The drafts and flutters that had been barely contained within her body blew through her flesh. Suddenly Sheehan's hands were drenched, with what he could not name. The smile in her eyes was rapturous. Where her skin had been hot and wet and cold and white, all turned into an ecstatic blankness. He pressed his hands deeper into her back, wanting to hide his face in her neck. But her neck was no longer there as he understood it; there was only the consistency of muscle and feathers. He meant to look into her eyes, to check on their sentience, but instead he saw what could not be real: the drapes cloaking the windows had been peeled open. A thunderclap shook the cottage. The blast nearly threw him off the bed. But it was not a bomb, a flash and concussion that stole time and distributed bodies. This was too slow, disciplined and controlled, a sound that restored time to the light.

The wind in his face was not wind, but the effects of a tremendous fanning; and the sensations against his body were not the result of a deliberate desire, but a symptom of proximity. What he felt may have been the chance encounters between different realms. A feather fell from the giant body hovering above, and came to rest on his chest. When he cleared his mind, he saw the neck of a magnificent bird reach for the still closed window, beyond which the heavens waited in their heady radiance. Then he saw the face and neck of that bird arch back down toward him. She beat her wings with a gentle assuredness, so that she neither threatened the human being below nor appeared as if she was threatened by him. Sheehan immediately thought of opening a window—the door, even—and raised himself to do it. But the bird maintained her distance, as if to tell him there was no need; she wished to stay awhile.

Sheehan lifted his arms, and the bird descended until it was close enough for him to embrace. She was whiter than his wife's denuded flesh, whiter than any cloud, than all the ivory he had once lived only to caress, but had denied himself this most instinctual of his needs, because of what the war had done to him, eroded his ability to sense its patterns, and to delight in its answers. The bird's head was crowned by an array of short, downy feathers. Sheehan watched them curl and sway, so precisely sensitive they were to the currents the creature's birth had portended. The eyes and beak were thrilling in their luster and darkness. Sheehan could not fathom why, or how, but laughter began in his chest as he touched the bird's feathers, as he smoothed them. He likely had only a few moments to learn their flow and direction. Now it was his throat that had turned useless as his hands had been, for it could suppress nothing. Sound rolled out, drafts of laughter. The great bird reacted, stretching out her neck as if she could laugh, too, and then bending her head to meet Sheehan's own.

Sheehan now felt himself lighter than air, coreless and hollow: how this grand animal must feel when it first resolves to fly, the joy and weightlessness when the wind is underneath it, but no longer upon it. He jumped onto the bed, standing at the bird's level, as if he intended to follow her out the window. The bird dipped its crown to ruffle Sheehan's chin, for its eyes to pass as close to Sheehan's as possible, and then it shifted its focus: first to the pillow where only moments earlier its precursor had rested her head. Sheehan's eyes dutifully followed. There was a note there, one of hers, but before he could read it the bird had raised itself before the now open window. Sheehan kept his eyes on the magnificence he had married: the span of her wings, the translucence of her body. Sheehan lifted a hand—to wave, not to beckon. The bird thrust herself through the window, and in her wake, the note on the pillow rose to catch Sheehan's notice.

It read:

> Fever begins in birds,
> in flocks or cosseted by
> the precocious yet delicate
> ambitions of those who believe
> they will tame creatures before
> their disappointments can first
> tame them. When I was a child,
> I was told never to touch a bird,
> so as not to confuse it about its
> purpose, so I left the speed and
> industry of birds for others to
> master, like the dew that must
> moisten their songs to one
> another; or the insects that
> compete with them for nectar;
> or the plumes and diagrams

a flower gives off, in search of
a plough, or a lover. This is
how fever begins, in shaft
and follicle, the culling of
feathers for hats and cushions,
and from there it travels, much
as its precursors do, in darts
and arrows, and into the lungs
and other febrile organs. This is
not a fairy tale. This is a fable.
So let me go, love; let me
love what I have left, the rise
of fevered air into clouds and
relief; the floating life that will
not break, so long as I have this
love as my guide in the aftermath,
until we again meet.

Epilogue

THERE WAS NO need for Sheehan to speak once he arrived at Lord Thorton's estate; the servants had been instructed to immediately fetch Christopher or Lady Margaret should he turn up there. He arrived after the evening's cigars and cocktails, and appeared to have walked a longer route to the estate than should have been necessary. It was Christopher who acted quickly to send for an ambulance before he drove himself and Sheehan back to the cottage.

The ambulance driver and his assistant said nothing about the condition of the bed clothes, soaked as they were in an unfamiliar transparency. Neither did they remark on the body, which seemed empty and wet in comparison to any form of humanity. The medical examiner and the registry also

remained silent in their descriptions of the corpse, and offi-
cially listed the death of Eva Williams Sheehan as attributable
to suffocation, and/or drowning by consumption.

If anyone—or anything—knew what precisely happened,
it was the Great Snowy Egret espied around the cottage in
the days following, but no human can speak to birds properly. So no one could ask the bird what it was doing there,
without a body of water to scour for food or marshes for its
nesting materials. The Egret paced around the cottage and did
not appear lost so much as expectant, and it remained on the
grounds for several days, though Sheehan was immediately
evicted from the location.

After Lord Thorton's death, Christopher had the new
bride's body moved from the churchyard at the western edge
of the college to the estate. Mr. Sheehan could more easily
visit a private grave than one so public, given that he was
suspected in some way long after the death. He no longer
needed to leave white flowers at the doorstep of the cottage,
and became a frequent visitor at the proper resting place. At
the change of the seasons; and on the anniversary of her death
and their marriage; on cold spring days that reminded him of
how they had met; and on long summer evenings: the flowers
were no longer white or just cuttings, but those morning
glories, foxglove, and trumpet creepers he had planted. He'd
watch them fall away from the sunlight and into somno-
lence. Occasionally Christopher would join him at the grave,
although they did not speak, and Christopher never brought
any tokens of his respect. He left the tending of the grave to
Mr. Sheehan, who took up weeding, raking, and seeding the
area, although the groundskeeper would have gladly taken care

of it.

Suitable employment and lodging were found for Mr. Sheehan at St. Thomas Hospital, where he performed small repairs and tidied the rooms and common areas. He was invited to play and maintain the organ in the hospital chapel, but he declined, although he did live to play piano again. Once Lord Thorton passed away, Sir Christopher secured for him a position in the college infirmary. Mr. Sheehan was offered, but refused, all manner of a traditional room on the estate, so Christopher gave him an outbuilding to do with what he liked. Christopher's sisters assumed Mr. Sheehan to be one of their brother's compatriots from the war, someone he had rescued; they were gracious and fair when Christopher announced Mr. Sheehan had been invited to Christmas or some other family obligation. Christopher eventually started his own family, and Mr. Sheehan was there for the more important moments, in the back of the church, or some grand room, before he predictably slipped out early.

Mr. Sheehan maintained his position at the infirmary, such as it was. With what he could buy or find in materials, he made himself a kind of loft bedroom, and below that, a library and sitting room. He furnished the library with Miss Williams's books, which Christopher had managed to save for him, and he relished the shelves he had built to properly house the volumes. Because his home was one of the outbuildings, it could not be outfitted with a kitchen, although Mr. Sheehan did keep a few provisions on the shelves, especially those he was able to raise himself from the garden he started. He took his meals with the servants in the main house when it suited him.

And on the instrument that had so troubled him that one day, Michael Evan Sheehan made use of his renewed sense of touch, and eventually even his timing, although his playing was inexorably different. He had to learn to play through the calluses that came to bind his hands, so that everything he had once perfected—his posture, pace, resistance—had to be adjusted. He did not play regularly, but at random intervals that corresponded to no particular circumstance. He no longer played with any particular goal, but to summon something within himself: a memory, a moment, an instant when time might end, and there would be nothing left to do but listen. At first, it was said that he played just as he spoke, in his snippets of obligatory greetings and courtesies: "Please," and "Thank you," and "Good morning," or "Good evening." But as the years stretched beyond what any of them expected, it was Lady Margaret who, believing herself to be the one person to have truly heard Mr. Sheehan speak, thought that his playing was not like his diction but the quality of his voice, if he would ever see fit to give people more of it: low and restrained, briskly eloquent, and, if not sweet, than sympathetic, to other sounds—of people, of the house, its guests, residents and servants, of nature, wind through branches and grass, and birdsong especially—that surrounded them.

Source Material

THE HAWKMAN WAS primarily inspired by a reading of the Grimm Brothers' fairy tale "The Bearskin," in its original German, in which it is known as "Der Bärenhäuter." The Grimms' stories often share elements of metamorphoses between good and evil, man and animal, and the impoverished to the unaccountably wealthy and powerful. These transformations are often linked to love and marriage; "The Cat Skin" is another example. Similarities may lead readers to believe that *The Hawkman* is a retelling of the more popular "Beauty and the Beast," but "The Bearskin" is the controlling tale here, as it explored one man's journey from desperation to deviltry, and the consequences it had for those who helped him come back to himself.

The fictional Michael Sheehan's experiences at the front and in German prisoner of war camps are loosely based on the recorded experiences of Lance Cpl. F. W. Harvey of the 2/5th Battalion, Gloucestershire Regiment. In the Great War, English-speaking prisoners of war were relatively rare compared to French and Russian prisoners. For the sake of authenticity, I wanted to use the record of a documented English prisoner. Harvey's book, *Comrades in Captivity: A Record of Life in Seven German Prison Camps* was highly influential. I have added and subtracted certain details about the execution of the war and the treatment of English and Irish soldiers in POW camps to serve the plot. Locations and approximate chronologies are also based on *The Story of the 2/5th Battalion Gloucestershire Regiment 1914-1918* by A.F. Barnes. Both books have been reprinted by many publishers since their original publication. Barnes's book is available through The Naval and Military Press Ltd. of East Sussex, England. *Comrades in Captivity* was originally published by Sidgwick & Jackson Ltd. of London, in 1920.

Other books that were consulted for information are Stanley Weintraub's *Silent Night: The Story of the World War I Christmas Truce* (Plume/Penguin Group 2002); *The First World War: A Photographic History*, edited and with an introduction by Laurence Stallings (Simon and Schuster 1933); and *A Mammal's Notebook: The Writings of Erik Satie*, edited by Ornella Volta (Atlas Press 1996). By happy accident, I also listened to Dan Carlin's six-part podcast, *Blueprint for Armageddon*, sometime during the years of the writing of this book, and it surely had its influence.

Acknowledgments

JESS WINFIELD SUGGESTED that I write a fairy tale, so this book would not be here without him. Dan McLaughlin was just as encouraging with this project as he's always been, and he deserves much gratitude. A conversation with Ellen Kushner about the purpose of fairy tales inspired the ethos that I hope is apparent in these pages. I wish to thank Brett Cott for research materials, and Victor Greenberg for his knowledge of history. The fine eye of Jim Meirose was instrumental in getting through the revisions. It should go without saying that I am indebted to Elisabeth Fairfield Stokes, Michelle Hoover, Patricia Horvath, Kate Southwood, and Michelle Valois, but I'll say it anyway.

Without the editing team at Amberjack Publishing, this novel would have been a far slighter, much less mature work, so I'm also grateful to Cherrita Lee, Kayla Church, and Dayna Anderson.

Finally and mostly, I thank Patrick J. LaForge and Eva LaForge for the trip to Ireland and anything and everything that can be thought of, forever and always. I love you both so much.

About the Author

JANE ROSENBERG LAFORGE was born in Los Angeles to a pair of political and news junkies. As a child, she grew up in Laurel Hills, a suburb adjacent to the storied, some say enchanted, enclave of visual artists, hippies, rock musicians, and Hollywood actors known as Laurel Canyon. This milieu shaped her lifelong fascination with history, politics, subcultures, and folklore. She also studied ballet, which introduced her to the world of fairy tales and legends of supernatural transformation.

Jane's first professional writings were as a journalist. Her reporting took her throughout California, Maryland, and upstate New York. She enrolled in a graduate creative writing program in order to write a novel based on a court case she covered. Her studies led to a career as a college English instructor and writing literary criticism. She has published articles on fairy tales and the influence of African folklore on contemporary authors. As a college instructor, she has taught composition, children's literature, and African American literature.

After the birth of her daughter in 2000, Jane found little time to write at length and began exploring poetry. In 2009, she published her first chapbook of poems and later brought together all her interests to write *An Unsuitable Princess: A True Fantasy/A Fantastical Memoir*. *An Unsuitable Princess* was an annotated fairy tale with poetry that told the story of her adolescence as a Hollywood outsider. All together she has published four poetry chapbooks and two full-length collections. The most recent is *Daphne and Her Discontents*, an examination of the Greek myth of a girl who turns into a Laurel tree—which gave Jane's childhood neighborhood its name—to avoid Apollo's advances.

Jane now lives in New York with her husband, Patrick; daughter, Eva; and their cat, Zeka.